He couldn't turn Josie loose.

Lost in that darkness with her, he knew she was his anchor. Her hand brushed against his forehead willingly, even as she heard his terrible cry. Her fingers were warm in the zero cold of his agony, even while she trembled against him.

Her touch kept him from disappearing into that wild, whirling darkness. But her touch had also focused those images. Sharpened them into crystal pieces of pain that sliced through her, too. And while he sought rest in her green eyes, peace in her sturdy refusal to bend under the weight of her loss, he'd brought his darkness to her.

He'd thought to protect her, to find out the truth of what hovered around them, but he'd endangered her. With the last remnant of strength he had, he shoved her away.

Lindsay Longford, like most writers, is a reader. She even reads toothpaste labels in desperation! A former high school English teacher with an M.A. in literature, she began writing romances because she wanted to create stories that touched readers' emotions by transporting them to a world where good things happened to good people and happily-ever-after was possible with a little work.

Her first book, *Jake's Child,* was nominated for Best New Series Author, Best Silhouette Romance and received a Special Achievement Award from *Romantic Times* for Best First Series Book. It was also a finalist in the Romance Writers of America RITA Award contest for Best First Book. Her Silhouette Romance novel *Annie and the Wise Men* won the RITA Award for the Best Traditional Romance of 1993.

DARK
MOON

LINDSAY
LONGFORD

Published by Silhouette Books

America's Publisher of Contemporary Romance

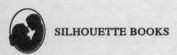

SILHOUETTE BOOKS

ISBN 0-373-51187-6

DARK MOON

Copyright © 1995 by Jimmie Morel

All rights reserved. Except for use in any review, the reproduction or utilization of this work in whole or in part in any form by any electronic, mechanical or other means, now known or hereafter invented, including xerography, photocopying and recording, or in any information storage or retrieval system, is forbidden without the written permission of the editorial office, Silhouette Books, 300 East 42nd Street, New York, NY 10017 U.S.A.

All characters in this book have no existence outside the imagination of the author and have no relation whatsoever to anyone bearing the same name or names. They are not even distantly inspired by any individual known or unknown to the author, and all incidents are pure invention.

This edition published by arrangement with Harlequin Books S.A.

® and TM are trademarks of Harlequin Books S.A., used under license. Trademarks indicated with ® are registered in the United States Patent and Trademark Office, the Canadian Trade Marks Office and in other countries.

Visit Silhouette at www.eHarlequin.com

Printed in U.S.A.

CHAPTER ONE

It was the sudden silence that made her look up.

Struck by the stillness, Josie paused. Pebbles of dirt spattered from her trowel to the ground as she raised her chin. Dust spiraled up, gritty against her mouth.

She tilted her head, listening.

And heard nothing.

Her fingers tightened against the leaf of the tomato seedling. Uneasy, she rested her trowel on the ground.

All morning she'd been distantly aware of the occasional trill of a mockingbird or the squawks of a blue jay in the pines at the edge of her property, the bird noise a numbing background sound in the July heat.

But now, this *silence*.

Abrupt and absolute.

Only the stifling darkness of the woods in front of her. Darkness and stillness and the heavy drumming of her pulse in her ears.

Over the pungent scent of the bruised leaf in her hand came a musky scent mixing with the smell of dry soil.

Heat pressed in on her, trickled down her spine.

Something there, just at the edge of her vision. A shape, a form, unmoving in the shadows of the woods.

She blinked, clearing the haze of perspiration from her eyes. Shades of darkness slid into focus, and her heart stuttered and skipped a beat as she saw him.

Ears folded over and stub of a tail jutting out, the dog paused at the edge of the woods and stared at her. Heavy bodied and blunt nosed, he watched her, an intimidating intelligence in his unblinking yellow gaze.

Predator eyes.

Kneeling in front of the straggling tomato plants, Josie gripped the trowel stuck in the sandy soil of her garden and didn't move.

The dog fixed her with his murky yellow eyes as he slowly lowered his muzzle.

Understanding pierced her heat-stunned brain. Rabid, heat-mad, whatever—the animal was readying himself for attack. Josie swallowed, the sound loud in her ears.

Balancing herself, she flattened her free hand in the dirt, dropping the seedling uprooted by the force of her grip. One broken leaf lay like a green arrowhead against the clumps of earth.

With her barely perceptible movement, the animal, a good two feet or more at the shoulder, stepped forward, his long, sloping shoulders moving with massive power.

Fear sharpening her senses, Josie studied him. He was almost 130 pounds of tight, hard muscle from shoulder to flank. But his eyes— Josie shivered.

His stubby tail, upright now, wagged once.

She might have thought it was a sign of friendly greeting.

She knew better.

Friendliness was not in those eyes.

Not friendliness at all. Something else entirely.

Threat glowed deep in their muddy depths.

An instinct she hesitated to trust whispered, *Evil, evil.* Another voice, one she knew damned good and well not to trust, murmured seductively, *Run!*

Sweat dripped down into her eyes as she edged back slowly on her heels, unthinking, reacting at a primal level. Keeping her gaze on the ground, avoiding direct eye contact, she kept the animal in peripheral view.

He lifted his snout, sniffing, and cocked his head, watchful, waiting. His front paws alternated in place, a curious, prancing dance, before he drifted out of view. She carefully turned her head, and through a blur saw the dog pace three steps east along her yard toward the clothesline where her sheets hung limp and still, and then three steps west, observing some boundary invisible to her, a boundary only yards away as he guarded her. His mouth was partially open, his tongue lolling to the side.

Her knees ached with the effort she made not to leap to her feet and run. Behind her, the house might as well have been miles away, light-years from where she knelt shaking and sweating in the dirt.

Smells rose to her nostrils, the salty smell of sweat on her arm, the dry tickle of dirt, the fetor of animal excitement heavy in the still air.

The only moving thing in her universe, the dog stalked slowly in front of her.

Emerging from the darkness of the woods like a shadow, another dog eased to his left. Then a third, both dogs staying slightly behind the lead dog, and all three fixing her with that stare that sent a slide of ice bone-deep.

The trowel was greasy with sweat—slick in her bare hand. Her vision hazy, she saw the first dog stop. Watching her steadily, intently, he closed his rust-colored muzzle.

In all that thick silence, Josie could have sworn she heard his powerful jaws snap. He was thinking, reaching a decision. That, too, she would swear.

If she could wipe the sweat from her eyes, she could— *run!* Deep in her brain Josie heard the treacherous voice growl.

She thought about it. Her muscles tensed, needing the release of action.

No.

She didn't dare take off in a race for her house. At gut level, she knew the pack would be on her before she could reach the safety of the porch.

For seven days, the male and four companion animals, all with distinctive rust circles over their eyes, had appeared in the woods, each day moving closer to her yard, her house. Closer to her.

She'd seen them at night, too, their shadows slipping silently through the trees bordering her property, merging in and out of the deeper darkness of the woods before disappearing.

Roaming through her house during the quiet hours as heat and night sounds seeped in through her open windows, she'd had an odd empathy for the animals, longing herself for the cool darkness of the woods, desiring an end, whatever it was, to the waiting that filled her days and kept her wandering through her heat-blasted house at nights. In those unending hours, she'd envied the pack's oneness with the dark.

She hadn't seen their eyes at night, though—only the heavy bulk of their bodies loping smoothly and silently before disappearing. She hadn't been prepared for the brute intelligence that held her captive now.

Across the span of arid yard, the lead animal lifted its lip in a silent snarl. Like sentinels, two more dogs appeared noiselessly, fanning out behind the triumvirate. Sweat trickled into her mouth.

Knowing better than to move in any way that would seem a challenge, she edged backward, still on her knees, inching her way to the house. Passive, she let her body language acknowledge their dominance.

It wasn't enough.

Again, the alpha dog lowered his head. The animals behind him shifted, restlessly pawing the ground.

In that instant, Josie knew she had no choice.

They were going to attack her if she stayed.

They would attack if she ran.

She had no possibility of reaching her house. Aroused by the chase, the animals would close on her in a frenzy of bloodlust.

In spite of the heat, terror struck her with utter, immobilizing cold.

And in that tick of time when the world hung motionless,

everything suspended, even the drop of sweat poised at the tip of her eyelash, she wondered if this cold stillness was how it had been for her daughter. For the other children who'd vanished.

She couldn't breathe, couldn't move. From the hidden spaces of her fears, that unguarded thought slipped fully formed into her mind. Had Mellie been this cold, this terrified? Unbearable, that sly thought. Oh, Mellie, she thought, the ever present grief stone-heavy in her chest. *Mellie.*

Thinking of her daughter, Josie blinked, and her vision cleared. The earth turned, slowly, with an almost audible hum, and she heard the chambers of her heart open, close, heard the swoosh of her blood through her veins.

And with the roaring of her pulse in her ears, she knew she wasn't going to be one more victim. She had too many questions she wanted answered.

She owed Mellie those answers.

The first dog lifted one paw and bowed his massive back.

The hot, dusty air carried his low growl to her, the rumble coming from deep within his massive chest, the vibration palpable in the earth under her palm. With one hand Josie gripped the slippery trowel, and with the hand pressed against the earth, she scooped up a fistful of dirt and crouched, her legs shaky as she prepared to leap to her feet and run the sixty yards to her porch.

Incisors showing in a fierce snarl, the huge dog flexed his haunches and laid his ears back. As his powerful neck stretched forward and he lifted his forequarters, Josie saw a darker shadow glide from behind a clump of moss-hung trees, shadow separating from shadow.

The coarse hair on the dogs' backs stood upright. All five animals growled, a low rumble that raised the hairs at the back of her own neck. Primitive, that response, electric.

Now or never, she thought. Rising jerkily to her feet, she flung the handful of dirt and the trowel toward the dogs now in midleap. In that instant of furious motion, she saw a long arm lift, a hand held palm out, unspoken command in the thin, outstretched fingers. Control in the index finger pointing to the ground.

And faster than she could think, everything happened, changed, in a burst of sound and images. A buzzing loud as a swarm of drought-ravaged hornets in her ears, the yellow-eyed dog twisting in midleap, stopping and then hunching low to the ground, his stub tail between his legs. A drawn-out whine as he slunk off, disappearing as quietly as he'd first appeared, the other animals vanishing behind him.

Sweat streaming down her back, into her eyes, her heart pounding so hard she thought she'd throw up, Josie had an impression of a lean form dressed in jeans and a faded, dark shirt, had an impression, too, in that charged moment of dark, haunted eyes.

Clearing her vision, she blinked, and the tall shape vanished as silently as the animals.

From far away came the beginning chatter of a blue jay, and then, the melody hastily cut off, the woods were quiet once more in the heat, a silent, waiting presence in front of her.

Josie pressed a hand between her breasts. Her chest hurt. She'd been holding her breath and hadn't known it. Gulping, she inhaled. The air was so hot and heavy with dust that she could feel it coating her lungs, her throat, as she took rasping breaths. The muscles of her legs quivered and shook, straining as if she'd run ten miles.

But remembering those moments when she'd kneeled and seen the dogs coming toward her, been their prey, Josie forced herself to stand upright, anger bubbling sludgy-thick in her throat and stomach as she surveyed the hushed woods in front of her. Secrets there in the thick pines, the undergrowth.

Danger.

Secrets.

Grit clung to her damp hands, and she wiped them down the sides of her shorts. Mixed with her perspiration, dirt smeared the frayed denim.

"Damn!" Shaken and frightened, Josie glared toward the pines. She'd had enough of secrets and unanswered questions to last her the rest of her life.

Stuffing her trembling hands into her pockets, she considered the situation. Man and dogs had all disappeared in the same direction.

"Ryder Hayes," she murmured, misgivings underscoring her words. Her neighbor. If *neighbor* was the right term for someone she'd never met. Their two houses were the only ones on either side of the woods, and they were miles from town. No one ever casually strolled near her place.

Josie rubbed her eyes. The man must be Hayes. His property lay to the west of the woods and north of Angel Bay, the town. The dogs had to be his. No one else's. She scuffed her toes in the dirt as she sorted through her confused memories of the past few months.

Seven or eight months ago, she didn't know exactly when, he'd returned to the old house that backed onto the Angel River where it flowed into the Gulf of Mexico. She hadn't seen him.

Until now. She was dead certain that intense, solitary figure was Ryder Hayes, those terrifying dogs his. Keeping her gaze on the woods, she backed up. She wouldn't let him get away with letting his pets—*pets!* she thought, outraged—roam uncollared and uncontrolled.

God knew what those beasts were capable of.

What if she'd been a child?

Sweaty and shaky, Josie shivered as the memory of those yellow eyes glazed her burning skin with ice. "You and your damned dogs can all go to hell, Ryder Hayes." Alarm still whipping through her, she clasped her arms around her

waist and swore, the words shocking her with their violence.

She hadn't imagined the feral calculation in the dogs'
gaze. No. Despite everything she'd been through in the past
seven months, she was firmly in command of her imagination. She jammed her hands deeper into her pockets, closing her fingers around the fragment of rippled green glass.

Unlike her emotions, the touch of the weathered-smooth
glass caused no pain. Christmas Eve, Mellie had handed
her the lumpy package wrapped in a piece of the Sunday
comics. "Magic, Mommy," her six-year-old had said, blue
eyes solemn but still not hiding her excitement. "From the
woods." She'd waved her arm vaguely toward the trees
and then stuck her thumb into her mouth, her eyes growing
wide, her bowed pink mouth becoming an upside-down U.

Mellie wasn't supposed to go into the woods by herself.
Ever.

Christmas.

January.

And now this hellish July.

The shard of glass was cool against her palm, as cool as
the translucent watery green of its tint.

A blue jay chattered angrily. In that instant when sounds
rushed in, anger battered at her, anger at a world that no
longer made sense, anger at the animals that had reduced
her to a quivering heap in her garden.

That image of herself wasn't one she liked at all. She'd
be damned if she'd stay cowering inside because of a pack
of animals. She didn't like being helpless. Being a victim.

Damn Ryder Hayes. His animals could—

Fury gave her the strength to turn her back on the trees
and shadows and tear into her house, the screen door of the
porch slamming behind her. She'd rip a piece off Hayes's
hide, she would. She wasn't going to let him get away with
that kind of carelessness.

But she wouldn't face Ryder Hayes's dogs without some

kind of protection. Wild, spooky as hell, they were only animals, after all. Nothing more. She could deal with them.

Yanking open the drawer in the kitchen, she pulled out a key chain with a silver cylinder of capsaicin attached to it. She needed something else. Staring wildly at her kitchen cabinets, she threw open a door and whirled the carousel of spices so hard that a bottle of cinnamon flew off. She snatched the can of black pepper and stuffed it into her shorts pocket with the silver capsule. On her way down the sagging back steps, she grabbed her garden hoe. Silt from her morning weeding still caked its metal edges.

The *whang* of the slamming door echoed in her ears as she left her yard.

Skirting the southern edge of the woods, she went up the west approach, following the faint path in the low brush. Even with her arsenal, she lacked the nerve to take the shortcut through the woods.

In January, though, she'd run screaming like a madwoman through the moss-shrouded pine trees, the palmetto bushes, and wax myrtle. She hadn't gone into the woods since.

January.

Mellie.

And the six other missing children, the latest a nine-year-old boy.

And only five bodies.

Oh, Mellie, Josie thought, and her throat closed tight. She scrubbed her face hard with her fists, a desolation beyond words cramping her breathing.

Looking down at the dirt path, she realized for the first time that she'd left her house barefoot. She was so used to going without shoes, she hadn't even thought of them in the flush of anger. Stupid. Anger had propelled her down this path. Driven by the hot rage that boiled through her as hard as fear had earlier, she hadn't thought clearly.

She'd had only one idea in her mind. Hayes's beasts might be responsible for—

Off to her right, the woods had grown silent again as she neared Hayes's mansion. Eerie, that sense of a gathering intelligence. Half expecting to see one of the animals, Josie raised the hoe and looked behind her. Whirling, she stumbled as she looked up into one of the live-oak trees a few feet into the woods.

Narrowing her eyes, she realized the tree was dead, leafless. What she'd taken for leaves was a thick colony of birds. Every branch of the tree was covered with silent, watching grackles, their black plumage blending into the shadows, their bluish purple heads turned in her direction.

Her heart fluttered against her ribs as she squinted at the tree. She was close enough to see the bronze necks and throats, the yellow irises of their eyes.

Not a wing fluttered. Not one bird made a sound as she took another step down the path, but their yellow eyes followed her every movement.

"Scat, you stupid birds! Leave me alone, you devils!" Spinning in a huge circle, she waved the hoe in their direction, her voice shrill. In a huge, dark cloud, the birds rose, silent as ever, their wings beating as one. Wheeling left, they spread out, their shapes black Vs against the bleached white sky.

Then, as if directed by one mind, they hovered over the treetops, above her.

Josie shuddered. "Go away!" she shouted, waving the hoe toward the sky. "Shoo!"

And still they floated over her shoulder, their presence up there in the sky following her, the silent sweep of their wings drifting across the white-hot sun.

There was something chilling about the sight of the heavy clump of birds moving as one. Unnerved by their silent passage but not understanding why, she broke into a run. Even Ryder Hayes was preferable to this storm cloud of grackles. Gasping for breath in the heat, she came to the turn in the path that led either to Angel Bay or to the Hayes property.

The sickly-sweet branches of a drought-pinched oleander whipped against her shoulder as she pushed them aside and came to the shell drive leading to the Hayes house. Her breath rasping deep in her lungs, she paused. The edges of the crushed shells were sharp against the sole of her foot as she hesitated.

Tilted closed, the louvers of the wooden shutters gave the house a hostile, secretive appearance. In the smothering heat, the house seemed to shimmer in front of her, illusive.

Someone was watching her.

The hairs on the back of her neck rose.

She spun around.

The grackles had flown away.

Nothing behind her but the path.

No dogs there.

No one, in fact, merely that sense of being observed. She looked around and saw nothing, no one.

To her left, the distant curve of Angel River.

And in front of her, the house.

She hadn't seen it in years. The paint on the tall white columns flaked to gray underneath, and dead vines crawled like spiderwebs against the blank wall of the right side. Decay, rank and ripe, lay heavily over the house.

Walking slowly up the driveway, Josie kept one hand in her pocket tight around the pepper can. With her other hand, she clutched the hoe like a weapon. Shells popped and cracked under her feet. She kept her eyes moving from left to right, half expecting the pack of dogs to come around the corner of the house, to leap at her from the bushes massed at the edge of the porch that circled the front and sides of the house.

As she made her way up the center of the steps, she thumped each one with her hoe, announcing her presence.

The smell of rotting wood and insects filled her nose as the wide steps squeaked and splintered. She watched carefully where she placed her feet and tried not to think of what might have taken root or made its home in the recesses under the raised porch. Once more she wished she'd taken the time to slip into a pair of shoes.

Clutching the hoe like a walking stick, she cursed the stubbornness that kept her moving toward the front door of Ryder Hayes's house when what she wanted was to turn and run as fast as she could away from the oppressive gloom of this house. Her lungs were constricted, leaving her dizzyingly short of oxygen as she trudged across the warped expanse of porch.

Her stubbornness would be the death of her someday. Anybody with half a brain would know when to quit. But she hadn't had a choice, not really. Not with those dogs running wild—

She shut off her brain. She wouldn't think of the children.

A prickling awareness made goose bumps on her skin, stayed with her.

Taking one final step, she swallowed as she paused in front of the huge, heavily carved front door and raised her fist, pounding on the grinning faces, the grimy wreaths and grapes chiseled into the wood, unleashing her frustration and terror and grief against the unyielding mahogany.

The door should have creaked. It should have groaned. There should have been cobwebs hanging from the frame and a humped Igor to open the portal a crack.

Instead, the door swung inward, and a gaunt figure appeared in the dim foyer, shading his eyes against the sunlight. A draft of air coiled around her ankles and up her thighs like the brush of an unseen, cold hand.

The door had been opened so silently that she hadn't heard it, and her fist, still raised to pound against the door, slid against the cool cotton shirt of the man who leaned against the doorjamb. Her knuckles brushed against the thin black T-shirt, against the cords of his stomach, and she heard his swift intake of breath. His head snapped up and his dark gaze met hers.

Ice and heat burned her fingertips.

Josie jerked back, one heel scraping against a splinter. She couldn't help her reaction. Power rising toward her, threatening to swamp her and suck her under, sweeping her out beyond safety. Coming from him.

Slumped against the door with his aloof burning gaze meeting hers, he looked too weary to speak, too weary to live, and yet waves of energy came from him, battering against her, and she took another step back, stunned by the force of his presence.

"What do you want?" Exhaustion made his low voice gravelly and he shaded his eyes again, taking a step back.

Josie gripped the hoe and stepped forward. The man looked ill. "Ryder Hayes?"

"Most of the time. Usually." He sank more heavily against the frame as he glanced at her hoe. Slurred in a rough drawl, his words sounded as if he'd dragged them up from some dark cavern within himself. "Unless that's a weapon?"

"What?" Josie frowned.

With a barely perceptible movement of a long index finger, he pointed to the hoe she held in a death grip. "Have you come, lady of the moss green eyes, like some medieval villager with torch and hoe, to burn me out?"

"I don't know what you're talking about." Confused, Josie reached into her pocket for the cylinder of capsaicin.

"I see. Not a weapon, then." He shook his head and pulled himself upright, almost disappearing behind the shield of the door. "Sorry, but I'm not interested in buying farm tools."

"Good. Because I'm not selling anything."

"Of course you are. Everyone's selling something."
Cynicism curled the edges of his words.

"I'm not. I'm here to see Mr. Hayes." Josie thumped
the hoe emphatically. "Are you Ryder Hayes?"

"I'm afraid I am." Slavic cheekbones sloped down to a
full, sharply delineated mouth that curved down at the corners. "Not that I seem to have any choice about the matter."

"Then I've come about your dogs, Mr. Hayes."

"My dogs?" Straight white teeth flashed under the hood
of his hand as his mouth stretched in a yawn. "I can't help
you." He edged the door shut.

"You know good and well what I'm talking about."

"Do I?" His voice became only a drift of sound.

"The dogs that almost attacked me this morning. Those
beasts. Your pack of dogs."

White lines scored his beautiful mouth, nothing more
than a minute pull of muscle. He lowered his hand and his
dark eyes met hers again, eyes so tortured that Josie
dropped the hoe and stretched her hand to him. Clattering
to the porch, the hoe fell between them and she bent down
to pick it up as he said, "I have no dogs."

"I saw you with them," she insisted, stubborn in the
face of his denial and confused by the torment she'd
glimpsed.

"Did you?"

"Near my house. In the woods," Josie said.

"Perhaps you imagined you did." His voice was remote,
disinterested, but underneath the polite dismissal she heard
a disturbing note that kept her standing on his porch.

"I don't imagine things. I know what I saw." She
gripped the hoe until her hand hurt.

"Unlike the rest of us, then? How fortunate for you. To
know what's real. What's not."

"I saw you. You stopped the dogs from attacking me."

"Did I? Fascinating."

Wanting to shake him out of his indifference, needing to make him admit the truth, Josie reached out and grasped his arm. With her movement, the capsaicin cylinder flew out of her pocket and racketed across the porch into the grass. His forearm was all muscle and bone under her fingers.

"Hell." He doubled over and groaned, yanking his arm free and brushing his hand across his eyes. His hand trembled. "Damn."

"Are you all right?"

"I suppose it depends on your definition." He straightened and stepped away from her, putting the edge of the door between them before she could help him.

"Do you want me to call a doctor? Are you sick?" she repeated, concerned about the pallor that swept over his face.

"Sick?" His laugh was humorless and sent a ripple of shivers along her spine. "Spirit-sick, 'sick almost to dooms-day,' as the poet put it, but, no, lady green eyes, I don't believe I need the services of a physician. Thank you for your concern." Preparing to shut the door, his narrow, long fingers gripped the edge.

Glimpsing the strained white knuckles that tightened as she watched, Josie had the strangest impression that he was falling over the edge of a chasm and holding on with the last of his strength, but she couldn't let him escape without settling the issue of his animals. "Wait!"

"I thought we were through. Wasn't that all you wanted to know? About the dogs?" he drawled, his voice bored.

"They're dangerous. You were there. You saw them start to come after me."

"So you said." A flicker of pain stirred in the depths of his eyes. "And I've said, they're not my animals."

"You controlled them," she said flatly. "They obeyed you."

"Ah." The sound was long, drawn out, a whisper of

something disturbing in the heat. "There is that, isn't there?"

Josie frowned. Standing in front of him, holding her ground against his clear if unexpressed wish that she leave, she had the sense that she was leaning forward into the winds of a hurricane. Pale and gaunt faced, he was like the swirling winds of those storms, the power sweeping out around him, bending everything in its path. "I haven't seen them since then, but you have to keep them locked up. It's not safe to let them roam around." Uneasily she looked over her shoulder and off to the woods behind her and to the left.

"They're not here," he said, and his voice was gentle. "I don't have…pets."

Odd, Josie thought, the way he echoed her earlier thoughts. Stubbornly she persisted. "I want an explanation." She tapped the edge of the hoe against the porch boards.

"So do we all." He smiled at her, a faint stretching of facial muscles that moved like clouds across the gulf. "Want explanations. For something or other, don't we?" His gaze locked with hers.

"I want your dogs to stay away from me," she insisted. "Sooner or later, they're going to hurt someone. I don't want them anywhere near my property." As she glared into his hooded eyes, cold waves rolled over her, sapping her strength and dragging her down to darkness. Dismayed by the lethargy sliding through her bones, Josie struggled against the waves of passivity. She banged the hoe again. "Those creatures are as dangerous as a loaded gun. And you know it, Mr. Hayes."

"I never said they weren't…dangerous. But I can't control them."

"You did earlier."

"Yes, well, miracles do occur." His words were ironic and fraught with a meaning she couldn't interpret.

Josie fought the apathy, fought against the rush of sounds and darkness that enervated her. "Then find another way to make a miracle."

"I wish I could." Low and filled with suffering, his drawl wrapped around her, and she felt the beat of his anguish with each beat of her heart. "Believe me, I wish I could."

His words turned to vapor in front of her, a cool mist surrounding him and brushing against her flushed skin as he continued, his words growing fainter with each syllable. "You need to be careful, Josie Birdsong." His image blurred.

"Conrad," she whispered. "Josie Conrad." He knew her middle name. Her mother's name. He couldn't know. But he did. Josie was drowning in cold and darkness and she was terrified, reaching out for his hand. "What's happening?" she moaned and gripped his fingers, their strength solid in the rolling darkness.

And in that moment as her hand curled around his, from somewhere deep in his house, she heard the cry of a child. Sharp, distinct.

And then gone. Silence.

All rational thought vanished with the sound of that child. Josie yanked her hand free and shoved against the door. Down the dark corridor where she sank, she saw a white flutter, a hand, a face. A shape in the dim hallway of the house. *Mellie*. Oh, God. "Mellie," she cried and pushed against the force of Ryder Hayes closing his door in her face. "My daughter's in there! You have my daughter in your house!"

"No!" he muttered. The hard planes of his face contorted, the angles sharp as a knife, the lines around his mouth white and deep with torment. "No one's here. No one."

"Mellie!" she screamed and slapped both fists against the door panels.

His face twisted, and he threw up one hand to shade his eyes, his expression hidden. "For God's sake, go away!"

In that brief glimpse of his expression as he slammed the door, Josie saw the horror in his eyes. She didn't understand it, but she knew with absolute, unshakable certainty that his horror was real.

With the slam of his door, cold and darkness vanished. All around her was heat and silence, thick and heavy against the ice that encased her shaking body.

She heard the metallic click, the rattle of a chain, as he shot the bolt.

Motionless on a current of air, a solitary grackle hung in the pale sky.

The house with its shuttered windows and locked door loomed in front of her. Hostile.

"Mellie," Josie whispered, tears mixing with the dirt on her face.

Bracing his back against the door, Ryder ground his fists against his eyelids and sank to the floor, facing the narrow hallway that led from the front of the house.

He should have stayed away from the woman. Should have stayed away from Josie Conrad. *Birdsong* came the whisper. *Birdsong*.

But he'd been drawn to her by a power stronger than his intelligence, stronger than his will. He'd gone that first night and watched her small, strained face float above candle flames through the darkened rooms of her house.

And he'd returned the next night.

The night after that.

"Damn, damn, damn." Banging his fists against his face, he swore, the stream of curses no relief to the grinding agony inside him.

He should have been able to resist.

But he hadn't.

No, he should never have gone to Josie Conrad's house.

Not that first time when he'd watched her from the woods and seen her pacing hour after hour in the candlelit rooms of her house. And especially not today.

It was growing worse.

Something had happened while she stood in the doorway. She'd seen something. She believed she'd seen a child.

He groaned, a raw, animal sound of pain.

He was losing control.

Rising in one jerky motion, Ryder stood and turned around, facing the direction she'd taken. Through one of the louvers in the small window next to the door, he watched her slender figure as she vanished down the path. Her moss green eyes had been unbearably sad. Lost. Underneath her reckless courage, she'd been lost.

As he watched, a long braid of shiny black hair swung like a metronome against the pink of her blouse. The end curl of the braid hung like a comma past the waistband of her baggy shorts. A strip of smooth, tanned skin showed above the waistband and pink blouse edge.

He wanted to run the back of his finger along that small strip of satin skin, wanted to touch his tongue to the tiny dimple at the back of her knee and see if it truly tasted of honey and flowers. He wanted— God in heaven, he *wanted*—

The wooden louver cracked between his fingers, the sound like a gunshot.

A bead of blood appeared along the side of his palm as he stared down the empty driveway. Ryder leaned his forehead against the shattered strip, pressing hard, reminding himself.

He had to stay away from Josie Conrad. He would make himself leave her alone.

If he could.

Like an echo to the tattoo beat of his heart came that whispering thread of sound.

Birdsong. Birdsong.

CHAPTER TWO

Josie never knew how she returned home. She knew only that she was there, the desperate green line of her garden an oasis in the brown of dead and dying grass. She couldn't remember walking back down the path at all.

But she remembered very, very clearly the sound of the bolt slamming shut against her. Remembered, too, the suffering in Ryder Hayes's face, the sense of power that came from him and pulled her beyond resistance. Step by step, she tried to analyze what had happened and couldn't, no matter how hard she tried. She struggled to make sense from an incident that made no sense. She'd been frightened. Oh, yes, Ryder Hayes had definitely frightened her.

But not until that darkness had come from him, a cold, chilling shadow that swept over her like huge, enveloping wings.

And in those moments she'd heard a child's cry. She'd glimpsed, vaguely, indistinctly, a hazy shape drifting away from her down the long hallway.

Or had she?

Putting her hoe back on the porch, she frowned. She must have been in shock over the incident with the dogs. Or dizzy with hunger. Low blood sugar could account for that enveloping darkness that had claimed her.

Odd, but it had seemed like a *claiming*. A moment utterly beyond her experience.

Remembering the texture of Ryder Hayes's arm against her hand, she shivered. The hard muscle of his forearm had flexed, tightened at her touch.

But his skin had been so cold.

She'd had the most surprising urge to rub her hand over his arm, to warm him.

In the closet she'd turned into a bathroom, Josie splashed tepid faucet water against her face as she tried to recall if she'd eaten that day and couldn't remember eating anything since the bowl of cereal the evening before.

The water spotted the white sink, sending iridescent reflections against the white, the shimmering drops like the flash of colors in the black feathers of the grackles.

Josie stared at her startled eyes in the spotted mirror above the sink and then passed her wet hand over the image in the mirror. Water splintered across her reflection. For a second she'd seen Mellie there, Mellie who lifted herself up to the mirror to see if she was "bootiful" today.

Memories. The unending heat.

Sighing, Josie pressed her palms to her burning eyes. Maybe she was fooling herself. Maybe she wasn't coping as well as she thought she was. She'd been in the sun all morning and then stormed along the path in the heat of high noon. Heat could make a person do strange things. Imagine things.

Her fingers rested against her closed eyes.

She hadn't seen the colony of birds on her return. It was as if the curious massing of birds had been a dream.

They had been real, though.

The slow pursuit of the birds had been as real as the feral dogs. But like her conviction that the dogs were watching her with an evil intelligence, her panicked flight from the birds made no sense to her, either.

She wasn't a woman given to wild imaginings. She'd coped with the reality of blood and bones in the operating room and dealt with prima donna orthopedic surgeons. She was faced with reality every moment of her life. She *liked* reality.

Or she had until the reality of Mellie's disappearance and what it meant.

Had she heard a child's voice, though? Really? Had she actually seen a small form in that chilled, silent hallway?

Yes?

No?

But something had happened.

Cooling her feverish skin, Josie slicked water down her arms. She couldn't begin doubting her own perceptions. She was a trained observer in the operating room, competent in emergencies. Grounded. As she'd told Hayes, she wasn't a woman given to hysterical imaginings.

Before he'd strolled out of her life and Mellie's with a charmingly regretful smile on his face, Bart had always mockingly teased her about her sense of responsibility, but she'd sensed the knife-edge of truth in his teasing, the stab of hostility behind the charm.

"No imagination, no sense of fun, Josie," he'd said, shrugging. "How can I be tied down to a woman who lives by schedules and lists all the time? I'm a restless kind of guy, Josie," he'd said, throwing his duffel bag over one very broad, very restless shoulder, "and you're, well, doll, you're so predictable. And I like spontaneity, know what I mean, sugarbabe?"

Oh, yes, she knew. But *someone* had to worry about schedules and bills, and babies needed order, routine, and—

Josie breathed deeply, stopping the bitterness welling inside. No, she wasn't a woman given to fancies.

She could've been mistaken about—

Flipping water at her throat, she paused and considered possibilities. It made more sense to her that thrown off-balance by the power of Ryder's presence, she probably had seen nothing more than the flutter of a curtain in the shutter-induced twilight of that house, the yowl of a cat becoming a childish cry, the product of her own need.

But with one more child missing, she had to tell Jeb Stoner what she'd seen, no matter how flimsy the evidence. He was the detective investigating the disappearance and deaths of the children. He was the one who'd taken all the information about Mellie. He should know. It was his call.

The police could add Ryder Hayes to their list of suspects. They could search his house. If they found nothing…

She let her face dry in the air, welcoming the illusion of coolness as she scooped out the water from the sink into a can. She would pour the water on her garden tomorrow at daybreak.

Sooner or later, someone would slip up. She would find out what had happened to Mellie.

That was the day she lived for now. That fierce determination to look into the face of the person—

Josie smacked her hand against the sink.

No, she hadn't seen her daughter in that long, shadowy hallway. She'd given up hope that Mellie was out there, somewhere, desperate and frightened.

Now, all she hoped for was that someday she would *know*.

The drought would end.

The killings would end.

She would find out what had happened to Mellie.

In the meantime, she put out raisins for the mockingbirds that sang at night and pans of water for the drought-stricken animals that staggered and crawled to her yard.

While she endured the slow passage of heat-heavy days, she planted seeds in her scrap of garden, saving water to dribble on the parched earth that rolled up around the drops of water and coated them with dust.

And, always, she waited.

But a child was missing again.

The shrill ringing of the phone shattered her thoughts.

She went into her kitchen. "Hello?"

Humming silence. "Who is it? Hello? Who's there?" she repeated, her heart speeding up a little. A click. Static. Josie replaced the mouthpiece of her squatty black rotary phone, the old-fashioned relic of a phone Bart had hated, gently onto the base. A bad connection. A storm some-where buzzing along the electrical wires.

She always hoped, somehow, though, that the phone would ring and it would be Mellie.

Facing the woods in back of her house, Josie lifted the phone again and dialed the number of the police station. The line was clear.

Five years he'd been gone, and she hadn't missed him, not after the first year, anyway, and then only because she wanted him there for Mellie, for Mellie to have a father's hand to cling to as she took her first step. Josie couldn't help the sliver of resentment over the intrusion of those old memories into her chaotic thoughts today. One more thing that made no sense, she thought as she waited for someone to pick up the receiver at the other end.

Something moved in the woods.

Holding the phone, Josie leaned forward, straining. Only a wisp of cloud passing over the sun.

No one there.

Ryder Hayes. That was why she was remembering Bart. Two very different men, but in those few moments with Ryder, she had been edgily aware of him. Uncomfortable, but caught in the spell of that disturbing, heated awareness, she'd been at a pitch of awareness she'd never experienced.

She bent down to pick up a white dust ball.

The voice rasped in her ear. "Stoner here. Whaddaya want?"

"Josie Conrad here, Detective," she mocked. "And what I want is to see you. Today, please."

Listening to the faint drone that translated into words, into meaning, she waited. "I know, but— It's about my neighbor, Ryder Hayes. Please," she said, her voice rising and sinking in the late-afternoon quiet. She twined the cord in large loops around her elbow and hand as she listened. "All right. If you can't, you can't. Tomorrow afternoon will have to do.'' Carefully she placed the dumbbell-shaped receiver back on its hooks.

Tomorrow.

But there was another night to endure.

Just before supper, the phone rang.

Again the click and then staticky squawks.

''Hello?'' Josie said irritably, thinking she heard someone say her name. ''Hello? I can't hear you. Can you speak louder, please. We have a bad connection.''

The static grew louder, hurting her ears until she dropped the phone. She'd been getting a lot of interference on her phone line lately.

Maybe she needed a new phone.

When the long summer twilight ended, plunging the earth into dark, she lit the candles and opened a can of tuna, breaking it up into chunks with her fork as she chopped up celery and stirred in yogurt. Sitting down at her empty kitchen table, she made herself eat, but she turned on the television.

Under the intensity of the surge-dimming studio lights, the weatherman wore rolled-up sleeves, a gleam of sweat and an apologetic smile as he slogged manfully through the news that one more hundred-degree day had made it into the record books.

''Sorry, folks, looks like there's no rain in the forecast for this week. We've had reports of brush fires in some outlying areas, so keep an eye open for smoke, hear now?'' he admonished as he concluded and turned to the anchor.

''Joel, thanks for that report!'' The brunette with the stiffly sprayed hair beamed at him. The tiny line of perspiration along her upper lip caught the light as she spoke. ''But at least it will be another record day for the beaches, right?''

Joel nodded as the camera closed in on his sweating face.

''It's been an interesting weather year, hasn't it? The January freeze and now this drought?'' The anchor's expression was professionally concerned, her eyes drifting to an offscreen TelePrompTer.

"None of our computer projections suggested this kind of summer, that's for sure, Janet." Joel patted his shining face. "And, no, we don't have an explanation for it. Not yet. Maybe it's a sign that the world is ending." His laugh was too hearty. "No, but really, folks, we think it's probably related to the volcano eruption or to those huge gamma ray explosions reported by the NASA observatory and—"

"Fascinating, Joel! I know our listeners will stay tuned for more background." The anchorwoman's chuckle was feeble. Joel had had too much airtime. Her voice dropped to a really, really serious register as she interrupted, "On to local news, Joel. Young Eric Ames is still missing. The search has been expanded to Manatee and Sarasota Counties—"

Josie got up and silenced the perky voice with a flick of her wrist.

Later, she lit the candles lined up along the screened-in porch one by one, a ceremony of remembrance and sorrow, their light a token in all the darkness.

Once, sometime after midnight, an animal shrieked, caught by unseen talons. For an unsettling instant, she had the fancy that she could hear the frantic beating of that distant small heart, feel its fear pumping through her veins.

Standing and pacing on her porch, back and forth, back and forth through the night, she watched the candles and their flickering reflections in the panes of the open windows, until the last candle sputtered out, leaving her alone in darkness.

In the teasing cruelty of the cool that came shortly before dawn, she had the dream again.

Even dreaming, she knew she slept, knew she wandered in some limbo of the soul.

And in her dream she heard the ringing of the phone and knew if she answered it she would hear Mellie's voice.

* * *

"Mommy!" Ahead of her, Mellie danced from one foot to the other. "Hurryhurryhurry! You'll be too late, Mommy!" Her short, sturdy legs were covered with bits of moss and leaves. Behind her and to her right, a tall shape hovered, its edges blurred and unrecognizable at first. Twisting on her bed, Josie moaned. This time, she recognized the form.

Ryder Hayes, stalking through her dreams, his face turned away from her, only his lean shape betraying him.

"Mommy!" Impatiently, Mellie waved Josie to her. The bangle bracelet, nothing but imitation gold, glittered with her movement. "Now, Mommy. Now!" She stamped one yellow-sneakered foot on the ground and turned to run.

The shape drifted with Mellie, tracking her.

Hayes? Or someone else?

Her blood quickening, Josie twisted in her sleep.

"Mellie, wait!" she called out. From the corner of her eye, Josie saw the shadowy figure stalking beside her now, moving with the easy fluidity with which Ryder Hayes had disappeared into the woods, and she wanted to turn and *look*, really look, see if its eyes were the haunted dark of Ryder Hayes's, so that, waking, she would *know*.

But Mellie was vanishing ahead of her and Josie couldn't take time to linger. She couldn't lose sight of her daughter. If she did— "Wait for me, sweetie!" she called. Changing, swelling to an enormous shadow, the form brushed against her, closed her in its darkness as she screamed, "Mellie!"

She knew she screamed. Her throat was raw with the effort. But the words never came out. Strangled in her throat, they woke her every time. "Wait," she whispered now, the early-morning sunlight a pallid yellow that hinted of the heat to come.

The phone was still ringing.

With a shaking hand, Josie reached for it.

She expected static.

''Mrs. Conrad?'' Low, the voice slid over her skin like the tickle of a feather.

She thought he hesitated momentarily over her name. ''Yes, Mr. Hayes?''

''You shouldn't go to the police.''

''What?'' she whispered, stricken.

''Don't go to the police with your story about what you think you saw in my house. You'll look foolish if you do. Your daughter's not here. As far as I know, I've never seen her.''

Josie couldn't speak.

''Nor are those dogs my pets. Don't make a fool of yourself, Mrs. Conrad. Take my advice.''

The click as he hung up sounded like a threat.

Leaning her head on her hands, Josie sat at the edge of her bed.

He'd known she was going to the police.

He'd told her she would make a fool of herself if she did.

She pulled on clean shorts and a long T-shirt that she clipped into a wad on one side. Purple, orange and red, the ring made the shape of an exotic flower when she pulled the fabric through it. A gift, too, from Mellie.

Josie didn't like feeling threatened by Ryder Hayes.

Would Stoner have called Hayes? Would Stoner have had any reason to warn Ryder Hayes? Complications. Puzzles within a puzzle, but she hadn't changed her mind about talking with Stoner.

As she poured a glass of milk and snagged the piece of toast that popped up, she heard the heavy thump of the weekend paper landing at her front step. Carrying the milk in one hand, she walked barefoot over the wood floor to the front door. She would read the comics, the sports pages, the editorial.

She couldn't read the front-page headlines anymore.

Opening the inside front door, she reached for the latch on the screen door.

Even without his implied threat, Ryder Hayes made her uneasy in ways she couldn't identify.

He had been in her dream, an unsettling darkness moving through the mist toward her. He'd become the haunting shape in her dream. The figure was always there, just out of sight, and each time she had the dream, she was left frustrated, feeling that if she could only once remember to turn and look straight at that shadowy shape, she would know—

She flicked the latch up as she glanced down at her stoop.

Through the glare of sunlight coming through the mesh of the screen, she saw the rattlesnake coiled on top of the thick mat made by the folded-over newspaper.

Stretching toward her and following the movement of her arm behind the screen, its head was flat and triangular. The ropy body was thicker than her arm, its diamond shapes iridescent in the sun. Underneath those gleaming coils, showing in patches, the headline caught and held her gaze. Her eyes fixed on the words and she read them in a blink as the snake's body thrust forward: 'Angel Bay Child Remains Missing.'

With both hands, Josie slammed the wooden door. Glass shattered on the floor, and milk splashed up her legs.

The force of the snake's strike thudded against the screen, his fangs breaking through it, catching on it, scraping the inside door. Trapped high off the ground in the mesh of the screen, his heavy body thrashed against screen and wooden door.

Covering her mouth with a shaking hand, Josie stretched out a leg and dragged a chair to her, bracing it under the doorknob. Shuddering, she snapped the lock and retreated to her kitchen, gagging as the rattlesnake battered at her door, its thrashing smacks shaking the doorframe.

She sank into an aluminum-and-plastic chair at the table.

The door shuddered with the heaviness of the snake's body smashing into it. She couldn't think what to do.

A plan. She needed a plan. She couldn't deal with that reptilian body only a cheap wooden door away. She couldn't cope with it. Not now. Not with her dream waking her with its sense of evil pervading her world, not with Ryder Hayes's phone call.

No, she couldn't face that enormous creature thumping with intent against her house.

On the other side of her front door, the snake's body made a hissing sound as screen and wood slid against one another with the heavy flailing.

Pulling her feet up beneath her, Josie locked her arms around her knees. "Enough, oh, please, enough," she moaned, rocking back and forth, the clunking sound of aluminum against her floor riding under the agitated whacks of the snake's body. "I can't do this. I can't." She gagged, dry mouthed, nausea growing with each bump and whack against the door.

But of course she could, and so she stayed curled into herself for long moments, gathering her strength, preparing one more time to do what she had to do. Reaching deep into herself she disciplined herself to ignore the nausea and weakness dissolving her bones.

Finally, unlocking her arms, she stood up and went to get her knee-high boots, thick leather gloves and hoe.

If she'd had a gun, she would have used it.

But she didn't. She had the sharpened hoe, and, tears streaming down her face, she used it finally, after long minutes of walking from side to side, nerving herself to approach the thrashing snake, not recognizing herself in the woman who, screaming and cursing, slashed and sliced at the reptile until the huge body lay in pieces, separated from the head hooked into the screen.

Tasting bile, Josie got a bucket and scooped up the remains of the snake. She had to use the hoe to knock the head off, ripping the mesh as she gouged at it. Gagging again, she looped the hoe edge under the curved fangs and lifted the head into the bucket. Sliding the metal end of the hoe under the metal handle of the bucket, she carried it to the steel garbage can at the back of her lot. Metal hoe clicked against bucket handle, clicked with each shaking step she took.

She left the bucket beside the garbage can. She'd done as much as she was able to for the moment. She slipped the hoe free, and the bucket tilted, wobbled. Nausea rolled up as she saw the bloodied heap mixed with chunks of newsprint.

She ran. Dropping the hoe, she ran for her garden, but she didn't make it. Three feet away, she doubled over, retching, the harsh sounds tearing through her until she was spent and empty.

But she stayed upright.

Later she would remember that she wasn't driven to her knees.

She coped.

Reminding herself of that truth over and over, she summoned the strength to retrieve her abandoned hoe, to hook up the hose to the outside spigot and waste precious water flooding down the concrete stoop and screen door until no trace of the snake's presence remained except the gaping mesh flaps hanging like pennants from the edge of the screen door.

She felt as if the snake had exuded evil, its poisonous molecules oozing from it to her, lodging in her clothes, her hair. If she could have, she would have stripped naked and bathed outside.

Instead, methodically, systematically, squandering water with a vengeance, she sprayed herself with the hose first and then went inside, cleaned up and changed into a cotton dress. Keeping out the clip that had been Mellie's present,

she first washed it and then threw her shorts and shirt into
a garbage bag.

Her hands never stopped shaking.

Bart would have been surprised.

Shuddering, she knotted the bag with one vicious twist
and dropped it into the trash. She wasn't overreacting one
little bit, she told herself firmly and marched out her front
door.

A tiny clink as the toe of her shoe nudged a small cylinder wedged into the crack between two of the walkway
bricks.

The red-pepper capsule.

Stooping, she picked it up. Drops of water glistened
against its shiny surface. The force of the water from the
hose had forced it into the space where two bricks hadn't
quite met.

It must have been on her stoop. Under her newspaper.
With the rattlesnake on top? She recalled distinctly the clattering sound the cylinder had made as it rolled off the edge
of Hayes's porch.

Driving into Angel Bay over the bridge that crossed Angel River, she could see the roof of Ryder Hayes's house
to the north.

At the Hayes property, the river swung in before taking
a wide curve out toward the gulf and the bridge from the
mainland to the offshore islands.

Devil's Island was visible from the Hayes property, then
Santa Ana and finally Madre Mia, which, over the years,
had become Madder Me for Angel Bay natives.

He had come to her house this morning, and she hadn't
heard him.

She'd heard the newspaper delivery boy.

But not Ryder Hayes.

Every self-serve newspaper stand she passed on the way
to the police station had black headlines that leapt out at
her, and she kept her eyes fixed straight ahead. Just before

she walked up the steps into the station, she felt a tickle of awareness at the back of her neck, and, frowning she stopped and turned to look behind her.

A shadow vanished behind the corner of the dry cleaners.

An effect of the hazy heat?

Or someone hiding from her? Ryder Hayes?

The deep tolling of the bell from the Baptist church down near the river rang out, the sound long and sonorous, throbbing in the air around her.

She squinted toward the corner and saw nothing except the blaze of sun and the haze of heat rising from the sidewalk.

The door to the police station opened and Jeb Stoner poked his head out.

"Hey, Miz Conrad, come on in out of the heat. I've been watching for you."

"Thanks." Josie cast one quick look at the empty street behind her and followed the sandy-haired detective inside. She wanted to ask him why he'd been waiting for her, but thinking about that uneasy awareness she'd had, she allowed the moment to pass. Maybe she'd ask him later.

Inside he motioned her to his desk, letting her precede him. Like a rag doll, he flopped into a cracked vinyl swivel chair behind his desk. The chair creaked and groaned under his slight weight. "Can I get you some station-house gunk?"

"No. Thank you." She folded her hand over the clasp of her purse hanging from its shoulder strap.

He always offered her coffee, and she never accepted. He never suggested a Coke or a glass of water. Josie wasn't sure whether he didn't remember or whether it was his way of making an awkward joke. Either way, she had grown tired some months ago of the pro forma offer.

"I don't drink coffee."

"Yeah, right." Everything he said to her came out

sounding as if he didn't believe her. It had been that way from the first.

Conveying the impression that he had all the time in the world, he fanned himself with a sheaf of papers as he waited for her to begin. She'd discovered it was one of his techniques. Most people found it hard to sit in silence. She wasn't one, but she had business and she wanted to get on with it, not play head games.

"Detective Stoner, something strange happened yesterday."

He leaned forward and slipped into a cracker drawl. "Miz Conrad, if you only knew, sumpin' strange happens in this town every day." He tapped his fingers on his desk. "We haven't found that boy. Eric." He looked away from her.

"Yes. I know."

"I'm sorry. I know you hope we'll find him alive. We sure as hell want to." Continuing to avoid her gaze, he sighed.

"Detective—" she paused, not quite sure how to say what she wanted to "—Ryder Hayes is a sort of neighbor of mine."

"What kind of neighbor is that? A 'sort of' one?" The chair creaked and squeaked. "Do you know him?"

"No. I met him yesterday for the first time." She lifted the flap of her purse and her fingers brushed the edge of the capsaicin cylinder. "Look, I think I heard a child in his house. Crying." She stared at the floor, at the black pattern of scuff marks against the linoleum, the coffee stains on the side of Stoner's desk. "I know it sounds unbelievable, but…"

There was a long pause.

"And when would that have been, Miz Conrad?" he asked gently. He picked up a pen, put it down carefully. "Yesterday?"

"Yes," she said slowly, puzzled.

"You were pis—ticked off with him, weren't you? About the dogs you thought were his?"

"What?" Josie spoke very carefully, not ready to uncork her temper but well and truly pis—ticked off now. "What are you talking about?"

"Um," he said, stretching out his short legs and watching her from half-closed eyes. He was a man who sat tall and stood short, a disproportionately long torso giving the illusion that he was taller than his five foot nine. As he pivoted under his desk, his feet brushed against the sides of her shoes. Josie tucked her toes under the rung of the metal folding chair as he pa-dum-dumped in a negligent rhythm on the arms of his chair. "Well, it's like this, Miz Conrad. Hayes came in earlier today."

"What?" Josie's fingers tightened on her purse.

That was why Stoner had been watching for her, to "handle" her with official soothing.

"He said we might expect a call from you. He wanted to touch base with us first."

"He's been a busy man, Detective." The red-pepper spray at her house. The visit to the police. Oh, yes, Hayes had been very busy. She wished she knew what else he'd been doing during the long hours of the night after she left his house. She shut her eyes for a moment, collecting herself. "What did he have to say?"

Stoner's voice was pleasant. "He thought you might be...upset, is how I think he put it."

Josie leaned forward and gripped the edge of the scarred desk. Ryder Hayes had been one jump ahead of her. He'd been busily creating a picture of her for the police. A picture she didn't care one damned bit for. "Listen, 'upset' doesn't begin to describe how I felt about his dogs—"

"They're not his dogs, Miz Conrad."

"So *he* says." She stood up, angry with Stoner, with Ryder Hayes, with herself. "But the dogs were on my property. For all I know, they might be responsible for what's happened to the children. They're dangerous. They went toward his house, and I believe they're his. And when I went to his house to—'' she paused, wondering what word was best to use ''—to talk with him about the situation, I think I saw a child crying in the hallway of his house.''

''A child?'' Stoner brushed his hand against the edge of an envelope.

Leaning toward him, both hands flat on the desk on either side of her purse, Josie added, ''You should consider adding him to your list of people to investigate.'' She whirled away, whirled back in anger. ''Why did he come here, anyway? What did he give as his reason for making a Sunday-morning visit to the police station? Don't you think it's a little peculiar? Just a tiny bit suspicious, Detective?'' Josie was so angry she thought her eardrums would burst with the force of her blood pounding in her head.

She wanted to scream at the stolid-looking detective, shake him, make him get up and go immediately to the Hayes house, and yet Stoner sat there rocking and watching her with that bland expression that told her nothing.

''Calm down, Miz Conrad,'' he said, rocking forward and leaning his elbows on the desk.

''Calm down?'' She wanted to screech at him, pull her hair out by the roots. Instead, she controlled her voice.

He motioned toward the chair. ''Yeah. Take it easy and set a spell longer, hear?'' Light blond hair grew thickly along the length of his fair, sun-spotted arms.

Like fur, Josie thought irritably. ''Why should I? You're wasting my time, Detective. And telling me nothing. *Nothing*.''

''Sit down, Miz Conrad.'' The casual tone disappeared. Command deepened his easy, light voice into something else. ''Please.''

Josie recognized an order. She sat.

Stoner templed his fingers, pad to pad. He avoided her

eyes. "I know you think we haven't done enough to find your daughter."

Not answering, Josie sat there, tension pounding in her head. He was right. She didn't believe they'd done everything they could have. If they'd looked harder, spent more hours, searched— She wound her fingers into the braided strap of her purse.

"However," Stoner said, letting his hands fall to the desk, "we've done everything we can. We've sent out APBs, we've distributed pictures to the restaurants along the highway, we've followed up every lead we've been given." His voice was weary. "You know that. You've been in here twice a week, checking."

Josie nodded, her throat spasming against the words threatening to spill forth. She couldn't afford to alienate Stoner. He was her only link to the search for Mellie. Stoner was willing at least to talk with her. Over the months, the other detectives had passed her along to him, tired of her calls and visits. "Yes," she managed to say at last. Clearing her throat, she continued, her voice rising with frustration, "But why won't you follow up on Ryder Hayes? How can you know he's in the clear unless you've searched his house?"

"We searched his house earlier today."

"What?" Josie sank bonelessly against the chair.

Now Stoner looked at her. She thought it was sympathy that darkened his eyes, but astonished by what he'd said, she couldn't tell. "This morning. After he came in and volunteered that you might call or swear out a complaint. He invited us out to search his house."

"But—"

"If he'd had anything to hide, he would have taken care of it before he showed up here, but, Miz Conrad, I swear on my mother's grave, there's been no kid at this house. And there aren't any dogs anywhere around. No sign of dogs on his property. We checked. *Nothing* that would signal that a pack of dogs had been there at all. *No* sign of a kid. There's nothing in that whole blamed house except dust and his magic stuff, a slick kitchen, and one room he sleeps in. We looked. Top to bottom. Everywhere.''

''Everywhere?'' she whispered, stunned. ''What if you'd looked last night?'' She should have insisted that they initiate a search earlier. Why hadn't she?

Because she'd been disoriented by the strange experience in those last moments with him. So bewildered that she'd felt as if her whole world had flipped crazily upside down.

''If we'd looked last night, we might have found indications that animals had been there, that a kid had been on the premises. We might have found something. But we didn't go out there last night.'' He turned his head from side to side and Josie heard a pop of vertebrae. ''Wished to God we had. We didn't, though. One more dead end.'' The thick hair on his wrist sparkled in the sunlight as he reached toward her and she jerked away.

The heavy glass ashtray was too near her elbow. Spraying ashes and matches, it fell to the linoleum floor. ''Sorry,'' she muttered and made no move to clean up the mess.

Neither did Stoner. ''Look, I know you're distraught—''

''No, Detective, I'm not *distraught*. I'm angry. You can't even begin to believe how angry,'' Josie said, clipping her words out. She wasn't about to allow him to label her and dismiss her. She knew how the bureaucratic mind worked. If Stoner could stick a label on her, he would be able to get rid of her more easily. She wanted him to take the memory of her face home with him every night. She wanted him to think about Mellie's small face in the dark of the night. ''I want my daughter found. I don't know anything about Ryder Hayes. But I saw the dogs. They were going to attack me. Maybe he had nothing to do with them, as he says. I don't know. But I'm not so *distraught*—'' she made the word into a blasphemy ''—that I'm losing my grip on reality. I'm the last person in the world who would do that, believe me." She spoke fiercely, willing him to understand. "I'm not going off the deep end. I want my daughter back. But I don't think that's going to happen. So I want to know what happened to her, that's all!"

"We're doing the best we can." Stoner's face was obdurate.

"Right," she said and stood up so abruptly that the chair skidded away. "Fine. Ryder Hayes is as innocent as a newborn babe. He doesn't have a pack of killer dogs hanging out at his house. Splendid. I'll sleep much better tonight, Detective. Thanks." When he grimaced, she knew her irony had been too heavy-handed, but she didn't give a damn. She only wanted out of the stifling atmosphere created by Stoner and his bureaucratic mentality.

She was glad Stoner didn't follow her to the door. She might have said something she would have regretted. She was ready to pick a fight, ready to vent the rage and frustration and grief that pooled in her and grew deeper and stronger by the day.

Outside the station, she blinked in the brilliant sunlight. Everything was glazed with white-hot light and Sunday-morning still. In half an hour, the churches would empty and the streets would be filled.

Head down, she walked to the parking lot. She'd lied to Stoner. She *was* losing her grip. Exhaustion and the constant drain of not knowing about Mellie were taking a bigger toll than she wanted to admit. That, and her refusal to go anywhere, see anyone except the detectives on the case.

She had to organize her life. If she didn't, she'd never make it through whatever was going to happen. She had to keep strong for Mellie's sake.

The car was idling next to hers, a low purring that she didn't even register until she reached into her purse for her car keys, and then she looked over.

The silvery car was backed in so that its driver's side

faced forward. Her car faced the chain links at the edge of the parking lot.

Breaking the glittery silver expanse, a darkened window slid down.

Blinded by the blaze of sunlight in front of her, Josie couldn't see the face inside the shadowed interior. But she recognized the voice and the lazy grace of his movements as he leaned forward, dipping his head.

"May I have a word with you, Josie Conrad? A moment of your time?" Ryder Hayes said politely, the cool smoothness of his words spreading over her suddenly flushed skin like melting ice cream.

CHAPTER THREE

The sidewalks down both sides of the street in front of the parking lot were empty. Heat shimmered over the surfaces.

The concrete seared the soles of Josie's flats.

Washing into the noon heat, the chill from Ryder Hayes's expensive car eddied around her ankles. His house had been cold, too.

She was fenced in between the wire chain in front of the hood of her car and the partially open door on the driver's side of the ghostly silver sports car.

It glittered in the heat.

Josie didn't back away, but her pulse swung wildly for those few seconds as she looked into the car and couldn't see his face.

"A moment of your time, Mrs. Conrad?" he repeated, shifting toward her. "No more than that. A small request it seems to me. Between neighbors, at any rate." His head angled in her direction. His hair absorbed the light, turned the glare into shades of darkness.

Josie could see the square of his chin, the harsh bones of his cheeks.

But not his eyes.

"I don't think so, Mr. Hayes," she answered in the same vein, her voice as exquisitely polite as his, denying the frantic pumping of her heart. She turned her head, looking back toward the police station. Where was Stoner? He'd been Johnny-on-the-spot when she'd arrived. Where was he now?

"You and I need to discuss some things."

She extended her key. "Unfortunately, I'm on my way

home.'' She wanted to inhale the words, take them back, as he shifted again. ''I mean,'' she added, spacing the words, ''that I have errands to do.'' She hoped the words didn't sound as contrived to him as they did to her. She stuck the key into her car door and opened it. ''People are expecting me.''

''Yes, I thought so.'' He shoved his door farther open, completely blocking her. ''That people were expecting you, that is,'' he added, irony shivering along his dark voice.

His exquisite politeness exposed her lie as the pathetic thing she'd feared it was, but doggedly Josie stuck to it. ''Friends who are stopping in for dinner.''

''I'm sure your friends won't mind waiting a few moments. Since I'm sure they're such close friends.'' The smile that curved long furrows into his lean cheeks mocked her. He glanced at the police station. ''You decided to swear out a complaint, after all.''

She edged closer to her car. ''Of course I did,'' she said. ''What did you expect?''

There was a long pause, and then he smiled. ''I expect you're lying, you see.''

She must have blanched because he nodded.

''But you intended to swear out a complaint. If I hadn't already entertained the gentlemen in blue. And in suits. I wasn't sure, but I thought you would, in spite of my call. It seemed the most logical action for you to take. That's why I approached the police first. It seemed...easier. A preemptive strike, if you will. I like to avoid trouble when I can. You should have taken my advice. You would have avoided complications for yourself.''

''I don't know what you mean.'' Her knuckles hurt with the strength of her grip on the car. The edges of her consciousness were darkening, thickening, closing in. She had to get away from him. Josie inhaled slowly, pushing back that terrifying darkness.

She should never have pulled her car in right to the edge

of the chain-link fence. "Would you mind shutting your door, Mr. Hayes? I'd hate to scratch the finish. I'm sure it's expensive."

"Yes, in fact, it is." His teeth flashed in the dim interior. "Very."

No matter how she tried, Josie couldn't see inside his car. Her eyes couldn't adjust quickly enough between the blinding light bouncing up from the concrete and the cool shadows of his car. She examined the side of the police station. In this new building all the windows were shut and sealed against the heat and humidity, thanks to the central air. The old police station had made do with tall windows, taller ceilings and lots of fans.

This was supposed to be an improvement.

Unless you were in the parking lot wondering if anyone would hear you if you screamed.

Josie studied the ground, trying to decide what to do. A chameleon on the raised concrete next to the fence lifted one translucent green leg. She could always hop into her car and back out, ripping his door off in the process.

If she had the chance, she thought as one sneaker-clad foot came into view. She looked up and saw only the edge of dark slacks that tightened across a muscular thigh.

"A penny for your thoughts." A copper coin spun into the air and she looked skyward. The coin gleamed as it tumbled to the ground, clinking as it landed.

"You can't afford them. They're worth more than a penny."

"Of course they are. I should have known." Still in the car and facing her, but with one foot on the concrete not far from her own, he dipped slightly forward in a seated half bow and his long fingers flashed in front of her eyes. A shower of copper pennies whirled and fell around her. One coin bounced off her shoe and rolled on its edge across the concrete. "So, lady green eyes, many pennies for your thoughts."

"You wouldn't be interested," Josie said, staring at the bright copper as it vanished under her car. The coin looked newly minted.

"I assure you I am." A second leg joined the first. His feet were slightly apart, his arm resting casually across the top of his open door, masking his eyes still. "I'm exceedingly interested in your thoughts, you know." And he came out of the car, his lean body moving in one flowing motion.

And this time, she did step back, as far as she could, slam bang into the side of her car. She was better off not seeing his eyes, she realized. She wanted to look away and couldn't. Caught by the dark blaze of their intensity, she stared and tried to swallow, the air growing thin and cold as she fought for breath while the rumble of his car's idling engine became the thrumming pulse in her veins.

As if from a distance, she felt the stir of air as he stepped to the side, heard from afar the soft snick as he closed his car door, his gaze never leaving hers.

She was free.

And still she couldn't look away from the tormented dark eyes of Ryder Hayes. More disturbing, much worse, was her realization that she didn't want to look away. Wanted, instead, to step into that darkness and linger there, offer solace where none was asked for or wanted.

Ryder Hayes wanted something, all right, but it wasn't consolation. Shaking free of the spell, she gasped as air flooded her lungs and she pressed back against the blistering metal of her car.

"What's the matter, Josie Birdsong?" he said, still several feet away from her, although she felt as if he were enveloping her in darkness and cold.

Or heat. Held by the intensity of his dark eyes, she could no longer distinguish between heat and cold. In his presence, ice burned hot.

He took a step forward, stopped, slid his narrow hands

carefully into his pockets as he scowled. "Am I frightening you?"

His question released her. "Yes, Mr. Hayes, you are. And I don't like men who try to push me around, so step back. I want to go home, and you're in my way."

"Is that how it seems? That I'm bullying you?" he asked with only the slightest interest. But he stepped back.

"Yes." Josie slid onto the hot seat of her car and grasped the door handle, ready to slam it at the first opportunity. "Maybe you're even trying to terrorize me. I don't know for sure. I can't quite decide, but, yes, you're definitely bullying me."

He frowned. "Possibly I am. I'm not really sure myself what my intent is." He leaned forward, touching the roof of her car. His arm blocked her exit as surely as had his car door. More so, she realized, since she didn't think she was capable of running her car over his lean body. "What I do know is that I need to talk with you."

"What you need is your business, Mr. Hayes. Not mine. And I don't need or want to talk to you. Especially not right now," Josie said through dry lips. She wasn't frightened anymore. Disturbed, oh yes. But not afraid. At least not when he wasn't holding her captive with his dark gaze. She half turned in her seat. The angle of her view hid his neck and face from her, but her eyes were on a level with the narrow silver buckle of his snakeskin belt. Remembering, she shuddered.

"What's the matter?"

Above the gleam of his leather belt, the dazzling white of his cotton shirt moved back, away from her, and she grabbed the door. His narrow fingers closed around the rim, stopping her. "Let go," she said. "Now."

His fingernails were clean, square cut. "One minute. Sixty seconds. Here. At your house. Or in the police station if it makes you more comfortable. Your choice, but it's important, Josie Birdsong. To both of us." Soft, implacable, his voice made it impossible for her to leave. It held a knowledge that he had no right to. In its way, it was as much of a threat as his hand holding her door, preventing her departure. "Your choice," he repeated. "Not mine, not what I want at all."

Josie didn't understand. He was asking her to meet with him.

"But we have to talk. As soon as possible."

Not responding to his demand, Josie lifted her head. "How do you know my mother's name?" He'd used it earlier, at his house. Even Bart hadn't known.

He shrugged, one powerful shoulder scarcely moving. "Magic."

Her heart stopped. Literally. And then it lurched forward. "Magic?" she whispered. Mellie's word.

Not touching her, he waved his fingers in front of her and a pale pink tea rose appeared. "Illusions, that's all. Nothing more. It's only magic until you know the trick. The gimmick. And everything has a gimmick, Josie Birdsong," he said, his voice taunting her. "Everything has an explanation."

"Nobody knows my mother's maiden name," she said, more jolted by his knowledge than she wanted him to know.

"No?"

"No," she insisted, tearing her gaze away from his and switching on the temperamental ignition of her car. It sputtered and died. "No one in Angel Bay knows. It's never come up. I've never told anyone here, not even the bank. How could you know?"

"Magic, then, I reckon," he drawled, a flavor of grits and redeye gravy turning his smooth voice rough. Before she could stop him, he stuck one long arm in through the open window and turned the key.

The engine purred like a tiger under his touch.

"Magic, Mr. Hayes?" Josie said, not hiding her derision.

"Luck." He shrugged. "Or skill. But everything has an explanation. If you look for it." He ran his flat palm along the frame of the car window. "And that brings us full circle, Mrs. Conrad. When can we meet to talk?"

"I'm not going to meet you. Not here. Not anywhere," she insisted.

"Yes, you will." He bent his knees and his face came into view. There was absolute certainty in his eyes. "You'll see me. And we'll talk. Tonight, probably." He shut her car door very gently and she barely glimpsed the rapid flick of his fingers through the window.

The rose and a handful of copper coins dropped into her lap, a waterfall of pink petals and golden red pennies, and that fast, he was inside his car, his sneaker lifting from the concrete, disappearing into the chilled interior as he pivoted and shut his door.

Josie turned to watch his car. Its silver vanished into the white dazzle of noon heat. She picked up one of the pennies and turned it over. Like the one lying on the parking lot and the one that had rolled under the car, this, too, shone as if newly minted. She examined a second, and a third. A fourth. Curious, she opened her door and peered underneath the car, retrieving the penny there and looking at its date. All were 1962 mints. The year of her birth.

As he'd said, everything had a gimmick.

Tucking the pennies into the space in the armrest, she lifted the rose. Merely touching it released its wild, sweet scent into the car. Its pink petals were warm and supple against her palm, like fingers brushing over her skin, growing warmer as she held them against her.

All the way home, Josie smelled the rose. With no air-conditioning in her car, the heat intensified the fragrance until she couldn't smell anything else.

When she arrived, she took the rose and put it into a clear glass bottle and placed it in her bedroom. Instantly the room filled with its subtle sweetness and she changed her clothes with the scent filling her lungs. The copper coins glowed next to the bottle.

Josie had no intention of talking with Ryder Hayes about anything. She didn't know anything about him. She didn't want to know anything more about him than she already did. What she already knew was disturbing enough.

She touched the rose and one petal curled, drifted to the dresser top.

Could he be involved in the children's murders?

He'd known her mother's name. Somehow he knew about Josie's Seminole background, that she was a remote descendant of Josie Billie, one of the old medicine men, a heritage so distant that Josie rarely thought of it herself. Didn't want to, if she were honest with herself. But that door opening on the past was one of the reasons she'd been so startled when he'd used her maiden name.

"Magic," Ryder Hayes had said.

"The wind," her mother had said when Josie was little. "The wind whispers everything."

Josie pulled on faded shorts and headed outdoors, away from the tender fragrance of Ryder's magic rose.

It might be real, but its hope was an illusion.

Later in the afternoon, the phone rang.

Rushing in from the garden, her hands grimy with dirt, she picked up the phone in time to hear the soft click as someone hung up.

A nuisance, but she couldn't change her number.

Not while there was a hope that Mellie would phone her. No real hope, an illusion she couldn't shatter. Not yet. Sometimes hope was a necessary illusion that kept the heart beating.

In a lingering flare of orange and neon pink, the sun paused at dusk before finally surrendering to a velvet black night.

Ryder had said he would see her at night.

He was wrong. She had no intention of wending her way

to his decaying house. Not in the daylight. Certainly not at nighttime.

By candlelight Josie sat at her kitchen table and lifted a spoonful of mango and yogurt, put it down. The yogurt gleamed faintly in the candle glow.

She wasn't hungry. She didn't want to turn on the television. Didn't want to hear about the missing boy. Eric. "Eric Ames," she whispered fiercely. The child had a name. Eric. She didn't want to sit on her porch.

She wanted—

Something.

Restless, the weight of her loneliness and grief pushing her into aimless motion, Josie prowled like a jungle cat through the four rooms of her house, from rose-scented bedroom to the living room where the lock she'd snapped in the morning was still in its slot. She took a quick shower and turned on a fan to circulate the muggy air as she pulled on thin cotton underpants and a loose cotton blouse over her damp skin, skin that hummed with electricity, as if there were a storm on the horizon. She peered out her window, hoping for a storm. For rain. For an end to her waiting.

The trees in the woods were motionless.

There were no yellow-eyed dogs hiding in the darkness watching her.

No storm in that clear, dark sky.

Only the occasional warble of a mockingbird, the dry croak of a frog carrying from the edge of the river where it curved away from her house.

She found herself in her bedroom, lifting the flower, stroking it across her neck, down to her breasts, over the skin of her wrists.

He'd said he would see her tonight.

Finally, sighing, she went to her porch. As she lit the candles there, she wondered if Ryder had planted a suggestion in her brain that was making her so fidgety.

Maybe he had.

She swept her hair off her face, the heavy weight too much in the heat.

And still her skin hummed, as if answering *something* that whispered to her on a windless night.

When she unlatched the screen door of the porch so that she could take the evening garbage out, she turned on the floodlights all around the house. She went outside toward the garage. She wanted to put the bucket with the snake in the metal garbage can that clamped shut, safe from marauding dogs and raccoons. All day she'd avoided that final cleanup, but she didn't want to wake up in the morning and find pieces of the reptile scattered about her yard.

As she approached the garage, she saw the empty, overturned bucket.

There was no trace of the snake she'd killed, no bits of paper, no trampled bits of earth where a ransacking animal had feasted. Alarmed, Josie paused and looked around, the light hairs on her arm rising with her uneasiness. *Nothing*. It was as if the snake had ever been.

The empty, shiny interior of the bucket gleamed mockingly at her.

She couldn't look away from that empty bucket.

Holding her bag of garbage out, a shield against the sight of that shiny metal, Josie backed away. Halfway to her porch she froze as she caught the minute change in the shades of darkness at the edge of the woods.

Bugs swarmed around the bright porch light, banged against the wide bulbs, clustered there until the swarm grew too thick, and heavy bodies fell to the ground.

And then he came out of the woods toward her.

She gasped and the handle of the garbage bag slipped through her fingers. Keeping his lean form in view, Josie took slow steps away from him, her breath rattling in her ears.

She'd misunderstood. She'd thought he meant she would come to his house. Stupid of her. But she'd had that sensation of being drawn, of being almost hypnotized, and so she'd misunderstood.

On one side of the screen door, her mouth going dry with something beyond fear, she faced him, the hook-and-eye lock nothing more than the illusion of a barrier.

In a glance, Josie took in his appearance. Ruffled, his hair looked as if he'd dragged his hands through it repeatedly. He hadn't shaved since she'd seen him that afternoon, and a faint beard shadowed his pale skin. His jeans rode low on his hips, and his black T-shirt was tucked into the waistband. A silver snap caught the light from the floods and sparkled momentarily as he stopped, one foot on the lowest porch step.

He nodded, as if he, too, felt that humming. "May I come in?"

"No." Josie saw the pinpoints of the candle flames deep in his eyes. "Absolutely not. I'd be crazy to let you in."

"Yes." He nodded. "Right now I'd have to agree with you. You'd be crazy to let me in." He took one step more, his sneakers soundless against the wooden step. That must have been how he'd approached her house this morning, soundlessly leaving the capsaicin and disappearing back into the woods.

"Stop," she said, her voice cracking. "Don't come any farther. I mean it."

"I wasn't going to," he said mildly, and settled down on the steps, his form a shadow flowing over dark water. "I told you. I needed to talk to you. That's all. And you're right to be afraid," he added, tilting his head to look up to her. "It's a frightening world we live in," he said, and his voice sighed away. "I'm afraid, too, Josie Birdsong, if you want to know the truth."

"What do you mean? Why should you be afraid?" Her voice was too tight. Tight with fear and that humming that strung her tight as a violin waiting for the stroke of the bow to make music. "I don't understand you, Ryder Hayes," she said, and realized only as she spoke that she'd called him by his given name.

Some boundary had been crossed.

"I don't understand myself, lady green eyes."

The birds had ceased their music and there was a stillness, a waiting that made Josie's knees tremble. She tugged at the tail of the blouse. "What do you want to tell me?"

"I'm not sure." Ryder watched the futile twitch of her slim fingers against the edge of her blouse. Sitting on the porch below her, he saw the narrow edge of elastic on her panties. Each movement she made sent a faint drift of roses toward him.

Regardless of what he'd said in the police parking lot about meeting her, he'd tried to stay away from Josie Birdsong.

He'd failed. He should have known he would. Her long, tanned legs were behind him. If he leaned back, all the way back, his head would be against her knees. He wanted to rest against her. He shut his eyes. He was so tired he couldn't think straight anymore. That was probably why he hadn't been able to fight the pull that drew him through the woods to her candlelit porch.

Even her legs smelled of tea roses.

He leaned his head against the frame of the screen door.

He thought she'd be less skittish if he weren't looking at her, but her sudden jump as he moved told him that she was as aware of him as he was of her.

And equally reluctant.

He wondered if she'd laugh at him if he told her she terrified him. He didn't dare touch her.

Just being near her, even without touching, the feelings, the images were gathering, and he didn't know what they meant, what was going to happen next. He'd been right. Josie Birdsong held the key.

But unlike her, he hadn't lied. He was afraid.

Because he didn't know what door the key would open.

"I didn't have anything to do with the disappearance of that boy," he said finally, not expecting her to believe him. "No matter what you think."

"All right. Fine. You've told me. Now leave."

"I can't." He'd been right about that, too. There was loneliness in Josie Birdsong Conrad. It lay underneath the breathiness, underneath the determination not to let him frighten her. He admired her courage, admired it while recognizing that her courage might not be enough to save her. "Can't leave, Josie. Not yet."

"Of course you can. It's easy. You just stand up and walk away. Easiest thing in the world." Her voice trembled.

The air around her rippled with her movements. He could feel those minute vibrations against his own skin. Even with his back to her, he knew what she was doing. He didn't have to see her.

"You don't need your hoe, Josie. I'm not going to breach the sanctity of your porch." He shifted so that he could look at her now, could rest in the play of candlelight and shadows on her smooth, tanned skin.

She was a woman of sunlight and earth, rooted in the realities of life.

While he—

"I know you're not. You're going to leave. And then I'm calling the police."

Steel in that magnolia voice. He liked that, too.

"Oh, Josie, if I wanted to, I could have already been in your house any night now for the past two months." He flattened his hand against the screen. It bulged toward her. "You leave your windows open, your locks are a joke and you sit out here on this porch half the night." He shook his head, and the effort to move was almost too much. "Your locks aren't even worth my trouble." He'd mastered locks and tumblers so superior to her pitiful pieces of steel and rusted metal that even if she'd shut her windows and locked them, too, he could have been in her house in the space of a breath.

"You're a locksmith?"

Ryder almost laughed, but the need pouring through him left him without even the energy to smile. He felt as if he were dying of the need to touch her, to feel just once more that satin skin against his fingertips.

He wouldn't, though. He didn't dare. He thought he still had that much control.

But still he lifted his right hand and grasped the scratchy metal door handle. "No," he said. "Not a locksmith. But I could be. Could have been," he corrected himself. Too late now for that kind of life. "I'm an illusionist. I make my living with tricks."

"A magician?" she asked in a thin, high voice.

"No. An illusionist. There's a difference. But possibly only in my mind. At any rate, will you sit down? Please? It tires me to look up at you."

She stiffened, ready to say something scathing, he was sure.

"Besides, the view from where I am is…well, I appreciate it, lady green eyes. I'm not sure you would, though," he concluded and leaned against the thick wooden support of the door. "No, don't go, not yet," he said as she backed up toward her kitchen door. He knew it had a heavier wooden door, cheap stuff, really, like her front door. No real obstacle.

She stopped.

"Josie, come here, I want to show you something."

"I'm fine where I am," she said in a muffled voice. "No, stay there. Outside!" Her voice pitched higher as he rose.

But she needed to understand what was happening, needed to comprehend why he was afraid, and he didn't know how to make it clear to her except by showing her. He'd told her he wouldn't open her screen door. He wouldn't.

But she would.

And so he looked at her, stared deep into her eyes that were the cool, restful gray-green of moss. He saw her eyelids droop, open, droop. "Josie," he whispered, "open the door. Take a step closer and open the door. I won't hurt you. I promise," he whispered, his voice dropping lower and lower until it was only a drift in the air, a touch against her skin, her will.

Just as her movements, her breath, had been against him.

"Another step, Josie, one more. And then unlock your door. Lift the latch, Josie, slowly, sweetheart," he breathed, coaxing in words that weren't words, that he wasn't even sure he spoke aloud, but he knew that she heard.

She lifted the latch and opened the door. Her silky hair swung forward, a curtain over her wide eyes and full mouth as she bent to the latch.

"One more step, Josie. One more," he urged, luring her with sound and whispers onto the porch step, luring her outside her porch.

The screen door whispered shut behind her. She blinked and her eyes lost the dazed, unfocused look they'd had. He'd wanted only to give her a hint of the power that pulled at him, and now she was standing next to him, but he didn't touch her.

He wanted to. Wanted to take that last, small step forward and touch her mouth, wanted to bend his mouth to the curve of her neck and savor the scent of roses that lingered there.

He didn't, though. He reached down inside and dragged up enough control to stay those inches away from her.

"What happened?" Bewildered, she swayed and reached out for his arm.

He stepped back. Too quickly, perhaps, because she jumped and gasped, her eyes growing clearer by the second.

"I asked you to unlatch the door. You did," Ryder told her. He wasn't ready to tell her anything else. "I asked you

to come off your porch. You did.'' He let his voice fall
into a lulling rhythm and watched her swaying slowly. ''I
told you I wouldn't come onto your porch, Josie. I kept my
promise. All right?''

''All right,'' she echoed, but her eyes were enormous,
focused on him. ''You said you wanted to show me something?''

He jammed his hands into his back jeans pockets. ''Josie,
I heard a child crying when you were at my house yester-
day. You heard that sobbing, too. But you saw something.
I want to know what.''

''You heard the child?'' Her face grew luminous, glowed
like the warm candles lined up on her porch, dimmed. ''But
there was no one there. The police searched your house.''

''What did you see, Josie?'' He flexed his fingers, lifted
them free of his pockets. ''Tell me exactly. What did you
see?''

''Nothing.'' Her voice was flat. She was lying again.

''Tell me,'' he insisted. ''I have to know. There was
something there, wasn't there? In back of me?'' The last
of his energy swirled through him, draining away with each
second he stood in front of her.

Ryder hoped she would answer quickly, while he had
control. ''Please, Josie, tell me,'' he said, and touched her,
the tip of his hand brushing against her arm as she stepped
away. There was heat and warmth in the slide of her skin
against his, the texture of her skin like a warm nectarine,
that silky smooth.

And with that skim of his hand against her, she was there
with him in that fast-moving cloud, the images twisting
around him, torturing him. Faces, faces, anguished, blurred.

But her face was distinct, the restful green of her eyes
calling him, and he wrapped his arms around her, holding
on for dear life, for sanity, for his soul's sake. And, touching her, breathing in her scent, he lost control.

The images sharpened, piercing him. Children's faces.

One face, clear, bright, and he could see it while Josie was in his arms. A boy's pug nose. Blue eyes wide and terrified. "Oh, God," Ryder said, praying and swearing, the images ripping him apart. "God in heaven." Or hell.

Sand. Muddy. Blood, a thin red line that turned to black against the sand.

Like a thousand razors raining down, the pain sliced him apart. He couldn't bear the pain tearing at him.

And he couldn't turn Josie loose.

Lost in that darkness with her, he knew somehow that she was his anchor, that she was safety, but he was afraid for her because she felt what he was feeling and didn't understand anything that was happening to them.

And then, as the child screamed, Ryder felt Josie's hand brush against his forehead, felt her touching him, willingly, even as she, too, heard the terrible cry.

Her fingers were warm against his forehead as she brushed his hair back, warm in the zero cold of his agony even while she trembled against him.

Her touch centered him, kept him from disappearing into that wild, whirling darkness.

But her touch had focused those images. Sharpened them into crystal pieces of pain that sliced through her, too. And while he sought rest in her green eyes, peace in her sturdy refusal to bend under the weight of her loss, he'd brought his darkness to her.

He'd thought to protect her, to find out the truth of what hovered around them, but he'd endangered her.

With the last remnant of strength he had, Ryder shoved her away, breaking contact.

She was shaking so hard that he wanted to reach out and steady her, wanted to kiss her pale mouth into pinkness, but he moved backward, away from her, putting space between them, giving her a chance.

Josie felt Ryder push her away, felt the distance grow

immense between them, and came rushing back from the terrifying darkness he'd taken her to.

"What's happening?" she moaned, wrapping her arms around herself. "Please, tell me. What's going on?"

"I don't know," Ryder said, his voice filled with agony as he kept moving backward, away from her until he was swallowed up by the darkness of the woods.

Even though not a leaf moved, Josie felt as if she were in the center of a hot, roaring wind that blew against her, shoving her back to her porch.

CHAPTER FOUR

Ryder watched the cards in the mirror turn smoothly through his fingers. He palmed the six and regarded the mirror closely as the queen of hearts slid behind the three of diamonds, flipped, turned, and then, all so fast that he would have missed it if he hadn't been doing the trick himself, the queen slid in front of the king of hearts, right where he needed her for the finale of the trick.

Control. It all depended on his control. The tricks always had...control.

Slipping five cards out of the deck, he made one vanish with a wave as he picked up a second card, making it vanish and continuing until five cards had disappeared, leaving only his face staring back at him from the mirror. Then, his right hand rising and moving, the cards flashed in sight, one by one.

He frowned. He was too slow on the back palm.

Laying the cards in a circle, he flexed his fingers.

Josie Birdsong's hands were short, square, their competence witnessed by the garden she tended like a shrine.

Even now, hours later, he still felt the imprint of her small hand across his forehead like a brand.

Picking up the pack of cards, he worked them quickly, riffling the pieces, shuffling them overhand and finishing with a dovetail shuffle as he watched the mirror.

The lights of the rotating silver-ball chandelier sparkled on the shiny silver cards. In the depths of the mirror behind his reflection, the tiny specks of light glowed white and red and blue, flashing and twirling as his fingers manipulated the cards.

He shut his eyes, letting the pads of his fingers move

swiftly over the cards, concentrating on the rhythm, the count, the touch of the cards.

Her skin had been as slippery smooth as the cards turning and moving through his agile fingers. Lust, ugly in its nakedness, had pounded in his blood as he'd touched her. With that brief touch, he'd wanted her enough to take her right there on her candlelit porch, satisfy that rush.

But there had been the visions.

The images of the blood in the sand. The glimpse of a child's face coming into view as he'd held Josie close, her body soft, warm against the coldness that never seemed to leave him.

Over everything, driving him to her in spite of the images swirling around them, had come that sharp sting of sex, hot and needy.

In the grip of that sweetest drug, he'd forgotten all the reasons not to touch her, forgotten everything except the need to draw her closer, to fill the emptiness in his soul with her scent, with her.

There had been a poignant, aching hunger, too, a hunger that went beyond the barb of sex. The hunger surprised him. It had been so long since he'd experienced tenderness toward anything. Even now as he played with the cards, the remembered sweetness of that hunger seemed alien.

His, hers, he couldn't remember, but the hunger had its own kind of pain.

Caught between the rush of desire and the torment of the visions, he'd clung to her, his pulse beating thick and urgent in his groin, life pounding in him while the images of butchery behind his eyelids melted, merged, became one horrifying sight that faded with the brush of her hand across his forehead.

He opened his eyes and looked down at the card he held.

The ace of spades.

Death.

He'd meant to turn up the queen of hearts.

Fanning the cards across the mat on top of the folding table positioned in front of the mirror, he looked for his mistake.

He'd broken his focus and screwed up.

Control.

Shutting his eyes again, he brushed his fingers across the edges of the cards, letting the sensitized tips of his fingers speak to him, show him the card. He slowed his breathing and timed the pass of his hands over the cards.

Speed and dexterity were everything. Sleight of hand was harder than the illusions. With the illusions, once you knew the gimmick, the process, you worked on the presentation.

He had to practice all the time for the tricks requiring sleight of hand for their illusion.

Flying over the cards, his index finger stopped at one as he registered the subtle difference. Memory. Dexterity.

Control.

Yes, there it was.

He opened his eyes and looked at the gaudy red and gold of the green-eyed queen of hearts.

Josie's gray-green eyes held too much pain and loss for one woman to endure.

But he couldn't help her. He was the wrong man at the wrong time. He would only hurt her.

Stupid to think he could get away with going anywhere near her in the first place. He still couldn't explain what had pulled him to her cabin night after night even before she'd come pounding at his door. Stupid, hell, *dangerous*. To both of them.

He'd have to keep reminding himself of that fact. He would destroy her. Or himself.

He was no longer sure whether he cared what happened to himself, but he didn't want any more deaths on his hands.

With a flourish, he twirled the card through his fingers and presented it to the mirror, bowing to his grim-faced reflection. "And there you are at last, queen of my heart, love of my life. Found you, you clever little tease."

He slid the card into the pack, and then, folding the cards together first, he spun them into the air where they rounded the top of the mirror before coming back to tumble into the crystal case he held with in one hand.

As he lifted his arms up, flinging them wide, the box became a scarlet-and-gold origami bird that once more changed, this time into a white dove that fluttered and settled on the rim of the mirror.

He scowled as he saw that he was still too slow in this part, the lack of practice clear to him in the slight hesitation that would reveal the trick—

He arced the last card in a furious throw. The card clinked against the chandelier, sending it spangling and whirling in a kaleidoscope of rainbows.

The dove cooed.

"So, babe, was it good for you?" Annoyed with his clumsiness, he leered at the dove, his mouth in a sardonic twist.

Betsy lifted a wing and tucked her head under it, preening.

"Well, babe, it wasn't good enough for me. Not by a long shot. I messed it up big-time." Ryder turned away, pacing to the shuttered window and back, jamming his hands into his pockets and swearing in a long stream.

He was so cold, but a thin line of sweat ran down his spine. Lately he was cold all the time.

He couldn't stand the look of his face in the mirror any longer, couldn't stand watching the endless repetitions of cards flashing before him. Most of all, he couldn't stand the look in his eyes. The fear that shifted in and out of focus even as he watched.

The man he saw in the mirror couldn't begin to think about appearing on a stage anywhere, not even in front of a bunch of kids, much less an audience filled with paying customers.

He disgusted himself.

Holding his hands straight out, Ryder watched their faint tremble as he picked up the cards again and faced the unforgiving audience of the mirror.

In its depths, a tiger's eyes glowed hot yellow at him over the thick coils of a rattlesnake. He thought he heard the deep-throated roar of the white tiger, the dry rattle of the snake.

With the twitch of his hands, the cards snapped, flew helter-skelter around him and clattered in a silver rain to the bare floor.

Illusions.

Magic.

He'd said everything was a trick.

What if he was wrong?

Standing on the corner of Church and Palmetto, Josie was trapped behind the crush of people waiting for the rest of the circus parade to pass. Coming out of the library, she'd been caught in the press of bodies pushing closer to the street. A tall back cut off her view of the calliope wagon, but its raucous music carried over the applause and squeals of the children lining the street.

One little girl hunkered down at the edge of the near curb, her feet right at the edge, her whole body quivering. The seat of her purple-and-white-checked playsuit bounced, settled, bounced as the calliope and caravan of elephants came around the corner.

Clumped on top of her head with a rubber band, her straight brown hair hung in a skinny, limp ponytail above her freckled neck. She was Mellie's age, had ridden the school bus with Mellie.

Josie looked away.

Such a fragile neck, a small thing. Vulnerable enough to break your heart.

Clutching her purse to her breasts, its strap falling toward the ground, she refused to allow herself the luxury of thinking about vulnerability and heartbreak.

The man blocking her view turned and moved to the left, his powerful body throwing a long silhouette over the freckle-faced girl. His work boot trod on Josie's toes.

"Oof." She dropped her purse and bent to pick it up.

"Sorry, Miz Conrad. Didn't see you standing there." Ned Dugan dipped his bearded chin toward Josie as he reached for her purse with one thick arm. His thick fingers wrapped around the leather strap, he asked, "How you doing?" His voice dropped, became more private, taking on a secretive tone as he patted her shoulder. "Things been going okay for you, out there all by yourself?"

"Yes." Reaching for the strap, Josie tugged her purse free.

Ned had been Mellie's Sunday-school teacher for the last two years. "I know it's been real tough for you these last months. We sure miss Mellie."

"I'm fine, Ned. You're very kind. Thank you." Tension coiled in her stomach. She didn't want to talk about missing Mellie. She didn't want Ned Dugan patronizing her with his concern.

He bent lower, cupping his hand around Josie's shoulder. She stepped back.

And felt foolish as his forehead wrinkled in bewilderment.

Ned was Ned. A toucher. A comforter. He took his religion seriously. Today, though, he seemed too earnest to her, too solicitous. Had his concern always been so intense? Or was she becoming irritable with everyone? Whichever it was, he was making her uncomfortable. She didn't want him touching her.

Shaking her head free of the antipathy springing up inside her, Josie dug deep for the fast-disappearing strands of civility and made herself smile. "Tell Lettie hello for me."

"I sure will." He hesitated and then ran his hand through his beard, tugging at the springy light brown hairs. "She'd love to see you sometime." The curls wrapped around his fingers, moving with a life of their own, like a nest of small, twining snakes.

"Yes, well, one of these days."

Ned was a good man.

Everybody said so.

Still, Josie couldn't help her involuntary withdrawal.

He'd been the first one to visit her after Mellie's disappearance.

He'd stayed too long, his tenor voice rising and sinking, rising until she thought she'd scream when all she'd wanted was to be alone to think and grieve, to let silence enter her and give her the peace his droning voice denied her, a peace she had yet to discover.

"Miz Conrad, you give me a call now, hear? Like I told you before, if there's anything Lettie and I can do, you let us know. You can count on us. Anytime, understand?" A fleck of spittle dried at the corner of his mouth.

"Yes, Ned, I sure do. I'll call if I need anything. Immediately. I will." Josie found herself nodding her head so vigorously that her braid whipped around her, threatening to fly up and slap her in the face if she didn't stop bobbing her head like one of those dogs on car dashboards. Anything to speed him on his way. Unable to stop, she found herself bobbing her head again, manufacturing an enthusiasm embarrassing in its phoniness. "Don't let me keep you," she added, using her elbows to work her way to the right, away from him, as he still seemed reluctant to turn around and leave her. "Bye, Ned," Josie said brightly, and seized the opportunity to slip through a momentary opening made as a teenage girl plastered herself against the frame of the earring-studded, too-cool adolescent male with the half shaved, half ponytailed hairdo.

"Sorry," she muttered in her turn as she bumped the cuddling twosome into an incendiary position.

"No problem, ma'am" came the boy's deep voice, and his studied indifference didn't quite conceal his delight.

The girl giggled. "Jimmy *Joe,* stop that! Right this moment. Or I'll tell your mama on you!"

"Go right ahead, darlin', 'cause I'm *not* gonna tell your mama on you," Jimmy Joe groused, his voice cracking this side of manhood.

Josie tried to work her way down the curb line, but she was stuck, the crowd shrieking as the horses came into view, their plumed heads held high, the spangled and glittering bridles winking and sparkling in the sun.

Uneasy, feeling as if someone were watching her, she looked over her shoulder.

She'd forgotten about the parade when she'd decided to see if she could find any information in the library about Ryder Hayes. Like a magnet, the thought had slammed into her brain and stuck there, tight, giving her no rest until she'd searched through the microfiche. Skimming them, she'd copied the articles, and her curiosity grew with each article about Ryder and his amazing illusions.

The articles troubled her.

She'd stuffed the copies into her purse and stepped out into the blaring tumult of the parade, her thoughts lingering on the man presented in the clippings.

That man pushed the limits.

Like Houdini, to whom he was compared, he used his own skill and agility in many of the spectacular feats, enticing the audience to a kind of bloodlust.

In the light of day her nighttime encounter with Ryder on the porch had been like a dream, all disconnected emotions, no thought, only those inchoate feelings, hot and intense and immediate.

Suddenly her skin rippled as if someone stroked it.

The tip of her braid moved across her breast as she turned her head and looked straight at Ryder Hayes. Even masked by the dark lenses of sunglasses, his gaze met hers.

Her nipple puckered as if he'd reached out and touched it with one long, clever finger, intimately, with purpose.

The din of the parade vanished, and there was a long moment of silence, of nothing except the sensation of his touch on her, brushing her skin into shivering awareness.

Bubble gum scents of cotton candy and the buttery tang of popcorn swirled and mixed with the richer, earthier scents of horses and elephants, mixed with the acrid smell of urine-soaked straw from the open-caged lions.

Holding her gaze, he pushed his sunglasses off his face and into the thickness of his hair. She thought there was an edge of mockery in his casual gesture, a note of teasing.

A statement of power and control.

He folded his arms across his white-shirted chest and then, looking away, Ryder nodded, releasing her.

Sounds rushed in.

The calliope passed with a rootin', tootin' blare, and an elephant trumpeted to her right, the sound shrill and savage.

Behind her, someone bumped into her and an elbow, sharp and heavy, jostled her. Off-balance, Josie jumped. Her foot slipped on the curb and she pitched forward toward the street.

"Josie!" A voice carried over the roar of the lion and the squeals of the elephant, and she twisted and stretched out her hand.

Later she would wonder whether she was reaching for the hand that went with the voice or trying to brace herself.

Her bare knees scraped against the concrete and her hand slid along the road surface, her palm stinging and burning as stones and grit shredded her skin.

His head lowered and his tree-thick legs swinging sideways, the lead elephant galloped toward her.

"Get out of the way, lady!"

"Holy sh— What the hell happened!"

"Nicki! Come back here!"

On her knees in the street, Josie saw a flash of purple and white as the girl darted off the curb.

The piggy eyes of the elephant were wild, rolling back in its head.

Nicki and Josie were right in the path of the rampaging elephant. Its ears fanned wide at the sides of its head and bounced with each lurching stride.

"Nicki!" The scream was as shrill as the elephant's piercing squeal.

Glancing back at her mother, the girl stopped. She looked up at the elephant and back, unable to move.

Josie scrambled to her feet. Suddenly the elephant halted, his head swaying. His thick legs swinging with a speed that terrified her, he galloped to the far side of the street, butting a man standing there, rolling him on the street as people screamed and ran.

Looping her arm around Nicki, Josie clutched the child to her as the elephant swerved back toward them, trumpeting and tossing its head.

"Come on, honey. Hold on. I've got you," Josie murmured as she felt the hot breath of the beast wash over her. She shoved the little girl behind her. Less than a foot away, the quivering end of the muscular trunk was like grasping fingers.

Something flicked against the end of the snout, fell to the ground. The elephant squealed again, its agitation at a pitch. It raised its trunk high, the convulsing end closing and opening, flexing.

In that instant, Josie turned and scooped Nicki up, running with her toward the curb and out of the elephant's path. As she ran, the elephant returned his attention to them and lifted one massive foot. Its trunk plucked a streaming tip of Josie's skirt and pulled.

"Run, Nicki!" Josie urged the girl. She tried to lift Nicki and toss her to the sideline, but burying her face in Josie's neck, the child clung to her, the tiny sobs louder than the elephant's squeals.

Bending forward, Josie struggled against the strength of the clenching trunk. The needlelike hairs of its body pricked her skin.

Something else snapped against the elephant's snout and fell, landing at Josie's feet.

Distracted, the elephant freed Josie from its grasp and sent its quivering, inquisitive snout toward the ground, searching for the red-and-gold playing card inches away.

The joker.

Josie lifted her head and saw Ryder Hayes, a hundred feet away, flowing toward her from his position across the street. Like the wings of a dark, avenging angel, the sides of his black linen jacket belled out with the swiftness of his stride. His right thumb was over a card, his index finger pressed along one corner, his middle finger somewhere under the card as he snapped the card toward the elephant's flank.

Irritated and confused, the joker still grasped in its snout, the elephant turned its head left, right.

Josie was afraid to move. Terrified that her movement would again draw the attention of the enraged mammal, she stayed still, her arms curled around Nicki as Ryder, his long legs scissoring the distance between them, came closer.

With each step he flung another card toward the elephant. Shoulder. Buttock. Leg. Flank again.

As Ryder strode toward him, the elephant backed up, advanced, its massive head swaying as it focused its attention on him, on the swarm of irritants he flung. But as Ryder continued moving toward it, the elephant began a steady, high squeal, backing away but still too near Josie.

The last card popped against the haunch of the elephant, spinning it away from Josie and Nicki.

With Nicki in her arms, Josie leapt for the curb and the nearby buildings.

Behind her, Ryder's lean arm fastened on her waist. Half lifting, half pushing, he carried her with him. Josie felt the flex and release of his muscled thighs against her hip, her rear end, their power a disturbing reassurance in the mad sprint for safety. His strength kept her moving even as the elephant pivoted and bumped into her, his head knocking her sideways.

Above her, the red madness in the elephant's eyes took her breath away. Ryder shoved her forward. "Don't stop, Josie, no matter what," he yelled. "Keep moving! Faster! Over there!" He pointed to the corner.

Over her shoulder she saw him turn and scan the chaos behind him as he urged her toward the wide sweep of the stone steps of the First Federal Loan and Mortgage. His narrow hand pushed against her ribs as he shoved her up the stairs of the bank where they stopped and looked down on the scene below them and to their right where people flung themselves under cars and behind light poles as the elephant lumbered first one way, then the other. A wake of screams and panic followed the beast.

The elephant handlers struggled to corner the beast, to bring his rampage under control. Horses were rearing, pawing at the air as their riders hung on with grim-faced determination. The lion cages rocked on their wheels as the elephant smashed past them, its frenzy intensified by the deep-throated roars of the lions.

"Mama!" Nicki leaned toward the white-faced woman who snatched the child from Josie's arms.

"Nicki, Nicki," the woman wailed. "I told you to stay on the curb! You never listen!" Her voice was filled with the terror of what had come so close to her daughter.

Ryder's arm stayed around Josie's waist. She felt the

cold press of each of his fingers through the thin fabric of her blouse. She wanted to lean back against him, absorb his strength.

She didn't.

She knew better than to depend on someone else's strength.

But, oh, she needed to lean against Ryder's hard chest and rest for a moment. Simply rest.

Instead, she straightened her shoulders, her eyes stinging at the sight of Nicki curled against her mother, the small child trusting in the adult strength.

The mother choked out "Thank you" in their direction, but her attention was all on the tear-streaked face of her child as Nicki sobbed in her arms.

A shot rang out and Josie flinched. Ryder's fingers dug into her waist.

A high-pitched squeal.

A second shot.

Screams.

As the elephant dropped, falling on its side, Josie felt the reverberation in her stomach, a sickness of the soul at the sight of the enormous body lying in the street, its huge front foot lifting and then dropping to the ground. A sound she could only describe as an unearthly groan came from the elephant as its huge head twitched, struggled to rise.

"Oh, no," she whispered, stricken by the creature's efforts.

"Don't look," Ryder said and cupped her head to him, bringing her around to face him where he tucked her under his chin.

Gratefully, Josie shut her eyes and breathed in the starchy scent of his shirt. His hand was gentle against her fevered neck, his fingers cool on her scalp where they stroked through the cap of her hair.

A final shot rang out.

"Shh," Ryder whispered over her head, his cool fingers

sliding through her hair, tangling with the welts of the braid. "Shh. It's over now, Josie Birdsong."

It was as if she were underwater, looking up at the phantom shapes of another world, the cool darkness moving in front of her, shading everything and distorting images until they seemed unreal, imaginary, while the darkness grew deeper, taking her down as Ryder held her close and stroked her hair with his clever fingers.

As he murmured something and shifted, she stepped into the wedge of his legs, seeking heat where there was ice, needing light where there was only darkness and confusion and that thread of sound calling her.

Her voice? His?

Someone else's?

Such a tormented sound in all the dusky clouds.

Lifting her head, Josie saw the spasm contorting his face, the thin, white line of his mouth. "Ryder?" She touched his cheek, traced the slope of its bones down to the corner of his mouth.

He didn't look at her. His gaze was fixed on his hands. "Blood. On everything. The clothes, the sand." Raising his hands, he backed away, staring all the while at his upturned palms. "Too much blood," he muttered. "There wasn't supposed to be any blood."

"Ryder, stop it," Josie whispered. The grimace on his face terrified her as much as had the wild eyes of the rogue elephant. "What are you talking about?"

"The boy."

"The boy?" she said through dry lips. "Eric?" Appalled, she couldn't look away from Ryder. The angles and planes made by his bones showed under his skin, and in the harsh light, the sharp bones of his face suddenly became alien.

Her earlier suspicions were right. Ryder Hayes was somehow connected to Eric Ames's disappearance.

"What is it? What's happened?" Josie took a step forward, one back.

She couldn't stay. Couldn't run. Not while there was a chance that he would tell her what he knew.

Not wanting to believe that he'd abducted the child, Josie didn't know what else to think. She couldn't believe that the man who'd rained pennies and roses into her lap, that the man who'd made it a point of honor not to force his way onto her porch could be capable of the kind of evil connected with the disappearance of the children of Angel Bay.

But people weren't always what they seemed.

A smiling face and charm could mask corruption and evil.

"Ryder!" Josie grabbed his hand, stilling its restless movement. "Are you on drugs? Are you having a flashback of some kind? Tell me what's happening to you!" she insisted, squeezing his hand so hard that her fingers ached.

A current of air moved, hot and dry, over her, the stirring of air that spoke of a coming storm.

Abruptly Ryder snapped his head in her direction and stared at her.

He'd looked at her with that same unfocused expression the day she'd gone to his house.

And she knew in that instant that something was terribly wrong.

His dark gaze was focused not on her but on some distant vision, some other place. Ryder was looking at a scene not visible to her.

Lifting their joined hands, he stretched them out, a triangular bridge from him to her, raising her palms with his, reaching out as if to touch something standing between them. His lips moved silently as he stood there, and she knew that whatever he was seeing, it was destroying him.

Over the bridge of their linked hands, Josie felt a current pass between them, growing more powerful the longer their hands stayed joined, and that current drew her closer to him, his agony mingling with her grief.

"It's happening again, Josie Birdsong." Ryder's voice grated against her. "It's your choice."

Josie almost dropped his hand. He knew she was there, but his gaze was still fixed on that other scene.

In the narrowing space between their bodies as the air darkened like a dust storm, she saw shapes form, twist.

Heard a faraway voice calling her.

Not his.

Palm to palm with Ryder, her hand burned with cold as his fingers slipped between hers, closing over them, and she couldn't free herself from a grasp that was as light as air.

She tightened her own grip and the voice grew more insistent, the shadowy shapes clearer.

This time, Josie knew she wasn't dreaming, knew she wasn't imagining anything, knew that Ryder heard what she heard, that he was there in the darkness with her.

She wanted to shut her eyes, to close them to the misty shapes in front of her.

She didn't.

Needing to know what was happening, she didn't look away from her hand linked with Ryder's. She saw their hands blur one into the other, a flamelike brightness where they touched in the center of the shadows.

"Get away!" The voice was childish.

Not Mellie's.

A boy's.

Josie trembled. Bending her fingers over the back of Ryder's hand, she gripped him and waited, her body vibrating like a tuning fork to the note Ryder struck.

She was cold, hot.

"You promised—" The childish voice rose higher. "I don't like you—" And the voice ended on a long, drawn-out breath, the sound as soft as a sigh.

The sound made her want to weep. She wanted to touch the misty form in front of her that broke apart and drifted like smoke.

Gone.

The sun blazed against the white columns of the bank's portico. Not comprehending, Josie looked up at the sky.

It was the same white-blue it had been for weeks. Cloudless.

She looked at Ryder.

Unsmiling, he was watching her, his narrowed eyes clear and guarded. His shirt merged into the dazzle of the bank's marble, but Josie saw that he had clasped his hands in back of him.

"Crazy world, isn't it, Josie Birdsong?" He leaned back against the building. "It was the same as last night, wasn't it?"

She nodded. "And at your house? I saw a child there, too?"

"I don't know what you saw. I know we heard the same thing. A child's cry."

"Yes." Rubbing her arms against the chill that slithered over her in spite of the blasting heat, Josie kept nodding.

"What happened in these past minutes doesn't make a damned bit of sense, does it, Josie? I don't have an explanation. Do you?" One thick eyebrow lifted as he braced one foot against the wall and balanced himself.

"No." She looked down at her empty hands. She'd dropped her purse. It seemed easier to think about the purse than what had happened. "I don't have an explanation." She couldn't allow herself to consider the possibility that exploded in her mind.

They had seen and heard the same things. Impossible. Nobody would believe her. She didn't believe it herself. Didn't want to. If they saw something that wasn't *there*— She shuddered. Impossible.

"This same kind of incident occurred before, but we

didn't talk about it last night, did we? We were…diverted, perhaps. Are we going to talk about these episodes today?'' The roughness and urgency were back in his voice, but he still leaned against the hot concrete wall, as casually as if he didn't give a hoot in hell what she answered. He folded his arms across his chest, locking his palms flat against his sides under his arms as if he were in a straitjacket. ''It's up to you. I don't care.''

''No?''

''Nope.'' His mouth twitched, thinned.

''What you're suggesting is—it's crazy.''

''I agree. But then we're both crazy, aren't we?'' He smiled, taunting her. ''I mean, since we both heard something. Saw something.'' Still smiling at her, he was a man with all the time in the world at his disposal. ''Didn't we?''

''If you're telling the truth.''

''Looking for the gimmick, then, Josie?''

She nodded.

''Smart. But then I told you there was always a trick, didn't I?''

She nodded again. ''You could have an agenda of your own. Something you wanted. You could be working a scam. You could have a mini tape recorder in your jacket to make me think I was hearing one of the children. You might be a con artist.''

''I could be. But what if I'm not? What then?''

Despite his nonchalant pose, Josie registered the tension radiating from his lean body, in his eyes, in the clamp of his hands under his arms. He was coiled, waiting. Her answer was important to him, but he was making himself wait, giving her time to sort through her thoughts. She rubbed her arms.

His easygoing manner was costing him. She saw the effort revealed in the aggressive thrust of his chin, in the tight line of his mouth even as it lifted in the semblance of a smile.

"So, Josie Birdsong, what's it going to be? A nice, civilized discussion of a fairly peculiar incident—" he broke off, frowning "—or three, actually. Can we manage that, do you think? Can you give me that much of your trust?" He rested his head against the bank, still watching her from under lowered lids.

Josie understood how important her answer was to him.

Not able to answer yet, she shrugged.

"We're alone, you know," he added gently. "No one's here. No one's going to think you've gone off the deep end."

Her chin tilted up. "I wouldn't care if they did. People will believe what they want to. What they think doesn't change anything. I learned that a long time ago."

"Did you?" The sympathy in his voice seduced her.

But she glanced over her shoulder, checking to see if Nicki and her mom had noticed anything.

When she turned around, Nicki and her mother had gone. She'd never seen them leave.

"They've been gone awhile."

"Oh." Her back to Ryder, Josie scraped a foot on the edge of the step.

"Josie," he said, and air moved against her, "I have to talk with you. There are things I need to know in order to understand what all of these incidents mean. If anything. But if you're honest with yourself, you'll admit you want to talk with me. You're curious about what's happening, aren't you?" He stood behind her and the smooth fabric of his slacks brushed the backs of her knees.

"What I heard— It doesn't make sense."

"No." He shifted and the material slid across her skin, mixing up her thoughts.

She gripped her empty hands together. "I *couldn't* have heard—"

"But you heard a boy's voice, didn't you?"

"Yes," she admitted and turned to him, her eyes filling

with tears, that forlorn sound wrenching her. "And I think it was Eric's voice!"

Ryder stepped back from her as she swiveled, her skirt whipping around his legs and tying them together. "So do I, Josie." He shrugged and his white shirt tightened across his chest, revealed the flat muscles of his stomach. "I've heard other things, too, a word here, a sound there. Nothing like what happened last night or today. Fragments. And I don't know where they're coming from."

"What do you mean?"

"The voices. The images. Every night. I *see* things, Josie Birdsong. I don't know if I'm making the pictures up. Or if I'm remembering something I don't want to remember." His voice broke off.

"Or?"

"Or if—" he ground the heels of his hands into his eyes "—or if something impossible is happening. And it seems that I can't find out alone. When I'm with you, there's a power—"

"I don't understand."

"Guess what, lady green eyes? I don't, either." And he laughed, the sound empty and humorless. "But I'm damned if I'm going to stand back and not find out." His expression was grim.

Josie understood that this time he wasn't giving her a choice. He would make sure that she helped him whether or not she wanted to.

No matter what he said, no matter what she wanted, he intended to use the power of his will against hers, to bend her, one way or another, to his design.

CHAPTER FIVE

"I found this at the curb edge. It's yours, isn't it?" As he opened her car door for her hours later, Ryder tossed Josie the green purse.

"Thanks. I dropped it." She waved her hand back toward the parade route. "It didn't have anything important in it. A few dollars. Not much more. Nothing important." Her eyes slid away from his. "I wondered if anyone would find it and turn it in. If I'd get it back."

Ryder sighed. If he weren't so tired, he could figure out why she was lying, but at the moment it didn't seem important, and anyway, he didn't have the energy. He had to concentrate on the remnants of those impressions. He didn't want them to fade away. Not before he understood them.

And he couldn't understand what was happening without Josie Birdsong's cooperation.

He couldn't think past that fact. Josie had to help him. Without her, he would never know what those impressions and images meant. Never know if somehow he had— Ryder swallowed and glanced back at the steps of the bank, over to the scene of the wrecked parade.

Although most of the spectators had wandered away shortly after the trucks and cranes disposed of the elephant's body and departed, a few spectators remained along Church Street. Yellow traffic cones and police tape marked off the area.

Josie had parked her car in the municipal lot, and he'd walked with her there after the police and reporters finished with them. She hadn't wanted him to, though. She'd made that clear without saying so. He'd asked for her trust, but she wasn't handing it out like candy at Halloween.

In her place, he wouldn't, either.

Not wanting to be blocked in by the parade, Ryder had left his car two blocks over in the lot on the river. Now, watching her slide into her car, her gauzy skirt riding up over one abraded knee, he regretted driving to town.

If he gave her too much time alone, she'd build on her doubts, reinforce them, not allow him to get close enough to her to see if he could figure out an explanation he could accept for what had happened each time he'd been with her.

She pulled her door closed and started the engine. "I'm going home."

"Not yet. Please." He reached in and switched off the engine.

"What do you want? Why can't you leave me alone?" Her voice was so low he barely heard it.

"I have to understand—"

She interrupted, agitation in the snap of her head toward him. "I don't know what to do, what to say to you. Today, last night—it's all beyond me. I can't handle any more. For all I know, you hypnotized me into thinking I heard something! I don't know! I don't care. I want my daughter back where she belongs, with me. That's all I want." Leaning her head on the steering wheel, she gripped the brown plastic of the wheel as if she would never let it go. "And I don't think that's ever going to happen."

"I'm sorry." Knowing the words were inadequate, he still said them. He had nothing else to give her. No comfort. No answers. Only more questions.

"Yes, well, so am I, and I can't do a damned thing about it." Lifting her head, she pushed her shoulders back, swung her braid away from her face and turned to him. "I can't help my daughter. I certainly can't help you, no matter what you think."

"How do you know?"

"Don't you get it? How much more clearly can I say it?

I don't give a damn whether or not I can help you! All I want is to go home and be by myself!'' She slapped the steering wheel.

"That's not a good idea. Not now.''

"But it's what *I* want. What I'm going to do. And don't you dare say I'm too upset or hysterical to stay by myself, or so help me, I'll—'' She switched on the ignition again. Her engine idled too fast, sputtered and chattered, but kept going.

Ryder couldn't let her leave without him. He thought about leaving his car in the lot and asking her to give him a ride home. He didn't think she would refuse him a lift. Anything so that she stayed with him.

Coming from somewhere deep inside him, the urge to keep her near him was overpowering.

Exhausted, he tried to figure out how to maneuver her so that she would give him the chance he needed. "Look, why don't you follow me home? You look as if you haven't eaten in days. You have to eat. I have some steaks—'' He stopped as she grimaced. "No, on second thought, that's not a good idea.''

"Not meat.'' She shuddered. "Anyway, I'm not hungry.'' The car engine coughed once, died. She didn't restart it. Her face had gone sickly pale at the mention of steaks. A faint green tinged her skin.

"Will you be all right?'' Despite his concentration on manipulating her into doing what he wanted, that strange tenderness he'd noticed before stirred again in him as he saw the effort she made to keep her head upright. She didn't look as if she had the strength to drive two blocks, much less back to her house. "By yourself?'' He held his hands up in surrender as she glared at him. "Not that you're hysterical or upset. Of course not. Any fool can see that you're not either of those. Or overwrought.''

"Good.'' She reached for the gearshift and the shiny line

of her hair over her ear caught his attention. Water smooth and glistening, a richness of texture and color.

Then, touched by the curve of her narrow shoulders under the brave green promise of her blouse, he added gently, "Maybe tired. Tired of carrying a heavy load by yourself. Anybody could understand how that kind of burden could wear a person out. Even a strong person."

A bead of perspiration formed at her temple, became a small magnifying lens to her glossy skin, and he touched the drop, lifting it on his finger where it gleamed in the sunlight, shimmered and trembled as he moved his finger back and forth, watching the play of colors until they vanished. Holding her gaze with every ounce of energy left in him, he delicately touched the tip of his forefinger to his mouth and tasted her.

The flavor of Josie Birdsong was a sweetness beyond anything he'd ever known. "Like wildflower honey," he murmured.

She flushed, frowned, looked away from him. Ran her hands over the steering wheel.

"I've been alone for a long time, Ryder—" she said finally, the words coming slowly as if she weren't sure what she was going to say, and her husky voice stumbled over his name.

"Alone can be okay. I've always preferred being by myself. But I'm learning it can be…lonely." In the past few months, he'd come to understand too well how empty alone could become. The taste of her lingered on his tongue, made him hunger for more.

"I never felt lonely or frightened until Mellie disappeared. And I can't change that. I can't bring her back, so I'll be as 'all right' tonight as I am every night. No night is better or worse. No day is better or worse!" She tipped her chin at him, her expression fierce and lost. "You have no idea what my life's like, do you? I wake up, go to work. Plant my garden. Try to keep it alive in a killing drought.

Most of all, I try to get through each day. And wait." A tiny sob escaped her. "Oh, God, I *wait*. Do you understand now? Until I find out what's happened with my daughter, my life just *is*. Nothing more." Unshed tears gleamed in the green of her eyes.

Thinking, Ryder flattened his palm against the hot metal of her car roof.

If he had Josie on his own turf, he could— What?

He blinked. Struggled to come up with a strategy in the face of her resistance.

She had to stay with him.

It was important.

The edges of several white pieces of paper were caught in the crumpled snap of her purse. Below them, indenting the leather, was the imprint of a horse's hoof. As he rubbed his forehead, she dropped her hands to the purse. Carefully, she turned it first one way, then the other, its green moving against the lighter green of her skirt.

He needed her. That was as far as his aim went.

His body craved her.

His palm flexed against the hot metal.

As if she'd heard the voice in his head, Josie glanced up at him, tilting her head. In spite of her spurt of anger, her tanned face was still drained of color, the two hectic red spots on her cheeks disappearing with the gleam of tears.

A green stone caged in gold lay against her bright green blouse with the rolled-up sleeves. Underneath the blouse, she wore a hot pink T-shirt, and, as he frowned, the physical need grinding deep inside him, a paler pink spread up from her neck over the contours of her cheeks.

Her face filling with that deepening pink, she turned her purse over, fiddled with the broken clasp, looked through the windshield at the bug crawling under the blade of the wiper. Looked everywhere but at him.

"Josie?" An idea nibbled at the fringes of his exhaustion. He was surprised it hadn't occurred to him earlier.

She traced the hoof imprint. "What?"

"Maybe we can find out what happened to your daughter. What do you think?"

"I think that's the cruelest thing anyone's ever said to me," she said and laid the purse on the seat. The strap coiled on the seat, fell over the edge. "Unconscionable. Heartless." Her eyes were bleak as she looked at him at last. "And I think you'd say anything to help you get your way, wouldn't you?"

"Yes." Bred-in-the-bone honesty made any other answer impossible. Honesty and the knowledge that frankness had a chance of persuading her when nothing else would. "You're right. I'm being cruel."

"Well." She shrugged, and her hands dropped helplessly to her lap. "That's something, I guess. For you to admit the truth."

He opened her car door and knelt down beside her. "But, Josie, suppose—no, wait," he urged, holding up his hand to stop her but not touching her. "Suppose for one second that maybe what we've experienced *is* real?"

Her mossy eyes widened and the black satin arch of her eyebrows rose.

"What if we *are* seeing something that's real?" He waited. The heat of her car engine rose up from under the car and around him, and he was still cold. "What *if*?" He touched the round shape of her bare knee lightly. "Can you take that risk?" He touched the center of her hand, closed her fingers over her palm.

She would have to make her own choices. As he had.

"Do you want to let that possibility—even though it's so remote as to be laughable—do you want to let that possibility slip through your fingers?"

Her hands lay still in her lap, empty, one fist closed.

"No." She opened her hands, leaned forward and restarted her car. "Get in, Mr. Hayes."

"Ryder," he said and stood up. "Josie."

She nodded. "Ryder." Leaning to the passenger side, she threw open the door of her car. "Come on before I change my mind."

"Whatever you say." He got in. He wasn't going to give her a chance to reconsider. His car could damned well stay where it was.

As they crossed the bridge over the Angel River, he leaned forward and turned on the radio. "I want to see if there are any—"

"Deaths," she said, staring straight ahead and clenching her fingers around the steering wheel.

"Yes." He spun the radio dial until he found a station giving the news and weather. Listening intently but hearing no new details of the catastrophe, he discovered that in the closed car, he was too aware of her, of her presence. Heat lapped at him, welcomed him and the space between them seemed to shimmer. He wanted to move closer to her, to the warm glow around her. Instead, he shifted in his seat, increasing the distance between them as much as he could.

The rattle of the metal grate reverberated through the car as she steered it easily over the bridge. Her hands were small and competent looking, the nails so short they were almost nonexistent.

"You're a good driver."

She wrinkled the straight length of her nose at him doubtfully. "I don't like phony compliments, Ryder."

"No, I meant it. I like the way you drive. It's…restful."

"Restful?" Her rounded chin tipped up. "Sounds to me as if you're handing out a backhanded compliment. I know I'm what's called a 'safe' driver, which translates as excessively conservative and boring." The chin angled higher.

"Hit a nerve, did I?"

"Not at all," she said. He might have bought it if she hadn't added, "Nothing thrill-of-the-open-road about my style."

Ryder gathered she wasn't talking about driving.

"Nothing exciting happens when I'm the chauffeur."

"Don't knock it, Josie. Fast and flashy aren't all they're cracked up to be. Flashy's usually all show, no substance." He laid his head back against the seat and shut his eyes, letting the radio voices drive out the impressions flowing between him and Josie. "Flashy's what I do. And it's all illusion. You can't trust illusions." He opened his eyes and caught her quick glance.

"You make your living fooling people," she said.

"I used to." He knew what she was thinking, wondering, but he wouldn't lie to her and toss out guarantees. She would have to decide for herself whether she could trust him. "What do you want me to say, Josie? Do you want promises of safe passage from me?"

"No. I wasn't asking for anything. I was reminding myself who you are. What you are."

"And do you know who I am, Josie?"

As she stopped at the light, she gave him a long, thoughtful look. "Not in the least. I'm not even sure I want to find out. But I don't care who you are as long as you help me find out about my daughter. Nothing else matters."

"And if you don't find out?" He gave in to temptation and twisted his finger into the end of her braid, lifted it, let it fall over her shoulder to her front. A warm, living thing, the strand caressed his finger, there and gone, a drift of silk. The swoop of thick black hair slid against her blouse, settled in a curve around her breast.

"If I think you've tricked me..." The light changed, and she shrugged. With the movement of her head, her braid circled the tiny point of her nipple like a lover's touch. "Don't play games with me, Ryder."

"Josie, playing games doesn't interest me at all."

"Ryder," she echoed, mocking him, "I think *all* you do is play games with people. Everything you've done or said since I met you has had another level to it, another meaning. There's nothing frank or straightforward in anything you say or do. You hide behind words, you disappear behind...coins, flowers, tricks with cards.''

"Then why did you decide to come with me?''

"Because I'm desperate.''

A distant pity stirred in him, but a well-practiced ruthlessness tamped down that dangerous emotion. She didn't need his pity. When he was with her, he couldn't let down his guard, couldn't let his concentration wander. "Do what you want, Josie.''

"I'm not sure anymore that what I want has anything to do with what happens.'' Resignation flowed through the warm velvet of her voice. "But right now I'm following a trail of bread crumbs through the forest, Ryder Hayes, and I don't know where you fit into the story.''

"Don't cast me in the part of your brother, Josie. That would be a mistake.''

Black eyelashes lifted and a glint of green flashed. "You're warning me against making another mistake?''

"My feelings toward you aren't in the least brotherly, Mrs. Conrad,'' he said mockingly. "And you know it, don't you?'' Restless, needing an outlet for the dark aggression riding heavily in him, he wound his fist into the flimsy cotton end of her skirt, pulling it tight against her thighs, her belly. "And I reckon some of those urges are percolating in your own sturdy little self, aren't they, Josie Birdsong?''

He ached to flatten his palm against the small curve of her abdomen and stroke the fabric, lightly, lightly, against her, teasing her with the glide of material until her green eyes lost their guarded wariness and turned soft and dazed, filled with him.

"If they were,'' she said, snatching the end of her skirt free, "believe me, I'd ignore them.'' She tucked her skirt loosely around her knees. "The only thing I'm interested in percolating is coffee.''

"I have a coffeepot," he offered slyly and watched that wave of pink move up her neck once more.

"You're playing games again, Ryder," she said, dismissing him.

"Of course I am. It's a way of passing the time until we get to my house." Forgetting, he reached into his jacket pocket for the deck of cards he always carried with him. "We can entertain ourselves, Josie, or we can get into the subject neither of us seems ready to discuss. Which is it? Do we have our consultation now? In the confines of your car?"

"How about a little peace and quiet?" Peevishly, she turned the wheel, steering them down the dirt road that meandered for about three miles before it ended at his driveway.

"Peace and quiet? You got it."

In the remaining minutes of the drive, he shut his eyes, seeking the still, silent place that he'd once found in the rhythms and pattern of his illusions, but he couldn't shut out Josie's presence, his awareness that she was only an arm's length from him. He could reach out and touch her.

She filled his senses. The scent of her, the rustle of her skirt against her naked legs, the whisper-slide of her braid across her breast. The remembered sleekness of her skin under his palm, the texture like a warm peach. She filled the pores of his body until he seemed to taste her in the very air he breathed.

He told himself the hunger was sex, lust, pure and simple.

The bead of perspiration from her temple had evaporated, but he touched his finger to his mouth. He inhaled. There, the faintest taste of her lingered.

Sex, lust. That was part of it. He understood those drives very clearly. They held no mystery for him. Sex made him want to run his hands over her curves and slopes and discover the supple muscles under the sleekness of her skin.

Sex made him itchy with the need to taste the darkness of her mouth....

The sexual pull was stronger than anything he'd ever experienced.

The hunger was new, a puzzle.

He couldn't explain it.

But he knew he didn't like it.

It threatened him in some indefinable way that made him want to lash out, push her away from him.

If he wanted to figure out what was going on, though, he needed her.

And he wanted her.

That was the catch.

Watching the slope of her neck merge into the curve of her breast, he understood finally that there was nothing simple about his feelings for the small, self-contained woman sitting next to him.

Nothing at all pure.

The indistinct shape of his house rose in front of them as she drove up the shell driveway.

Long afternoon shadows from the trees cast the porch into twilight. Grottolike, the dark spaces under the porch blended into the ground, and the house seemed to hover above the ground, insubstantial, a chimera.

For a disturbing second, he had the impression of figures moving across it, ghosts from a distant past.

A trick of the dimming light.

Illusions.

"Well, Ryder, we're here. Not to make a point of the obvious," she added, not moving, leaving her seat belt fastened.

"Not afraid to come in, are you?" he challenged. Curious, his hand on the door handle, he waited to see what she would do. "Afraid of goblins and ghoulies, Josie?"

"Are you?" She threw the challenge back at him. "Afraid to be alone in your big ol' falling-down house? Is that the reason you talked me into coming here? Is that the game? You're afraid of things that go bump in the night, Ryder, and looking for someone to hold your hand?'' Annoyance showed in the rigid line of her body as she stared at him.

''What if I were? Would you hold my hand through the night, lady green eyes? Would you keep my demons at bay?''

''Certainly not.'' She unsnapped her seat belt and removed the ignition key, clicking her purse for emphasis. ''And in spite of everything that's happened, Ryder, you haven't convinced me that you're not working some kind of con. I don't believe in ghosts, ghoulies or demons.''

''Neither do I, Josie.'' He smiled, amused at the momentary whimsy that had shaped ghosts from shadows. ''I never have.'' Though he'd pitched the possibility to her because he figured it would help sway her, he wasn't ready to believe in the tenuous shapes he thought he'd seen, the voices he and Josie had heard, the strange sense of dislocation he felt when he touched her. ''Anyway, if I did believe in ghosts, I'd like to think they came to comfort, not torment.''

''If comfort's what you need, then find someone else. I wouldn't be any use to you. I'm the wrong person.''

''I don't think so.''

She shot him a quick, suspicious look as she opened her car door. ''Believe me, I am. I have no comfort left to give.''

''Oh, Josie, still so little faith. You really do think I've lured you here under false pretenses, don't you?''

She exited from the car. The door slammed, sending the car rocking back and forth.

''I'm shocked,'' he mourned. ''Do you think I'd do something like that?''

''I don't have a clue what you'll do. Or not do.''

"Then I reckon you'll have to trust me, after all, won't you?"

"No," she said, regarding him intently, her thick eyelashes obscuring her expression from him. "I'll trust you as far as I can see you, and I'll watch your every movement."

"Ah, but the hand is always quicker than the eye, Josie Birdsong." The green stone dangled from his extended finger. "You mustn't forget that."

Letting the stone on its gold chain swing gently to and fro between them for a moment, she finally closed her hand around the stone and took it from him, putting the necklace into a pocket of her skirt. "Thank you for the reminder. I won't forget again." Shells crunched under her shoes as she turned her back on him and took several steps forward before she stopped.

Waiting for him, she slipped her purse under her arm and stared at the house.

Ryder felt her imperceptible tensing as he came up behind her. "Goosey?" He tugged the end of her braid.

"No. I told you, I don't believe in what I can't see. But there's an—" she frowned "—*atmosphere* about this house. Nothing spooky or frightening. It's a sadness, I guess."

"This place has a history. That's why I bought the property."

The rounded contour of her cheek gleamed with light as she looked over her shoulder at him. "That doesn't make sense. It's not an historic monument or anything important. Nothing more than a rickety old run-down house."

"I know." He stared at the immensity of his house, moved by the sag and tilt of it, the shabbiness and permanence of the structure as it melted into the woods, its back to the river.

"You must like old houses, then."

"Not especially."

"It would take a fortune to restore this place." She walked slowly up the porch and stopped at the heavily carved front door. "You'll never get your money back when you sell it." She wrapped her arms around herself, her green purse held close to her, its thin strap disappearing into the green of her blouse. "I can't imagine why you bought this house. You must have a reason." The soft mouth firmed in disapproval. "Or more money than you know what to do with."

"So practical," he conceded. "But you're fishing, Josie." He swung the door open. "If you want to know if I can afford to restore this house, ask. I'll tell you." Her prim dollars-and-cents approach to what had been an impulsive decision amused him at some level.

"It's not any of my business." She shrugged, her sense of insult showing in her scrupulously casual expression.

With the lift of her shoulder, her blouse pulled across the curve of her breasts. Ryder stepped closer, drawn to that delicate shape. Her shoulder dropped, and the fabric draped loosely once more.

In the gloom of the hallway, he leaned toward her, ran the back of his finger over her braid, following the dark satin to its end. "It's only a house, Josie, not a project. A place to live, that's all. Once upon a time, it was a sugar plantation. A thousand acres or so. Sometime in March 1856, a raiding party of Seminoles burned it down. The settlers killed the Seminoles. The Seminoles killed the settlers. The house was rebuilt."

"So much destruction." She laid her hand against the near wall, stroking the dingy paint.

"It wasn't unusual. It happened all up and down the Tamiami Trail, Josie. You should know."

It was the first reference he'd made to what he knew about her that she seemed to believe no one else knew.

"Why would I?" Her defenses were up again.

"Local history. I figured you'd heard the stories."

"Some." Looking straight at him, she dared him to cross the imaginary line she'd drawn in the sand. She wasn't going to give him an opening into her past.

He placed his hand next to hers, watching the shape of their hands side by side. He needed to have her by his side to find the answers he sought, so he didn't pursue the subject. Later, though, he would. One way or another, he would satisfy his curiosity. "I see. My mistake. Ancient history."

"A sad history, Ryder. Greed and death." Her eyes were luminous with distress.

"Most history is. One person wants, takes. Someone else loses, is shut out. Conquered. That's what human history is. Stories of greed and death and destruction."

His sympathy had been all with the Seminoles who'd been forced to retreat, retreat and retreat from their land. He understood the sense of displacement and bitterness they must have felt as they'd vanished into the Everglades.

There, in a land no one else had wanted until modern times, the Seminoles had changed, adapted.

They'd survived.

But they'd never surrendered.

"I don't like to think about the past," she said, flattening the specks of paint. "It's all about someone winning. Someone dying." She lifted a bit of the paint, dug it free of the wall. "The present's hard enough."

Her words hung between them in the hallway.

Lifting her hand from the wall, she made a sweeping gesture that included the river, the yard, the woods. Shivering, she said, "A dark and bloody ground. A killing place. I'd think you'd have a hard time sleeping here, knowing its history. Especially after you said you've heard voices." Mockery tinged her silvery voice.

Even through his slacks, he felt the brush of her skirt against him as she moved imperceptibly closer to him. "It's only a place, Josie. This house doesn't give me nightmares.''

She fingered the strip of peeling paint again, then brushed the flecks from her hands. "Doesn't it? Good for you."

He'd bought the house with his first big paycheck and slept very peacefully in the place until this January. Until that disastrous final show at the auditorium. After that, he'd run home like a dog with its tail between its legs.

There, sleep had fled, and he'd seen impressions, heard faraway voices, so faintly that he didn't know if what he heard was nothing more than the sifting of dust across his old floors.

And every day the newspapers were filled with stories about the five children who'd been killed, their bodies found weeks afterward.

Escaping the house, unable to sleep, he'd begun watching Josie on her candlelit porch, drawn to her like the fluttering, dying moths around her porch light.

Eric Ames and Josie's Mellie were still missing.

He and Josie believed they'd heard Eric's voice.

He wanted to know for sure.

"No," he said, his voice steady. "I don't need anyone to hold my hand in the dark," he said and reached around her to turn on the lights. "That's not what I need right now."

She blinked, the deep green centers of her eyes shrinking in the light.

He peeled off the strip of paint she'd been worrying and crumbled it, letting the bits flutter to the floor. "I'm not afraid of the dark or of this house, of what happened here over a hundred years ago, Josie. But the future? What's going to happen? Well, that terrifies me these days." Slipping off his jacket, he tossed it over the newel post of the winding oak staircase, its balusters and treads dull with old varnish.

As he did, a bulb in the too-small chandelier fizzed, a tiny popping sound, as it flickered and flared out. One by one, the bulbs spat and died, leaving the hall murky with shadows.

He heard Josie's gasp and reached for her hand. A fingertip brushed his as she whirled toward him.

"Nicely done, Ryder," Josie muttered. "Do you want me to applaud? I will, if you want. I mean, you were superb. Excellent scene setting. The story, the special effects. I bought the whole bit. Start to finish. Especially the story, but what was the point you were trying to make?"

"No point, Josie. Reckon you wouldn't chalk it up to faulty wiring?"

"Not on your life. Not this time." She stuck both hands in her skirt pockets, the strap of the purse slipping down to encircle her wrist like a bracelet. Her skirt hem lifted, floated, settled around her long, tanned legs. "But was the story necessary?"

"The story was true. The lights are…erratic in their wiring. It is, as I said, an old house and has its own personality." He motioned down the hall. "So, Josie Birdsong, won't you come into my parlor…"

"Said the spider to the fly," she completed, chin up and striding ahead of him, irritability spiking from her in almost visible waves. "And we all know what happened to the fly, don't we?"

"I was merely going to offer you a sandwich," he said mildly. "Cheese? Tuna fish? A glass of wine to drink?"

"All right. A cheese sandwich. Water, tea. Or can you snap your fingers and produce them right here?"

"Nasty, nasty," he chided.

"That's how I feel. Testy. Cranky. Nasty."

"You need food. Come on, Josie. You're tired and so am I. Right now, we're like flint and tinder, striking sparks off each other because we're running on overdrive. We'll do better with some food in us."

"This was a mistake. I shouldn't have come. Or not to-night, at least. You're right. I'm tired, and I don't have much tolerance for anybody or anything lately. Usually I'm not so—"

"Prickly?" he suggested. "Crotchety? Cantankerous?"

"Those, too." A faint smile tilted the corners of her mouth, giving him a glimpse of the woman who'd gone into hiding with the loss of her daughter.

That survival of humor in spite of everything she'd endured touched him in a way he couldn't have imagined.

He hadn't seen her smile before, the sweetness as poignant as an old photograph, and he thought with a pang that if their circumstances were different, Josie Birdsong could break his heart.

"PMS-y?" he offered politely, matching her attempt.

"Oh, drop it, Ryder," she said with a shrug, but her green eyes sparkled in a way that lured him closer. "Give me a sandwich, please, and we'll see if I'm more civilized then." As she shook her head, the tail of her braid swung like a metronome, the shining end clinging first to one side of her waist before sliding to the other side. "But I'm not guaranteeing anything."

"I didn't think for an instant you would." He led the way down the wide, long hall to the kitchen.

They passed magazines stacked on hall tables, boxes of hinges and gears, toolboxes. He wondered if she'd ask about the odds and ends stacked in the hall and visible through the open doors, but he didn't really expect her to ask any questions. He'd learned that much about her. She would observe, draw her own conclusions and keep her own counsel. Unlike him, she was direct, uncomplicated.

But after months of living across the woods from him without ever intruding on his life, she'd come banging on his door because she thought the wild dogs had something to do with the missing children.

Josie would be a fierce ally. An unyielding opponent. He wouldn't relish being on opposing sides from her.

"What do you think of my haunted house now that you've had a look at it?" He swung open the door to the kitchen and pushed the light switch.

Brightness flooded the polished gray Italian tiles of the floor, shone against the white walls.

Clicking on the five-inch television above the sink while he waited for her answer, he surfed through the channels until he found an all-news channel.

"I think your house is a lot like you," she said as she slowly pivoted, surveying the gleaming stainless surfaces of the kitchen. "Not quite what it appears to be." She crossed her arms across her breasts. "The kitchen goes with the car, of course. I think all the decay and overgrowth are a nice camouflage."

"What on earth would I need to hide, do you think?" He opened the double-doored refrigerator. "A simple guy like me?" Squatting on the floor to look into the deli drawer, he sneaked a peek at her.

Over by the window, she looked out at the backyard that rolled to the darkness of the Angel River. In the bright light, her cobwebby skirt became a tantalizing veil through which he could see the shape of her legs, the sweet length of her thighs.

She turned suddenly, surprising him with the swiftness of her movement. "I think you hope your house will keep everyone away from you. You're hiding something you don't like to think about, Ryder—something that really and truly does haunt you."

Moving swiftly toward her, Ryder tossed the white pages he'd taken from her purse in her direction. They fell in a flurry onto the floor, the table, her shoes.

"Did you have time to read all these articles?" he asked, the headlines and titles black against the gray tiles, stark on the stainless-steel table. He didn't know why her digging around in his past angered him, but it did. Reaching for control of the fury that ratcheted through him, drawing him as tight as a bowline, he touched the closest copy with the toe of his shoe.

Watching Ryder's tight, closed expression, Josie wanted to back away, not confront his anger. Staring at him, she clutched her purse, but she didn't back away. "They were still in my purse after you found it in the street. And I haven't turned loose of it since then. You took them out of my purse!"

"I told you, Josie. The hand is always quicker than the eye." His face blazed with resentment. A dull flush spread along the tight skin of his broad cheekbones. "Did you discover anything helpful?"

"One article quoted you. You admitted you killed a woman."

"Yes. The quote was accurate. I said exactly that. Do you have any other questions, Mrs. Conrad? What? Not fleeing toward the door?" He stalked her around the table until there was nowhere for her to go. "Foolish of you, wouldn't you think, Josie? To stay here with a self-confessed killer?"

"Is that what you are? A killer?" she asked, watching the glittering intensity of his eyes, seeing the confusion and pain there in the depths of their darkness.

He closed his hands around her neck, his thumbs resting gently at the base. "This is such a fragile, lovely little neck. So vulnerable." One thumb stroked the length of her neck, to her chin and back, a skimming touch that was as much caress as threat. "You're in my house, at my mercy. Why aren't you screaming, Josie Birdsong?"

His voice was sad and despairing.

CHAPTER SIX

"Should I scream, Ryder?" Josie murmured and lifted her hand, reaching past his anger. "Should I be afraid of you? I'm not, you know."

"You should be, Josie. I've told you. I frighten myself sometimes. I killed her. I was responsible."

From the recess over the sink, the reporter's voice snapped between them, broke the spell. "We're going live to Angel Bay for an update on this afternoon's tragedy."

Ryder flung his arms out and stepped back from her, dropping his head into his hands as he sank onto one of his shining steel chairs.

Caught by the flickering images off to her right, Josie turned away from him.

"The three people injured at today's Last Fling of Summer circus parade remain in critical condition at Angel General Hospital. At this point the cause of the elephant's rampage through downtown Angel Bay has not been determined. Circus officials maintain that the animal was not mistreated and that its handler is an experienced trainer with no history of complaints against him. One small child escaped injury when an unidentified woman pushed her to safety."

Quick cuts of the parade scene flashed as Josie stared at the minute screen. In one shot, she saw herself, her skirt tangled between her legs, her face hidden by Nicki's. Ryder was somewhere out of camera range, the bulk of the elephant screening him. In one shot of the crowd, she glimpsed Ned Dugan. Half turning away from them, he watched her and Nicki stumble out of the elephant's way, his profile unusually still in all the noise and confusion.

He hadn't stayed to be interviewed.

Neither had Nicki's mom.

Behind the reporter, Josie noticed Jeb Stoner on the sidelines talking to a short, thin man. Stoner's sweat-streaked back was to the camera, his head tilted attentively to the man in front of him. Something about Stoner's posture and the second man's face caught her attention. Approaching the screen, she tried to identify the man with the detective. Not one of the circus performers or people, he was vaguely familiar in the way everyone in Angel Bay was, and she should have been able to put a name to him, but as she leaned toward the screen, the camera came in for a close-up on the reporter, and she clicked off the television.

She'd heard enough.

Ryder dropped his hands flat on the silvery surface of the table as she turned and leaned against the sink counter, facing him as he spoke. "Three people injured. It's going to be a long night for their families."

"Probably." She sighed. "I'll call a friend of mine at Angel General. She'll give me an update. I want to know, too. We were lucky. They weren't. Fate's a double-edged sword. I wish we could have helped them, too."

Outside, from far away came the shriek of a screech owl. "Witches, my mother used to say. Evil spirits." She shuddered. "Old ways, old superstitions." She turned to glance out the window, not expecting to see anything, just suddenly edgy with her back to that darkness. Moving away from the sink, she traced the line of the counter, not looking at him as she said, "But you know all about my background, don't you? Somehow you found out. Why did you bother?"

Ryder's expression remained impassive, shuttered against her. "Tit for tat, Josie. Why did *you* go poking around into my past? I thought you said you weren't interested in the past."

"Unlike you, everything I found was in magazines and

newspapers. As far as you know, I might have read it already. What you did is in a whole different category. The two acts aren't at all the same.''

"Possibly not.'' He templed his fingers in front of him, interlaced them, stretched them out, avoiding her eyes.

"I don't understand why you're reacting so strongly. And to something that wasn't personal information.'' Josie shrugged, adding, "Unlike you, I didn't pry into anything private.'' Challenging him with a pointed glance, she let her gaze fall to his hands. Because their constant motion seemed to give them a life of their own, a life apart from whatever was going on consciously between Ryder and her, those narrow, clever hands were a constant source of fascination for her. "I didn't play private investigator.''

"No, you didn't. It felt invasive, though.'' His discomfort showed in the way his gaze met hers, slid to the side.

"You shouldn't have gone into my purse.''

"It was an irresistible impulse.'' He dropped his head and spread his fingers, staring at their shapes reflected in the table. "You were hiding something. I was curious. I'm always curious. About everything. A character flaw, Josie. One of many. It may turn out to be a fatal flaw.'' He lifted his head and raked his hands through his hair. The dark strands were stark against his pale face. Weary and drawn, his face looked as if he'd aged ten years. "At any rate, do you want me to apologize? And if so, for what? For prying? Or for trying to intimidate you? Your wish is my command.''

"For both reasons, perhaps?'' she suggested gently.

He watched her for a long moment, his expression unreadable. "Not for the failed intimidation, I think,'' he finally returned. "You're not an easy woman to browbeat, are you, Mrs. Conrad?''

"Then why do you keep trying?'' She really wanted to find out what was behind his constant goading. He'd piqued her interest. "If you know it won't work?''

"Hope springs eternal, I reckon." A flash of self-mockery lightened his saturnine features.

"What are you hoping for, Ryder? That you'll bully me into staying? Leaving? What?"

"I don't think I really know, myself. Both, maybe? Or maybe because you intimidate *me* in your own quiet, intensely feminine way. You unsettle me, Josie. I want to pull you closer and shove you away at the same time. Now there's a contradiction for you to consider." He lifted an eyebrow, ridiculing himself. "Why did you go snooping around in my life? Do I unsettle you?"

"You do." She nodded. "And I wondered why you worked so hard to keep me off-balance. That was one reason." Josie moved away from the sink. "The second was that I didn't know anything about you. I decided it was a good idea to find out what I could about my neighbor. Safer."

"Good for you. Knowledge is power. Forewarned is forearmed." He grimaced. "Did I leave out any cliché? And now, forewarned, do you feel more powerful?"

"I don't feel as if I'm a puppet whose strings you're pulling," she said. "That's a kind of power, I guess."

As if without his knowledge, his hands moved, tapped silently against the reflective surface, rubbed the steel finish. "Are we going to talk about it?" he finally said.

"The woman's death?" Not facing him, Josie braced her hands on the counter. She could still see him in the shining surfaces of the kitchen. Even sitting down and not looking at her, he disturbed the air between them in some indefinable way that sapped her will.

"What a nice, antiseptic way of putting it. But, yes, Josie, the woman's death. You obviously have questions about it. About what happened. Maybe we should deal with that first?" He pressed the tips of his fingers against the table, arching them like spiders, his hands poised so that it looked as if he were about to levitate the table using only the pads of his fingers. "We can talk about Sandi's death. Or we can talk about the peculiar things that have been happening—that would be my preference, actually. That was my original plan. I don't know what yours was."

She wasn't ready to talk about the reasons she'd come with him to his house. Not yet. She had to be sure about him, about his motivations for playing his games. Until she believed he wasn't setting her up in some way, she wouldn't reveal anything he didn't already know. She sensed that it was her only way of maintaining a balance of power between them. "All right. Let's talk about her. If you want to tell me about the accident." She turned around.

"Accident? Not quite as antiseptic a term as your first phrase, but, still, a pleasantly distancing way of removing cause and effect." Stretching his legs out, he slumped farther down into the chair as if the energy keeping him upright had abruptly drained from him. "Cause—me. Effect—" he shielded his eyes with an arm thrown over his face "—well, you read about the effect. An illusion went wrong. I lost my concentration. Something happened. I still haven't figured out what. Five people in the audience were injured. My assistant died."

"She was mauled by the tiger."

"Oh, yes. *Mauled* is an understatement."

"It was an accident," she insisted. "No one said it was your fault." His determination to see himself as a destroyer swayed her, elicited her sympathy when excuses wouldn't have.

"No," he repeated, his voice dead. "I told you. I lost control."

"Was the tiger yours?" Now she understood part of the torment that racked him, and pitied him. She did her own daily catechism of self-blame. "Did you train it?" She took three steps toward him.

"Not these days. Once I would have. The control issue, you see. But tigers are an endangered species. Most of us rent. The trainers come along with them. Except for Sieg-fried and Roy. Their situation is different. They raised their own tigers. White tigers.'' His words came out slower and slower, each syllable rusty with effort. "I'd worked with this tiger hundreds of times."

Bending down, Josie scooped the papers together. She held one toward him. "Nobody blamed you." The headline was large, centered over two columns of text next to a picture of Ryder in a tuxedo. "Lady or the Tiger: Illusionist Chooses Wrong Door." "The article says it was a case of bad luck. A mechanism jammed."

"I check the mechanisms before every trick. It's my job. I don't depend on luck. Unless I've stacked the deck first." His mouth twisted.

"What about afterward? What did you discover?" She wanted to press her hand against his agitated, twitching fingers, still them. They spoke to her in a sign language of their own.

"There was nothing wrong with the mechanism before or after the trick. The mechanism was fine. I lost concentration!" He jerked to his feet. "I didn't move fast enough! We'd timed the trick, performed it successfully for years."

"Then it couldn't have been anything but an accident. It wasn't a new trick. You were both familiar with every part of it. You must have been able to work it in your sleep."

"Sandi had enough time to make the switch. But this time—" he rubbed his eyes as he paced "—something dis-tracted me."

"You're a very…focused man, Ryder." She couldn't imagine his attention wandering from the stage, from what-ever he was doing. He was too intense. "Did you see some-thing in the audience? Hear a noise?"

"I don't think so, but I'm not sure. Everything seemed routine, the illusion going the way we'd always practiced it, but I must have taken too long with the patter and the setup. I'd moved to one side of the stage as Sandi's cage burst into flames. She disappeared. I was approaching the cage, moving through the flames and smoke, and then the tiger spooked. I heard him growl once. The smoke was there to cover Sandi's switch with the tiger, but suddenly, out of nowhere it seemed, the tiger came leaping out into the audience, snarling, his trainer behind him.'' Ryder groaned, the low sound filled with such pain that she hurt for him. ''I took off after the tiger, too. I never thought about Sandi. Somehow I got in front of him. I walked straight toward him. He kept backing up, slashing out with his paw, but he backed up. And the trainer got him. People were running, screaming, like today.'' He shuddered. ''But no one was killed this time.''

Josie had merely skimmed the old news reports. Back in January, she'd been numb with grief, moving through her days on automatic pilot, not able to do anything except get up and go to work and to the police station, or she would have read the papers and known who Ryder Hayes was when she first heard his name. ''Where was your assistant?''

''We found Sandi later. Her body was in the pocket behind the trapdoor. She'd been there with the tiger, but for some reason she hadn't been able to escape. To make the switch.'' Dropping his hands with a sigh, he squatted and shoved the papers together, handing them back to Josie. ''Somehow I was careless. And so I killed her.'' The edges of the white sheets shivered as a faint tremble ran through his fingers. ''That's my skeleton in the closet. Literally,'' he added as he looked up at her. ''One of them, at any rate. And then I came here. To more deaths. Those children. What if I'm responsible for them, too? Shh—'' He stopped as she interrupted him.

''What do the children's deaths have to do with you? You didn't kill them any more than you killed your assistant.'' She knew the absolute certainty in her voice momentarily stopped him.

The light washed out all the shadows on his face, turning it into a harsh mask. Tugging at the neck of his shirt, he frowned. "Until you showed up at my door, I was afraid I had, you see. I didn't know what else to believe." Tension radiated from his lean form, his rigid mouth.

Whatever he was, Ryder wasn't a killer. He wasn't trying to scam her. She'd seen the agony, the confusion in his eyes. They were real. "Why would you think such a thing?"

"Nothing else made sense to me. I don't do drugs. Nothing else explained what was happening to me. I thought guilt was making me crazy. But then you saw something in my hall. And today, after the parade, before we heard that child's voice, I saw, for one second, this clear picture of blood in the sand. Saw blood on my hands. Can you tell me where that picture came from, Josie? I've told you I sure as hell can't explain those voices, those images."

"But someone could fake it?"

"Hell, yes. I could figure out a way to create the same kind of effect if I wanted to. That's the easy part. But nothing I know about trickery and illusions explains how that voice and that shape appeared today. To you. To me. To us."

"There has to be a rational explanation, Ryder," she said, shying away from the implications of where he was shepherding her. "You're suggesting—what? That Eric's *spirit* spoke, and we heard it?" She shook her head. "That *spirits* are talking to us? That's impossible." She whirled away from him, unable to take in all the ramifications of what he seemed to be suggesting. "But what if they are communicating with us? What if they're evil?"

"I said I don't need anyone to hold my hand in the dark, and I told you the truth. I don't. But I need your help to figure out what's happening. I can't do it by myself."

"Because if I saw something, too, that gives credibility to the unbelievable? Because it will mean you're not crazy?

So you want me to believe that you and I are hearing communications from the ozone? From somewhere *beyond?*"

And if it were true? Oh, the infinite, blessed possibilities.

"From somewhere, at any rate."

She wanted to scream. Reality was not hearing voices, seeing things. "That's what you want me to *believe?*"

He shook his head abruptly. "No. I don't want you to believe anything. Josie, you have to understand. To me everything is a con, a trick. I've never taken anything on faith. All my life I've looked for the hidden wires behind the curtain. Mentalism? Psychic phenomena? Channeling? They're all hokum to me."

"But you're trying to make me think that some kind of psychic communication is happening. And I *can't!* It's too frightening!" Agitated, tempted by that slyly tantalizing hope, she wanted to weep with frustration.

"I don't want to talk you into anything. You don't have to do anything except tell me—like an observer, that's all— what *you* see. What *you* experience. But if I'm really seeing something that's related to those children, something I have no way of knowing, then I have to find out if it's real. I have to *know.*"

"That's what you believe? That there's a possibility that what happened was real? You're seriously considering this?"

"I don't know what I believe. Not yet."

"There must be some other explanation. You'll have me thinking I'm crazy, too." He was holding out a glimmer of hope where she'd had none, and it was a gift that could be the most brutal illusion of all. But it was that impossible hope that had led her to drive with him to this house. "You should know better than to believe that…that we're *hearing* that boy's voice. Seeing him."

"You're right. But you know what the real irony is, Josie? After all these years of fooling people, of providing the ultimate illusions, I *want* to believe that there's something authentic to these incidents. I need to believe in them.''

At last comprehending, Josie went to his side. ''If these occurrences are genuine, you think you can find out what happened with Sandi, don't you? That's your hidden agenda.''

He shrugged, not answering.

''And then you can finally find a way to forgive yourself for her death.'' She sighed. She knew how impossible forgiving yourself was because she'd never found a way to forgive herself for Mellie's disappearance. The what-ifs were unbearable. ''And that's why you want my help.''

Ryder was giving her a chance at redemption, a way of surviving the darkness.

If she went along with him. If she allowed herself to believe— But she needed more time to think.

Looking down at the copies she still gripped in her hands, Josie let them flutter to the table as she said, ''And you haven't gotten over the accident. You wallow in guilt.''

''Would you like me to tip my throat so you can go for the jugular next time?'' he inquired, a trace of venom in his polite tone as he shot her a slightly hostile glance.

''It's true, though, isn't it? You've shut yourself up in this house and you keep everyone at a distance. You don't want anyone to get close enough to find out what happened and offer sympathy or understanding. Is your hair shirt comfortable, Ryder?''

His eyebrows drew together with his scowl, and he stood up in one smooth, eye-pleasing uncoiling of muscle. ''I'm not punishing myself.''

''Whatever you say.'' Josie walked toward the refrigerator and paused with her hand on the cool metal of the handle. ''But I've always thought that if it walked like a duck, quacked like a duck—'' She understood too well the temptation to bury oneself in self-recrimination. It had a certain appeal. ''I'm sure you know best.'' Josie yanked open the door. "Do you have anything else to fix except sandwiches?"

"What?"

"I've discovered that being intimidated makes me hungry." Opening the door he'd slammed closed behind him as he'd stalked toward her with the pages he'd pilfered from her purse, she rested one hand on her hip while she surveyed the well-stocked contents. "Good grief. You could feed an army with this stash." She lifted out a package of deli meat and a lump of cheese, looked at the plastic fronts.

"I stocked up."

"This stuff's past the expiration date." Pulling out a container of cottage cheese, she looked at it in disgust, and tossed it to Ryder. "Is mold one of the major food groups I missed? Check the date on *that* lovely item. All this food, Ryder!" she said, exasperated at the waste, unaccountably vexed by his indifference to his own health. "Those steaks you mentioned earlier were nothing more than a figment of your imagination, were they?"

"I don't know. They were the first thing that popped into my mind. You might find some in the freezer."

She opened the freezer side, saw the huge packages of solid ice chunks piled one on top of the other. She poked one large rectangle dubiously. "Who knows what this is. Bet you haven't fixed a meal since you moved in, have you?"

"I've been busy."

"Active social life, Ryder?" she mocked as she pitched the deli meat, cheese and a carton of rancid milk into the garbage. "Hordes of weekend visitors, I suppose?" She knew what he was doing. She made herself eat because she had to, for Mellie.

"When I'm working, I forget about eating."

"I see. The lean and hungry look isn't just the result of a bit of extra self-punishment, then?" She covered her mouth. "Oops. Sorry. I forgot. You're not punishing yourself. That guilt load you're carrying has nothing to do with a refrigerator full of uneaten, past-its-prime food. You haven't eaten because you're just too busy practicing and working. *Very* praiseworthy of you.'' She nodded energetically, her attitude so cheerful that she figured it must be setting his teeth on edge. ''That makes sense. Planning a return to the stage soon, I guess?''

''No.''

''Hmm. These look safe.'' She carted a stick of margarine and a jar of jelly to the table. ''If you're not going back on the stage, why are you practicing?'' Pulling open sleek stainless-steel cabinet doors, she searched through cabinets stocked with cookware, boxes of cereal, bottles of wine that looked to her to be expensive enough to be in a wine cellar. ''Is there really any tuna fish here? A toaster?''

''And here I've been thinking you were such a *quiet*, restful woman,'' Ryder said, using the toe of his shoe to pop open a lower cabinet where a spanking-new, eight-slice toaster shone in all its chrome splendor. ''Silly me. The cans are over there. In the pantry.'' Nodding to a sleek door set into the wall in such a fashion that it seemed part of the room, he took the toaster and plugged it in.

Pressing along its edges, Josie popped the door open. ''Is there a secret panel behind the pantry? Seems as if being a magician, you should have one. So you could emerge mysteriously in some other part of the house while everyone thought you were safely in the kitchen.''

He shook his head.

Josie had no idea where the flood tide of questions was coming from. Part of her edginess came because she didn't want to consider the possibility he was holding out to her like a shining gold Christmas ornament. But the suffering in his eyes as he'd reluctantly detailed the events of his assistant's death left her vulnerable to him in a different way, made her nervous around him and kept her rattling on in an uncharacteristic fashion, unable to halt the torrent of words. "You could always build in a secret passageway in a house like this. It would be a good idea."

"Build a passageway?" His sigh was almost amused. "I figured you were a woman who didn't ask questions, Josie. What are you trying to do? Talk me to death?"

Surveying the high-tech chrome-and-white interior, she spoke to him over her shoulder as she removed a can of generically labeled tuna. "Intriguing contradictions in your food choices, too, Ryder. Makes me wonder which is the real you, which the illusion. The fancy wine? Cheap canned food?" She held the can out to him, but he didn't answer. "Actually, in answer to your earlier comment, I'm trying to feed us."

"Somehow that doesn't surprise me. Anybody who'd nurse a garden through a drought like this is into serious nurturing. Caretaking. But I can take care of myself, Josie. I'm not a kid." He stepped in front of her, his whipcord-tough body all adult male.

Involuntarily her gaze drifted across the breadth of his shoulders to his arms, his narrow waist, to the solid muscles of his thighs. "I can see you're not." She shifted to the side and he moved with her, making the distance between them seem too close, taking the air from her lungs. "No one would mistake you for a boy, Ryder."

"Good." His chest rose and fell in time with her breathing. "And I don't need a keeper." His breath fanned her face as he leaned over her. "It would be a mistake to let yourself think I do, Josie."

"I don't. I haven't."

"I need a lot of things, but that's not one of them. Least of all from you." He took one step closer, the toes of his shoes brushing hers.

And she felt the touch all the way through her body, a sharp, hot pang. "I understand."

"Probably not." He passed his long fingers over her face, her neck, down her shoulders to her breasts, not touching her, his fingers shaping the air that pressed against her flushed skin.

His eyes never left hers.

He had a way of focusing on her that made her skin too tight, made her womb ache with emptiness. He made her feel as if her body were soft wax, flowing toward him, waiting for his touch to shape it the way he shaped the air she breathed.

Seduction of a kind she'd never experienced.

Magical.

She swayed toward him and his eyes narrowed, darkened.

Illusive.

Reality was a hunger of a different kind. A different calling of the body, and she stepped once more to the side as his gaze dropped at last to her aching mouth. "I thought we'd both function better with some nourishment." She didn't recognize her own voice, so filled with yearning was it. A yearning beyond anything she'd ever known.

"I know what you're doing, Suzy Sunshine. You can drop it. I don't need nurturing any more than I need a keeper."

"Don't you?" she said softly, giving in to the pull, at last touching the deep lines beside his mouth. His skin was cool, firm, scratchy against her tingling fingertips, warming as she traced the grooves that seemed like brands of suffering. "Even once in a while?"

"No." He stepped closer and placed each hand on the counter behind her, enclosing her. "You know what I want, Josie." He bent his open mouth to her neck, to the pulse that thrummed there in invitation.

She jerked.

His lips were hot, hot, the tip of his tongue a spear of heat against her.

And everything was a blur of movement, of touch, of heat.

His hands, moving so fast, so fast, brushing her skirt aside, cupping her rear end, lifting her to the counter. His hands, sliding under her T-shirt, burning the length of her spine. His mouth, hot and wet, slipping down her throat, pushing aside the soft cotton neckline of her blouse.

Stunned by heat when she'd grown used to cold, she sagged against his body, melted into him in one shining moment of burning.

And craved more than that brief taste.

Frantic with need, Josie lifted against him, wrapping her arms tight around his wide shoulders, and it still wasn't close enough to ease the aching of her thighs, her breasts.

"God, Josie, please." He cupped one hand at the back of her head, the other clipped her heels behind his waist. "Damn, you can't know how much— God, Josie," he muttered into her ear, and his body moved against her, each stroke easing her pain, each stroke building the need.

She heard a groan and knew it must be her own, and the naked yearning in that groan shocked her. "This isn't me," she gasped through bruised lips, and raised her hands to the darkness of his hair, plunged her fingers into the thick strands.

"Then who?" he said, his mouth urgent against hers, his lips closing around hers as his tongue matched the rhythm of his hips against her.

"I don't know, I don't know," she cried. "I never knew." She angled her mouth under his, welcoming the urgency that matched her own. "So much pleasure."

"More. All you want. All you can take," he said, his voice dark and rough, all male animal demanding her touch as much as she needed his. "Whatever you want, Josie. Here?" He slid his open palm up the length of her thigh, pressing, circling, his fingers stroking where she ached the most. "Or here?" Through the cloth of her blouse, of her T-shirt, his teeth closed around her nipple, giving a sharp tug, a small bite, and all the while, his hand against the bare skin of her belly and thighs burned her.

She was jolted with such pleasure that there was nothing in her world except his touch on her body. No pain, no sadness. Only this pleasure. And in that instant of burning, she would have sold her soul, all for the pleasure that blazed through her and left her incandescent.

"Don't stop," she begged, pulling on his shirt, popping the buttons, as she felt him pull away. But he was only ripping his belt out of the loops, letting it fall to the floor in a coil of black leather that reminded her of something, the memory gone as he came back to her, the edges of his shirt draping over her arms, and she swept her hands over the smooth, hard muscles of his bare skin. "Please, don't stop."

"I can't." His voice was hoarse, unrecognizable. "Josie, I *want* you." He lifted her, and the gray-and-white colors of the kitchen, the tiles and shining chrome, blurred and whirled until, still locked to him, she shut her eyes against the dizzying light as he carried her down to the floor, his knee smacking the tile. "It's killing me, all this *wanting*."

His leg bent, he slipped off his shoes. Impatiently, Josie slid her toes along his socks, shucking them off. Against her feet, his were long, narrow, their high arches a delight to her sense of touch as she outlined their shape with her toes. His right foot flexed against hers, and with a motion so subtle that she was scarcely aware he'd done so, he wound his legs underneath hers, lifting her to him.

From outside came the shriek of the screech owl. The sound ripped through her, stripping away the cocoon of pleasure so abruptly that she was left on the brink, shuddering.

Opening her eyes, Josie saw Ryder's face above her, his eyes still closed, his down-curved mouth drawn tight into a grimace. His features strained with a need so elemental that it turned his elegant features savage.

She thought him lost to everything in the grip of his hunger. And in the seconds as her body returned to her and she knew herself as herself again, she envied him bitterly.

But it was too late.

Stranded on the shore, she had returned from some journey that had rocketed her to a place red-dark with pleasure and need.

The real world was a cold Italian-tile floor where she had almost…what? Made love?

Love had nothing at all to do with the fierceness of her longing for Ryder Hayes in those moments.

''Josie?''

Ryder shifted above her, but behind him, behind where all those gleaming doors mirrored them, Josie saw him, the back of his black hair, his white shirt, the white lace of her panties showing where her green skirt bunched above one carelessly sprawled leg.

Saw, too, the wild black of her unbraided hair spread across his floor in a wantonness she didn't know she possessed. The sight of the two of them, their bodies entwined, their clothes pushed aside in their haste, struck her as pagan. Frightening in its primitiveness.

She must have made a sound.

Watching her, Ryder went motionless. If she turned her head to the left, her mouth would brush his bent leg. He lifted slowly to both knees, his right palm still stretched across her abdomen, thumb and little finger resting on her hipbones.

As if he, too, were coming to himself, Ryder looked at his hand still spread across her stomach. He frowned. Lifting his hand from her, his fingertips lingering even as he withdrew his touch, he settled slowly back on his haunches. ''Did I hurt you?'' The dreadful tension that had distorted his features washed away, leaving him grim faced.

''No.'' Josie turned her head to the right. Flooded with embarrassment, her body still aching and unfulfilled, she couldn't bear to look at him, couldn't endure the sight of the two of them reflected over and over in all those shining cabinet doors. "No," she said, and shut her eyes, "you didn't hurt me."

"I scared you."

With each passing second, Josie felt her discomfort and humiliation growing. The image of herself lying on his floor, her skirt hiked up, her hair loose and tousled as he knelt over her disturbed her with its implication of domination and subjugation.

Victor.

And the vanquished.

Yet somehow it seemed more humiliating to struggle to her feet while he knelt there seemingly so self-possessed.

"I didn't plan this when I asked you to come here, Josie. Believe me. I didn't expect it. Finessing a lover is more my style, not...overpowering her. I'm sorry. If I could change what happened...God. To scare you like that. Damn." He flexed his hands, jammed them under his arms. His words came in fits and starts. "I can't believe—"

Near her, Josie saw one of his shirt buttons. The gleaming white circle was a reminder. She'd torn open his shirt in her frenzy to touch him. She'd touched him first, had traced the grooves beside the downward curve of his lips. He hadn't touched her until that moment. "You didn't scare me."

"I don't know what came over me. I've never been so—rough."

Out of control was the unspoken phrase that hovered between them.

"It wasn't your fault, Ryder." Smoothing her skirt down, she sat up and brought both legs to her chest. Wrapping her arms around them, she lowered her head to her knees and took a deep breath. She didn't dare stand up. Her legs were like overcooked spaghetti. "I don't know what came over me, either." She lifted her head and tried to smile. But that ability had left her, too. "Must have been the house." It wasn't much of a joke, but it was the best she could do at the moment, and she needed to take charge, to show him that she wasn't that woman she'd glimpsed in the reflections.

"Here." Rising, he held out a hand to help her up and then, with a look of misgiving, stuck it back under his arm. "I made a mistake bringing you here. I never thought—"

"Neither did I." Her legs still unsteady, she stood up.

Putting the table between them, he leaned against the refrigerator. "I couldn't stop, Josie. That's never happened to me before. I wouldn't have stopped."

"But you did." Shaking out the crumpled skirt, she tucked her T-shirt in with trembling fingers, rebuttoned her blouse and tied it at her waist. "You don't have anything to blame yourself for. You stopped."

"Only because you—" He glanced at the floor, touched a button with his foot, sliding the button back and forth with his toes, a tiny scraping sound in all the quiet. "All of a sudden you weren't there with me. What happened?" The button scraped a tile.

"I don't know. I think I heard…something." She struggled to recall what had intruded when she'd been senseless to everything except the exchange of pleasure. "An owl. Such a loud screech, as if it were in the room with me, and then everything changed. That was it. I heard the owl."

"Did you? I didn't hear anything except the sound of your voice, your heart thundering against my hand."

Forcing herself to walk toward him in spite of the mortification filling her, Josie said, "Look, Ryder, I don't have any skill at this sort of thing. I don't know how to make a sophisticated exit. What happened, happened. No one was hurt."

"Answer a question for me, first, though. Would you have stopped me, Josie? Stopped yourself if you hadn't heard the owl?"

Staring at the beautifully made button he edged back and forth, she admitted, "I probably wouldn't have."

"Do you make a habit of risky sex?"

Goaded beyond embarrassment, Josie raised her head and glared at him. "I shouldn't dignify that question with an answer, but you know I don't. It's an insulting question. How could you think that in this day and age I'd be so stupid? Are you? Do you make a habit of being…careless?" She put all the scorn she could in her question.

"Never. Not even once. Until tonight. And that's why I asked my question." One shoulder lifted in a shrug, he stuffed the tail of his shirt into his slacks, working the rest of the material in past the waistband of his pants as he continued. "My point is, lady green eyes, don't you find it a little…*curious*…that two people who usually act one way suddenly find themselves behaving uncharacteristically? Or is it your explanation that we're in the throes of some grand passion? Tell me, Josie, because the question enthralls me." Once more leaning against the refrigerator, he crossed his feet at the ankle and smiled so gently that anxiety knotted her stomach.

"What are you suggesting now, Ryder?" Aimlessly, unable to stand still, Josie wadded up the copies of the newspaper articles and crammed them into her purse.

"Let me ask you another question, okay?"

"Go ahead." But she delayed, rubbing her arms, trying to regain some of the warmth that had fled with the shriek of the owl. "Why do you keep it so cold in here, Ryder? Florida Power and Light must love you. Your bill has to be astronomical."

"The air-conditioning hasn't been turned on once this summer."

"Lucky you. But it's *cold* in here." She rubbed her arms again fretfully.

"I know." He hadn't moved, but the air stirred, seemed

to thicken. "I haven't been warm in so long I can't recollect when. Until a few minutes ago."

She remembered the chilly air swirling around her legs the day she'd come about the dogs, remembered, too, the cool touch of his fingers, his skin. Until tonight. There'd been no chill minutes earlier in the electric brush of skin against skin. Only that stunning heat.

"You're not hinting that you actually believe your house is haunted?" she asked. "Earlier, when you said that, you were joking, right?"

"I was joking, yes. And, no, I'm not implying I think this house is a halfway house for ghosts. But things are happening around us, Josie." Clipped, fast, his words pelted her like hailstones. "It's as though we're in the eye of a hurricane, everything dead-still around us, waiting for the big wind. For what will happen next. And every time we're together, the sense of being out of control grows stronger and stronger."

"That's ridic—"

He lifted his hand to stop her. "Wait. I'm not only talking about—this." He gestured to the floor, the scattered buttons. "More, Josie. The images grow more powerful, clearer, when I'm with you. I don't know why. But they do. And you share the experience with me. Every time we touch."

"But not—" She was bewildered. "We didn't hear any *voices*. We didn't *see* anything when we—" She halted, unable to complete the sentence since she didn't have words that defined what had happened to her, to him.

"No visions this time. No voices. Just this inexplicable hunger that turned us both mindless. Josie—" he leaned toward her, his gaze intense "—I don't know about you, but the house could have fallen down around us tonight and I wouldn't have known it. That damned elephant could have come charging through the door and I wouldn't have cared. What about you?'' he challenged.

And smiled, his mouth curving downward in satisfaction.

Josie could have slapped him. For the smile, certainly, but most of all for its curl of triumph.

CHAPTER SEVEN

Josie pulled out one of the table chairs and sat down, smoothing her rumpled skirt before she looked at him. Then, pulling that river of shining hair over one shoulder, she divided it into three thick strands, winding one over the other, her fingers moving quickly through the slippery strands as she faced him defiantly. "All right, Ryder. Since you've put me on the spot, you win. I wouldn't have stopped you." Her eyes were as green as the stone he'd taken from her, but unlike the stone, her eyes glittered with anger. "There!" She slapped the table. "Is that what you wanted to know?"

He didn't blame her. He'd pushed her to her limits. And he'd been pushed beyond every limit he'd observed throughout his life. "It'll do for a start."

"Does my answer give you some kind of masculine satisfaction? Feed your vanity? You looked so damned triumphant!"

Sensing her chagrin, he went to her in one stride and knelt down beside her. Her skirt puffed against his knees. "Aw, Josie, I'm sorry. And I don't have that kind of vanity. I've never been the kind of guy to notch bedposts. I'm not a scorekeeper. My damned curiosity prompted that insensitive, asinine, uncouth—" He let himself touch the light fabric. "Did I leave anything out? Any other tags you want to add? Listen, Josie, I smiled because your admission of your feelings escalates the whole mystery of what's occurring. I swear, I'm not trying to make you uncomfortable. Trust me on this, at least."

"Heaven help me if you ever really put your mind to it,

then," she said, her mouth pulled tight at the corners. "Because I'm *really* uncomfortable now, trust me."

"Me, too," he said. "I'm thirty-nine years old, and I've never been so careless with a woman in my life. Never wanted anyone so *feverishly* that I forgot everything in the immediacy of that urge to satisfy myself. I wasn't thinking about giving you pleasure. I was thinking about myself. Completely. Entirely."

The glitter was fading from her eyes. He had her attention.

"And I've never been that self-centered during love-making before, either, Josie. I've never—" he hesitated, searching for the right word "—never been taken out of myself to the point that I forgot about manipulating the scene, engineering what I felt, what my partner experienced." Trying to make her see how it was for him, he added, "Sex has always been like a game for me. A show, maybe."

"A show?" Finished with the braid, she flipped it over her shoulder. No longer confined by the rubber band he'd slipped off, the silky end unraveled, separated.

"With a supporting cast. Music. The whole bit. But the whole act *produced, controlled.* Josie, I wasn't seducing you. If I had been, I wouldn't have been so greedy. The scene wouldn't have gone out of control the way it did." He tapped the delicate roundness of her knee, wanted to let his hand linger. "Physical? Fun? Hell, yes. God knows, I sure enjoy sex. But everything under control."

"Sex without caring is so empty." She moved restlessly in front of him, her skirt catching on the corner of the chair. "But you said you like to be in control."

"Always."

"You've never been in love?" Her eyebrows drew together so silkily that the treacherous urge to touch her stirred again, making him shift as he knelt before her.

He understood what she was asking, but he didn't know

how to answer her. Pleating the fabric of her skirt in horizontal folds, he said, "I reckon not, Josie Birdsong."

"A solitary life, Ryder."

"I like being by myself. I like my life the way it is." At least he used to, before the images and voices. Before Sandi's death. "I've never felt the need of having someone to come home to. And if I had, I'd have bought a cat. Or a dog."

"So you've never been married," she concluded.

"Once." Inch by inch, pleat by pleat, the filmy cotton revealed her calf, its curving strength. He didn't touch her. "When I was nineteen. It lasted a year. I was bored, she wanted something I couldn't give. Love, maybe."

"Probably." Her tone was dry. "That's usually the reason for marrying someone. Love."

"Or sex. Or business."

"Such cynicism," she said, and her mouth softened as she looked at him in such a way that he thought he'd have to kiss its softness again, taste its honey.

Foolishness, of course.

"Sandi was important to you, though, wasn't she? She was more than your assistant."

"She was important," he admitted, sorting through the complexity of his feelings for the willowy red-haired woman who'd been with him for seven years. "We had an understanding. It was convenient for both of us. I cared for her. In my own way."

"But you didn't love her."

"No," he said, wondering for the first time why he hadn't. "She was sweet, funny. A walking, talking doll, but, no, I didn't love her, whatever that means. I should have." Like salt in a wound, the thought stung. "Maybe that's part of the guilt eating away at me. That I couldn't love her."

"And you were more important to her than she was to

you," Josie murmured. "That's part of the guilt, too, isn't it?"

He shrugged, wanting to drop the subject. "I can't change what happened, but I have enough guilt over Sandi to last me a couple of lifetimes."

Ryder couldn't handle the compassion that warmed her face. "What about you?" He let the pleats of her skirt fall as he stood up and walked to the window, looking out, as she had, at the July night. If she'd been in love with her husband, some part of her remained untouched by the experience, or she wouldn't have become wildfire in his arms. With his back still to her, he asked, "Did you love your husband?" He was intensely curious.

She nodded. "Yes. Of course." Frowned. "I thought so. I was sure crazy about him when we married. I must have. I know I loved Mellie."

Her sigh was the saddest sound he'd ever heard, and once again that errant tenderness stirred, touching him.

Ryder turned slowly, the tenderness taking root as he looked at her drained face. Tenderness was like the kudzu vine. It would take over if you gave it half a chance. "And that's why you were willing to come here tonight with me? Because of Mellie."

"A mother shouldn't have to outlive her child. I would have given my life for her."

The simple words devastated him.

"You would?"

She snapped her fingers. "That fast. Without even thinking. I wish, oh, God, how I wish, it had been me and not Mellie."

The clear spotlight of her words shone on his actions, his motivations, exposing them in all their selfishness.

Her love for her daughter was the lever he'd pulled to persuade her into coming with him.

He told himself he didn't have to feel regret for having used that lever, for having exploited her emotions. But looking at Josie's soft face, the deepening purple under her eyes, he couldn't convince himself he'd acted for the best, that he'd had her interests in mind.

He'd acted for himself. No one else.

Not even for the children.

That admission hurt.

He'd told her he could help her with her daughter in order to get what he wanted. He'd been playing a role, maneuvering her, for no other reason than that his curiosity spurred him on. He hadn't considered her well-being.

Not once.

The knowledge forced its way past his rationalizations, filled him with remorse.

Accepting the truth of his behavior in all its ugliness, he saw how flimsy Josie's defenses were. Prickly, independent, coping with a loss he couldn't begin to comprehend, she presented her picture of strength to the world, that strength a mask for the terrible fragility she hid with every atom of her being.

She wouldn't like knowing he saw past her mask. Wouldn't want his pity, but she stirred unaccustomed feelings in him that he didn't know how to handle.

Josie Birdsong Conrad would see an admission of weakness as a failure.

Because of his selfishness, he'd put her in even greater danger than he'd dreamed. He recognized, even if she still didn't, the power of what had whipped through him. The violence and the need.

The urge to mate with this woman and no other had overwhelmed him so fast it'd fried his brain. The need had been all hormones, primal.

Uncivilized, brutal.

He'd stopped.

But it had been a struggle. A closer one than he was comfortable admitting. He'd been ready to take her there on the floor, had seen her naked against the gray tiles, his mouth against her breasts and thighs. He'd seen his body thrusting into hers and her small heels riding against his hips.

And he'd wanted the reality of that picture more than he'd ever wanted anything in his life.

Even after he'd sensed her withdrawal, the pictures had pounded in his brain until he hadn't wanted to stop, not even with her lying still and cool underneath him, her mossy green eyes shocked as they met his.

Maybe regret wasn't enough.

"Josie, I'm sorry. For everything. For acting like a donkey's rear end. For what happened here." He gestured toward the floor. "It would never have happened if I hadn't persuaded you to come here today."

"You've apologized. Once was enough. We were both at fault, regardless of what happened."

"Hell, you don't know the half of it. I even left my car at the parking lot so that I could wheedle you into letting me ride with you. I didn't want to let you out of my sight, and I was ready to do anything to get you in one place long enough to talk with me. Well, I screwed this up right royally, Josie, and I'm more sorry than I can say."

"Regardless of what you think you talked me into doing, I made my own decision, and for my own reasons," she said. "You didn't trick me or persuade me or force me to do anything. Now go call somebody and make arrangements for your car to reappear." She paused, pursed her mouth. "You're awfully good at this guilt thing, Ryder. Must be a side effect of the magician business. I wonder, when it rains in Seattle, do you take responsibility for that, too?" A smile flashed across her face as quickly as the beat of a hummingbird's wings, leaving an impression of something rare and miraculous.

"These days, I might claim credit for the drought." He shook his head. "I knew what I was doing. You didn't."

"Oh, Ryder," she scoffed. "Come on, *please*. Do I look

that helpless? Now you've really insulted my womanhood. Or are you trying to make me feel guilty enough to sew on your buttons?'' Tilting her head and fluffing the gossamer green cotton skirt, she regarded him in much the same way Betsy sometimes did, ruffling her feathers, waiting patiently.

For some reason, the idea of Josie's sewing his buttons back on his shirt appealed to him. Maybe it was the thought of her small, capable hands working on his shirt, moving over it as they'd pressed against his chest. A prosaic act, tranquil. The kind of domestic act women had done for their men for centuries. A different kind of pleasure, and he surprised himself by asking, ''Would you?''

''Hmm.'' She lifted the toaster, put it down, twisted the cord. A tinge of pink touched her cheeks, vanished. ''Let's say I'd consider it. Since I tore them off, you'd be justified in saying I owed you. Probably.''

''I can sew, Josie,'' he murmured, watching the way her cheeks changed color, leaving that delicate pink against her tan. That fading rose tempted him unbearably, beyond his understanding. ''As well as you, possibly. In the early days I made most of my own costumes, designed and built the illusions until they became too complicated and expensive.''

''You said you didn't need a keeper. Obviously you don't need a tailor, either. You don't need anyone, do you, Ryder? Not really. Not for anything important.'' Her expression was contemplative, sad, as she wound the cord around the toaster and secured the plug inside the circle of cord. ''You thought my life was lonely, but I can't begin to fathom the level of your loneliness. Not to care or be cared for in that deepest sense. To miss out on that emotional connection with another human being in a way that lifts you out of yourself. You're the one who's led a lonely life, I think. Not to need anyone.'' She placed the toaster on the table, her hands resting on it.

Annoyed, Ryder thought she might as well be speaking a foreign language for all the sense her words made to him. Nothing was missing from his life. "I meant that I didn't want you feeling obligated, thinking you had to square accounts by repairing my shirt. I'll do it myself. Or I'll send the damned thing to the laundry. It's not a big deal. I was teasing you."

"Teasing?" Across the curve of her cheeks, her lashes cast shadows.

He wanted to brush them away, brush all the darkness away from her. Even nettled by her implications, he couldn't control the surge of feelings toward her. "Once in a while I tease."

"All right." She tipped the jelly jar between her hands as if she were weighing it. "Sometimes it's hard for me to know when you're playing games and when you're... teasing. Send the shirt to the laundry, Ryder. That's the best idea. And make that phone call." Steadying the jar, she stood up and pushed her chair under the table. Rocking the chair sideways, left, right, as if she were weighing something in her mind, she finally asked, "Do you still want me to give you my reactions and observations about our...ozone incidents?" Her spin on the phrase let him know she might cooperate with him, but she was still reserving judgment.

With the phone in his hand, he punched in the last number of the tow service and answered her while he waited for the phone to be picked up at the other end. "Nothing changed my mind. What made you decide to trust me? Because I can sew on my own buttons?"

"No. I think it was the fact that you didn't try to make me feel that I should sew them on for you. I wondered if you'd act like a jerk. You know, 'Oh, she was coming on to *me*. She *wanted* what happened.' As if everything were my fault. You could have done that very easily." She shrugged. "A lot of men would have."

"Would it have worked?"

"What do you think?" She smiled faintly at him.

"I could have wound up with the buttonholes sewed shut?"

"It's a nice shirt." Her gaze strayed to the gap in the front where he'd crossed the shirttails over, and his groin tightened with that inadvertent look. "I might have spared it."

"Custom-made, Josie." He held up a hand to stop her as the mechanic came on the line. Explaining quickly what he wanted done, he hung up and returned his attention to her. "Almost as expensive as my car, the door of which you were prepared to rip off, which, incidentally, I haven't forgotten." A button rattled under his foot.

"You're teasing me again, aren't you?"

Stooping down to retrieve the buttons, he glanced up at her. "You're catching on."

"In spite of an unfortunate fondness for game playing, Ryder, you're a fair man. Scrupulously so. That counts for a lot with me." She took the toaster to the counter and unwound the cord, plugged it into the wall outlet. "And since you think you can't find your answers alone, I'll help you." She opened a drawer flush with the cabinets, then another, searching until she located a can opener. "Now, let's eat and then see if we're both hallucinating or if there's a smidgen of truth to all this cockamamie psychic hoo-hah." Clamping the opener onto the can, she turned the knob. With her movement, the heavy braid unraveled a bit more, its gleaming color inviting him to brush the strands across his lips. If he did, he knew it would leave the taste of roses on his mouth.

Appreciating the sway of the braid across her back, the vulnerability of her bent neck as she concentrated on the task, he refrained from showing her the Swiss-made can opener in its specially made drawer under the counter. "Jelly and tuna fish?" he asked politely.

"Of course," she said, matching his tone and tossing him a quick look. "Do you have a problem with that?"

"Not at all. I'm sure it will be delicious." Giving her a small smile, he retrieved a bottle of mayonnaise from the fridge and offered it to her, lifting his eyebrow in a question. "Or was the plan to spread everything on the bread in layers?"

She gestured with the can of tuna. "Depends on that mayonnaise, Ryder, and how long it's been in residence. Does it qualify yet as an antique?"

He checked. "Nope." Handing her the bottle, he reached for bowls and plates, their sleek black shapes as smooth against his fingers as her skin had been.

Offering him her trust, she'd altered the situation in some indefinable way. In spite of everything, she was going to help him. Ryder sensed that in giving him her trust, she'd given him a responsibility he hadn't anticipated.

He didn't think she gave her trust easily.

He wouldn't treat it lightly. He would treat it as the treasure he suspected it was.

"Ryder?" She handed him the jelly. "Want to macho this jar into submission?"

"If I do, I won't insult your feminine sensibilities?" he said meekly.

Her eyes sparkled at him, but she didn't quite smile. "Oh, good. A man who knows his place."

"Barefoot." He looked down at his naked feet. "In the kitchen." He kept his face grave. "But even with magic, I can't manage the rest of it."

And then she truly smiled, a cheeky grin that cramped his chest.

"Ah, sweetheart," he said, stepping away from the enchantment even as his traitorous hand lifted to trace her mouth, "what a smile you have. You're a heartbreaker, you are, Josie Birdsong. You could bring stronger men than I to their knees."

Her voice was wistful. "My husband managed to resist. You're trying to sweet-talk me so that I don't change my mind again. You don't have to, Ryder." She dug into the mayonnaise with a large spoon.

"If I were going to sweet-talk you, I'd have done it the first time I met you instead of slamming my door in your face, Josie. You can take my comment however you want, Josie, but it may be one of the few times in my life I've said something without calculating the effect."

Startled, she let the spoonful of mayonnaise plop into the bowl.

"If he couldn't appreciate what he had in his life, your husband was a fool. I'm not. I see you for what you are. You're something special, Josie Birdsong. If you ever fall in love again, that man will know what real magic is. He'll know a miracle." He sighed and retreated another step, the tile growing colder with each step away from her, each step a pain.

Thumping the spoon vigorously against the bowl, she stirred the mayonnaise into the tuna and didn't answer him.

He walked away.

There was nothing else to do.

Except take her into his bedroom and love her all night long, show her the miracle of herself.

Enticed, Ryder stopped, almost did an about-face to go to her.

But he kept going. Retrieving his shoes and socks, he tucked the rolled socks inside and lined the sneakers alongside the others at the back door.

Later, taking a last sip of the wine Ryder had poured, Josie gestured with the translucent black glass in the direction of his bare feet stretched out under the kitchen table. "You said you're always cold. Why don't you wear socks? Or bedroom slippers?" She couldn't quite get past the picture of those graceful feet in something as mundane as slippers.

"I'm a very tactile person, Josie. I like the feel of the tile against my feet. My sense of touch grounds me. Maybe in the same way a blind person's other senses become more acute, my sense of touch tells me things. It's how I *know* something."

She remembered the feel of those arches against her own bare feet. The glass tilted in her hand. "That brings us full circle, doesn't it?" Centering the glass between them, she took a deep breath. "To what you want to *know*. To what neither of us believes can be possible. Yet both of us, for our own reasons, would desperately like the impossible to be real. More contradictions."

Sliding down to his tailbone, he nodded. "Yeah. So, here we are. Whenever you're ready. I await your command."

"Even the way you talk is a contradiction, Ryder. Do you realize that?" Josie knew she was delaying again. She'd decided that approaching the subject was sort of like waiting for bad news. Until you actually heard it, it didn't exist. In spite of Ryder's carefully contained impatience that was about as subtle as a highway billboard, she wasn't quite ready to *know*. "You have this formal way of talking, but then you sound pure grits and gravy. I don't get it."

He lifted his glass toward her in a mock salute. The light shone through the glass, showed the silhouettes of his fingers against it. "Short version, then, Josie," he said, turning the glass in his fingers, faster and faster until she thought the wine would slosh out onto the table.

"I'm...curious," she said, playing on the word he'd used. "But curiosity doesn't always have to be satisfied. Sometimes it's simply good old-fashioned, across-the-backyard nosiness."

Acknowledging her small barb, he smiled. "Be that as it may, my father was a Czechoslovakian merchant seaman, Josie, before immigrating first to England and finally to America where he became a citizen and married my mother. He was forty-five. She was eighteen and a Florida cracker. She wanted a hero, a savior. He wanted a maid. And someone to have sex with.''

"I see.'' Josie thought his cynicism might have been learned early.

"Do you, lady green eyes? How perceptive of you, then.''

"I'm listening.''

"You don't have to take notes. There won't be a test afterward.'' He drank the rest of the wine in one swallow, and Josie knew the memory was like the irritant in an oyster shell. "I was their lone offspring, despite my father's rigorous efforts. Following one of those efforts, my mother died. I was eight. A year later, I ran away for the first time. When I was thirteen, I ran for good. As far away and as fast as I could. Until then, for all the years I lived under my father's roof, he insisted we speak Czech at home. Never English. I was the class geek the other kids avoided. So I listened carefully to the teachers, imitated them, their manners, the way they talked. Quite the way to become one of the neighborhood guys, huh?'' He refilled his glass.

"I can think of worse ways, Ryder.'' Josie wished she'd left his past alone. She'd broken her rule, and his story made her want to weep for him, for children like him. Mellie had been so carefree, so— She stopped her thoughts before they fell into the groove of pain and stayed there. "What did you do? You're not a...*geek.*''

"I was the awkward kid in the too-clean clothes with the Old World father who yelled at any of the neighborhood kids who walked across his manicured yard. And inside our house, he ruled with the proverbial iron hand or, sometimes, the iron pot. If he felt like it. And he did. Frequently.''

"What did your mother do? Didn't she stop him? She must have.''

"She tried. It didn't do any good.''

"How could she stay with him, then? She should have left."

"She was a kid, too, Josie. With no resources, nobody to help her. She didn't know there were solutions for her. For me."

Understanding now how many skeletons clacked away in his closet, Josie reached out to touch him, but he withdrew his hand. "Oh, Ryder. How terrible for you, and for your mother. What did you do? How did you endure that kind of unhappiness?"

"Unhappiness?" He seemed bewildered. "I don't remember being unhappy. Or happy. Life was just what it was."

"What changed?"

"For a long time I was the goody-two-shoes Hayes kid who didn't have the hang of kid talk or kid play. Until I read my first magic book when I was nine. Magic opened doors for me. Made me the man you see before you," he finished, his mouth twisting with mockery. "Unless, of course, I'm surrounded by my magic paraphernalia, and then I may or may not be the man you see before you. Or anywhere else, thanks to the power of suggestion and illusion." He leaned across the table earnestly, his words beginning to slur with exhaustion and the wine. "Don't look so sad, green eyes. It's not the worst thing that ever happened. Not by a long shot."

"Bad enough," Josie said, distressed. It was hard for her to reconcile the power of the grown man with the idea of the defenseless child. "We have to pass a test, have a license to drive a car, but to raise a child, all anybody has to do—"

"Is what comes naturally," Ryder said. "And that's why I've always made a point of being very, very careful, Josie. About sex. I don't want to find out after it's too late that I'd be as lousy a father as mine. Understand now why my behavior surprised me so much?" He leaned back and topped off his glass, emptying the bottle. Bemused, he frowned at the two empty bottles. "I reckon I shouldn't have opened the second bottle." Yawning heavily, he rumpled his hair. "I didn't realize I was so tired. I don't as a rule have more than one or two drinks."

"That control thing again, huh?"

He nodded, the strands of his dark hair falling onto his forehead.

"You know something, Ryder?" Josie stood up and walked over to him, brushing his hair back from his face as she stood beside him.

"I know a lot of things, Josie Birdsong. Which particular something are you talking about?" He angled his chin toward her hand, and even though she'd told him to find his comfort somewhere else, and meant it, now she wanted to solace the child she saw lingering still in his dark eyes. Like the missing children from Angel Bay, the child she saw haunting the man wrenched her heart.

But, as he'd made dazzlingly clear, Ryder wasn't a kid.

He was an adult male who would take, and offer, comfort of a kind that neither she nor he could afford to risk. But, oh, the glory of that taking and giving. She tapped his cheek and reached for their empty plates. "Do you have any idea how late it is?"

"Not a clue." His sleepy smile was rakishly charming. "And I'm about two sips away from being drunk as a skunk, Josie."

"Good thing the bottles are empty, then." Snagging the bottles with two fingers, Josie twitched them off the table and over to the sink.

He applauded lightly. "Nice moves."

Looking back at him as she placed the bottles and plates down, Josie smiled. "You like the way I clean tables, huh?"

"Clever, Josie. You're catching on. Of course that's what I meant." He shut one eye and scanned her with a professional eye. "You're quick. You've waited on people a lot, haven't you?"

"Oh, yes." Not liking the sarcasm that escaped in her answer, Josie frowned as she scraped the plates and found the release lever that opened the dishwasher. "Been there. Done that."

"Ah. The ex," Ryder said.

"The ex," she agreed, not sure she liked the way Ryder's eyes narrowed, all the sleepy tigerishness suddenly gone.

"Want me to make him disappear, green eyes?" His words were cold sober.

"He did that all by himself." Josie wiped her hands on a square of toweling she found under the sink.

"If I dared touch you, Josie, if the situation were different, I could make him disappear forever for you."

She blinked.

"There are ways I could touch you, kiss you, ways I could make you want me until you'd never think of him again. What happened earlier tonight was simply a prelude."

A curl of pleasure rose from her toes.

"But I wish I could make the pictures of you lying there on my kitchen floor with your hair loose and wild disappear because I'm growing more and more certain each minute I'm going to regret for the rest of my life that I'll never have another moment like that. Josie," he said, and his voice grew somber, "I'm going to take that memory with me to the grave."

"Ryder," she said, more disturbed than she wanted him to know, "don't talk like that. We don't need the kind of complications that will come if we let ourselves drift into that kind of empty sex. And that's all it would be. For either of us. If you want the unvarnished truth, I was astonished that I responded to you the way I did, and, yes, I've never felt more alive during those moments, but, Ryder, right now

I'm so empty of everything except my obsession with my daughter that I don't have anything left to give. Not now. Perhaps never. And sex as a show, a performance—that isn't what I need. Or want. And I can't believe that it would be anything more than that for you.''

"Maybe you're right, Josie, and Lord knows, I could list a hundred reasons why we can't risk playing with fire, and have, but every time I get near you, those reasons fly out of my head. At the same time I know it would be a dangerous indulgence to ignore all those excellent reasons, I find I give in to the temptation.''

He rose and approached her. Carefully not touching her, he reached around her for the dishrag and returned to the table. The cloth flicked in his hands, the quickness of his movements cleaning the table in the time it took Josie to catch her breath. What he told her was so close to her own reactions, that she didn't know what to do, what to say.

"Aw, Josie, if the situation didn't have so much potential for disaster, I'd find the whole thing hellishly amusing, personally.'' Slouching with one arm braced on the table, he grinned and shook his head. "How about you, green eyes? Don't you want to laugh at the two of us? Isn't this a farce for the ages? Don't you imagine somebody up there is having a rare old cosmic joke at my expense?''

"No, Ryder, I doubt that anyone's laughing at us.'' Josie caught the dishrag as he flipped it toward her. "I think we're tired, we've been through a lot together, and we're—''

"Off-balance?'' Folding his arms, he leaned against the counter as she rinsed out the cloth.

"That, too, but I think it's more that we're both walking a fine line of guilt and exhaustion and stress. And confusion. We have all those emotions in common, and we've both let ourselves become isolated from other people. It's not healthy, Ryder. I think for the first time in a long time for both of us, we're reaching out for human contact in all the loneliness.''

"Maybe you're right." He tipped his head back, looking at the bright lights of the ceiling. "I hope you are."

"I am," she insisted.

"When you put it like that, it sure sounds simple, doesn't it?" he said. "Well, Josie, if you're right, all we have to do is stay a good ten feet away from each other and everything will be hunky-dory, huh?"

Her hands twisting around the dishrag, Josie nodded.

"Such an earnest little frown you have between your eyebrows, Josie. So determined, so fierce. And all I have to do to resist smoothing out that endearing worry line is to stay right here while you stay where you are, huh?" He smiled at her and ran his hands over his rumpled hair as he straightened and stifled a yawn. "Well, we'll see, sweetheart. We'll see. In the meantime, despite the increasingly late hour, let me escort you to my sanctum sanctorum, and we'll struggle against all these carnal urges as best as we can while we test a couple of hypotheses. All right?"

"I'm on vacation. My schedule's my own. And I don't sleep well at night, anyway."

"I know, Josie. I don't sleep well, either, and I've seen you, night after night, out there among the candles on your porch. The first time I stumbled out of the woods and saw your face floating above all those flickering candles, I thought I was seeing an honest-to-God, come-to-earth angel. It was an illusion, of course. You were wearing some kind of inky shirt, and with your dark hair, nothing showed in all that blackness except your face." His sideways glance was casual, but Josie didn't make the mistake of underestimating his throwaway comment. "Well, Josie, it made me feel like a lost sailor spotting a lighthouse on a stormy sea."

He motioned her toward the hallway and turned off the kitchen lights as they left.

Down the dim, wide hallway that led from the front door to the back of the house, Josie followed Ryder's wide back, the journey reminding her so strongly of her night dreams that her heart beat erratically, bumping between terror and exhilaration with each step farther into the recesses of Ryder's house where the shadows seemed thicker, palpable.

CHAPTER EIGHT

Josie gasped as Ryder pressed a switch, and muted, glittering lights filled the room, a slowly rotating faceted chandelier sending prisms of light into the dim corners.

The room was fantastic.

Ten, twenty—so many that Josie couldn't count them all, huge, six-by-six-foot squares of silk adorned the walls. One scarf had a picture of a man in a winged black cape waving a wand over boxes painted with mysterious symbols. In his chalk white face, the red of his mouth seemed perverse, the slash of black eyebrows menacing. The reds and golds of the silks were sumptuous, an invitation to the senses. Not all the scarves were picture designs. Stars and clear glass balls filled in the backgrounds of several, and some were blends of rich colors and gold thread in abstract designs swirling on black backgrounds.

And the mirrors.

In front of one mirror near the chair where Ryder stood was a square, open-bottomed table with a mat and a deck of cards.

In the others, Josie saw herself in a dozen pieces, her wrinkled skirt, bare legs, her wide eyes.

It was a wicked room.

A room that lured a woman, whispered to her.

It was a room that made a woman's clothes feel too tight, constricting. Made her want to slip out of them, drape herself in one of the opulent scarves, see her lover's eyes darken with an unnameable passion in the mirror.

It was a room that made her feel reckless.

Oh, it was a wicked room, and it spoke to the wickedness inside her.

It was the heart of the house.

Captured by the opulent images on the wall, she lingered at one scarf. An enormous green-eyed panther, mouth open in a ferocious growl, crouched in the foreground of one of the panels, while above him, the sorcerer arose from the sleek panther, one hand extended, palm down toward the head of the snarling animal.

A current of air moved behind the scarves, puffing the pictured animals and figures into a three-dimensional effect and rippling the fabric until the whole room seemed alive with creatures and magic.

Entranced, Josie studied the scarves. Reaching out to touch the one with the panther, she glimpsed Ryder off to the side of the room. "May I?" she asked, turning to see him standing near a winged burgundy velvet chair with a table beside it. "Is it all right to touch them?"

"Go ahead," he invited, and Josie's skin shivered at the abrupt roughness in his voice, the sound hinting of luxurious pleasures that matched the phantasmagoria surrounding them.

The silk moved under her light touch with a life of its own, the fabric a call to the senses. Following the lines of the panther's body, its powerful muscles, she traced upward to the shape of the magician's hands, the long, supple fingers, the pale face with its high cheekbones so like Ryder's. "It's beautiful," she breathed. "Gorgeous."

And she wasn't clear whether she meant the silk picture or the man.

"That's why I collect them. I like the look, the feel of them. They're not art objects, though. These silks were all used by magicians in their acts."

Again, she touched that hauntingly pale, silk face with its mesmerizing gaze. Cool, like Ryder's skin. "They must be valuable."

"Some are. Some aren't. The scarves are permanent, the

acts weren't. They were a fleeting entertainment, seen and gone, like magic itself.''

''Before television magic brought the whole world and its violence and reality right into our living rooms and bedrooms.'' She thought of the edited pictures from the afternoon's parade, the faces. The sounds.

''Television distances us. From reality. From pain. Everything is diminished, made trivial by that box. After a while, we're able to turn our backs on the suffering we see there. The marvelous becomes mundane, another hohummer, flip the channel.''

''We're overloaded with everyday miracles.'' Again Josie thought of the parade, the enraged elephant shrunken to a size smaller than her little finger. None of the smells and fear of that moment.

''But back then, the thrill for the audience was in being there, seeing and being amazed at what couldn't be. Ladies appearing and disappearing, turning into birds, tigers. A man in an iron oven cooking steaks and coming out unscathed, unburned. How could he have done it? Ah, Josie, that was the thrill of it.'' His eyes gleamed with enjoyment, and she thought it was a shame that she'd never get a chance to see him perform on a stage. ''They were *there*, you see. They could smell the meat cooking, hear the sizzle. A woman in a cage with metal bars vanishing in midair. Impossible. Real. Tricks.'' He shrugged.

''But everyone knew that they were seeing tricks.''

''Of course they did, but seeing's believing, Josie, for most of us, and we give great validity to what's in front of our noses and forget about what the left hand's doing. And the more people were fooled, the better they liked it. Nobody really wants to know the secrets. If you know the trick, there's no more mystery.'' He picked up the cards on the table in front of the chair, shuffled them, the cards flying through his fingers, his eyes dark and somber as he watched her trace the shape of the magician and his panther. "Most people prefer the mystery. I don't."

With the current of air under the silk, the haunch of the panther seemed to bunch against her fingertips, collecting as if he were about to spring out of the scarf toward her. But the magician's hand controlled the beast, reminding Josie of Ryder's motions toward the dogs from the woods. "Because the man who knows the gimmick is the man in control."

"That's about it." He moved restlessly. "I don't like being fooled."

"Nor do I," she said, reluctantly turning away from the scarf and wandering to the far side of the room where shelves filled the wall.

Stacks of *Magic Magazine,* their edges lined neatly. Hundreds of books, she couldn't begin to count them. The extravagance of the room made her breathless. Josie took a deep breath. Books on magic, biographies of magicians, books on chemistry and electronics and electricity. A set of schematics for illusions.

One book lay open to a diagram of pulleys and wires, weights and counterweights that made no sense to her but which intrigued her, hinting as it did of behind-the-scenes intricacies. Josie flipped the pages, fascinated. Wrinkling her nose, she turned the book sideways, trying to see if she could tell what effect the diagram would produce. "This is incredible. I had no idea so much was involved in producing a trick."

"Money, too."

She glanced his way. "Expensive?"

"An illusion like making the Statue of Liberty disappear can cost thousands and thousands of dollars. Six hundred thousand dollars isn't out of the ballpark. There are engineering people who work out the details once you come up with the premise. Their time's expensive. An illusion show's expensive to create. To produce. Some of us work

closely with the production, some don't. I like knowing
what's going on at every point." He walked over to one
of the shuttered windows covered by drapes and lifted it
up, looking outside. "Illusions are easy to learn to do,
though, not like the physical tricks. They take training and
stamina. Like Houdini's Metamorphosis, where you have
to change places, handcuffed, inside a bag. Speed's the key
there." He sighed. "The trick with Sandi was a variation
of the Metamorphosis."

Looking up from the book, Josie saw him slump toward
the darkened window and rest his forehead against the
pane. Even if he eventually discovered what had gone
wrong with that trick, he would always blame himself for
not being fast enough.

In the glass of the window, his gaze caught hers as he
lifted his head. The room was silent as they stared at each
other, only the sound of the wood in the highly varnished
floor creaking as she shifted, only the sound of his
breathing until he stepped back, facing her as he let the
shutters and drapes fall.

"With all this information, it would be easy to create
some of the things we saw, Ryder," she said slowly as she
returned her attention to the book she held, thumbing
through it, stopping as she saw a diagram that showed a
collapsible ring under fabric, the effect suggesting that the
woman was still there in the open cage while in the meantime she'd dropped down a trapdoor and was preparing to
appear inside a closed box on an open-legged table in the
center of the stage.

"Exactly. So let's see if we can figure out what we're
working with." He tipped his head toward a chair not far
from him. "Find a place where you'll be comfortable, and
then I want to listen to everything you have to say. Don't
skip any details. Just let me listen."

Taking her time as she stopped at first one item and then
another, the room seeming more and more like a treasure

chest spilling forth its wealth, she wandered toward the chair. "I don't think men have any idea how seductive that invitation is, Ryder. More enticing than they can imagine, believe me. Many a woman's been led astray by that simple phrase."

"Not you, though, Josie. You'd see through the ploy."

"I don't know. A man giving you his whole attention when sex isn't involved. A man *listening*. It's awfully tempting." Her sense of mischief prompted her smile.

"Stick out your tongue, Josie," Ryder said, startling her.

"Why?" She frowned.

"Thought I'd check to see if it's really razor sharp."

Giving him a reproving look, she wandered toward a series of black-and-white photographs on the wall near the couch. They were all signed photos of men whose names she didn't recognize. "No women magicians?" she asked, turning toward him where he remained at the wing chair.

"Not many women get into magic as the main performer. One or two. Mostly we're a boys' club, Josie." His mouth twitched, and she thought this time it was with amusement as he continued imperturbably, "Much as that pains me to admit to you."

"Hmm." She pointed to the forest green sofa. "Anyway, is this going to be like going to the psychiatrist? Do I have to lie down on that?" Its supple leather was piled with pillows, and a burgundy-and-green blanket draped one of its thickly padded arms. A thought nagged her. "Is that where you sleep?"

"Most of the time."

She wondered whether his bedroom resembled the kitchen or the room they were in, but she knew better than to ask. With its wealth of color and textures, this room swamped her senses, encouraging that side of her she'd discovered in Ryder's arms and leaving her vulnerable when she needed to be strong. If his bedroom was anything like this room—

She didn't think it would be smart of her to curl up cozily on that couch. Not tonight. Not after everything that had already happened. She sat down in the chair he'd offered and put her feet up on a low table covered with cardboard boxes, miniature screwdrivers and angled metal picks. "All right. What's the plan, Ryder?"

He draped his length across the sofa, taking several of the pillows in his arms as he faced her across their jeweled tones. "Well, first I want you to tell me everything that happened when you came to my door. Okay? Don't leave out any detail, no matter how unimportant."

"Everything?" Organizing her thoughts, she couldn't decide where to start.

"Pretend I don't know the first thing, Josie. Neither of us is sure right now what's significant, what isn't, right?"

Nodding, she leaned forward, bringing her knees up and doubling them, resting her chin on top while she considered the sequence of events that had brought them to this moment, to the illusory comfort and contentment of the two of them sitting among the exotica of his magic collection and props. "I wanted you to do something about those dogs," she began.

"Because you thought they were mine since they'd headed toward my house, right?" he said.

"They were too aggressive to be on the loose."

"Was this the first time you'd seen them?"

"They'd been roaming around my house for several days, but they hadn't been a problem before. This time they were different."

Half sitting up, he stuffed a pillow under his head and lay back, resting his head on his folded hands. "How so, Josie?"

"Different. Scary. Like…oh, I don't know. Like a pack with one idea in mind. Creepy. At first I was even afraid they were rabid."

"Go on, Josie. So you took off toward my house? Through the forest?"

"Are you kidding?" She gave him a swift, disbelieving glance. "Of course not. I didn't know where those devil beasts would spring up next."

"All right. What happened next?" he encouraged.

Throughout the rest of her story, he never moved. His gaze remained locked on hers throughout her recitation. Feeling silly, she even told him about the grackles, about what had happened afterward with the snake. Feeling even stupider, she told him, too, about the disappearance of the snake's body.

When she finished, he regarded her thoughtfully before saying, "I don't know anything about the snake, but I left the capsule on your doorstep."

"You could have given me the capsule yourself," she said, rolling her shoulders and loosening the tension that had crept into them with her story. Putting everything into words was a relief. She hadn't shared her worries and troubles with an adult since Bart had left. No wonder she'd begun feeling so disoriented, her thinking process slightly paranoid.

What was the old saying? A worry shared is a worry halved? She thought it was true. Sharing made the difference. She felt as if she'd walked out from under a burden she hadn't known she was carrying. "Why didn't you knock?"

"I came by early in the morning, right before dawn, Josie. Your newspaper hadn't even arrived. I thought you might be sleeping."

"I was." But Josie didn't tell him about the dream, about his part in her predawn nightmare and the ringing phone that had finally dragged her out of the sleep-drugged state. "You could have knocked, though." She wished now he had. The whole horrible business with the snake might never have happened. "I wouldn't have minded."

"Next time, I will," he said, and the rough note in his voice warned her away. "Are you up for an experiment, Josie? I want to try out something on you. You tell me if what you see in a minute resembles in any way what you saw in my hall, okay?"

Stacking the pillows in the corners of the sofa, he unfolded himself from the couch and went to an area where the room was divided by large folding doors. Pushing back the doors, he touched a panel of switches on the wall. As the lights in the room became a glow, Josie saw that the area functioned as a kind of workshop for Ryder. Long tables with orderly piles of machinery bits and mannequin parts lined one wall. Silvery mirrored sheets of glass rectangles leaned against another wall. Stars and comets flashed in silver and blue across the monitor of an elaborate computer area.

Like curtains drawn to the side of a stage, the folded doors framed the opening of the workshop, and though the lights grew dimmer, softening the edges of objects, Josie was able to see Ryder clearly.

Until he took one more step backward, away from her, and vanished before her eyes. There.

And not there.

The room was utterly quiet. Expecting to see him any second, Josie waited, letting the chill of the room seep into her.

Her stomach fluttered. Nerves. And the sense that she was alone when she shouldn't be. Ryder was there. She knew it. He'd *told* her he wanted to try an experiment. There was no problem.

Josie leaned forward, peering toward the end of the room. There was no unearthly mist, no laser light show. Nothing, in fact, to explain how Ryder had been there one moment in plain view and gone the next.

She rubbed her arms, the chill penetrating her light cotton T-shirt and blouse. "Ryder?"

There was no answer.

She was alone in a house where no one knew she'd gone.

And Josie decided after all that she did have an imagination, because she felt fingers brush her face, felt the chill touch of a hand on her neck.

The quick skim of fingertips was familiar, and she breathed a sigh of relief.

Expecting to see him, she twisted in her chair to look behind her. "Ryder! You're not being funny. I don't like this," she scolded.

But no one was there.

And then, as she squirmed in her chair to face front again, to face the direction in which she'd last seen him, she saw a pale shape drift toward her, becoming more distinct as she sat paralyzed in the seat.

But it wasn't Ryder.

It wasn't Mellie, either.

The diminutive form she'd seen, only a wisp of cloudy shadow glimpsed from the porch, was nothing like the figure becoming clearer with each second. As the figure moved toward her, Josie saw the transparent form of a woman, a woman whose hand stretched out, beckoning her as the apparition spoke.

The woman's voice was like a song, the soprano notes trembling in the air as the figure faded into the dim blue light.

Faded, changed slowly.

Became Ryder.

The lights blazed again, and Josie blinked, still caught in the spell the illusion had cast over her.

"Well, Josie, was that what you saw?" Stepping forward and leaving the doors open, Ryder grinned, his delight in her reaction plain in the careful smile he gave her.

"That was excellent," Josie said, leaning back in her chair. "You're really good. I knew you were up to something. I *knew* I would see *something*, and I was watching closely. The light was bright enough for me to see what you were doing, but then…you were gone. I'm impressed.''

"Good.'' He strolled toward her, elegantly casual, the pleasure in his trick translating into a male aggression that showed in the tilt of his head, the glint in his eyes. "It's a variation of Houdini's Arbor Illusion. The old version used sliding mirrors and struts to conceal the disappearance of the magician before he becomes the female figure, reappearing in a different place.'' His smile widened, and Josie was touched by his enthusiasm. "Anyway, I'm updating the concept, using holography and videos. It'll be more complicated when—'' He veered away from her toward the couch and collapsed among the pillows, his head thrown back onto the green leather. "If I were going to present it.'' He lifted his feet onto the table in front of him as he tipped his chin toward her and asked, "So?''

Shaking her head, Josie raised her eyebrows. "Your effect was different. Your figure was *bigger,* clearer somehow. I'll admit you had me going, but even so, I never thought for a second that I was seeing or hearing Mellie.'' Josie rubbed the cotton over her knees as she concluded slowly, "You know what it was? The figure I saw was definitely a child, with a child's way of moving. Kids move differently, Ryder. I don't know how to explain it, but they do. Little kids do that tippy-toe walk—'' Josie couldn't continue, not with the memories flooding her. She cleared her throat. "Not the same. I'm sorry.''

"Okay. Not a problem. I was working on some of the pieces of the equipment the other day when you knocked. I hoped maybe— Well, that's that, I reckon.''

"The cold fingers along the cheek and neck were a terrific effect. How'd you cause that? Can you create the same sensation for a large audience? If so, wow.''

Suddenly intense, he leaned forward. "Tell me about the cold fingers, Josie,'' he said so softly that she almost didn't hear him.

"Cold. The way your hands are most of the time." Josie shifted.

The calculating expression in Ryder's eyes made her anxious. She didn't think she would like what he was going to say.

"Josie, nothing in the effect I'm working on involves touching the audience. Nothing I did came anywhere close to you. Maybe a current of air?" He stood up and walked to the window nearest her, running his hand along the frame, his fingers seeking, searching.

"It's a drafty room." Josie turned to look at the subtle lift of the silks along the opposite wall. She shivered. "Your whole house is cold. Drafty."

"Yes." One hand still on the window, Ryder pivoted toward her. "I told you the house hasn't always been cold like this, Josie. The cold is a new...effect. But a cold hand? I don't know." He walked over to the windows near the bookcases. "Must have been an air current." Picking up a box of fireplace matches, he struck one and followed the outline of the windows with the long wooden match. The flame burned steadily.

"Ryder, I didn't feel a breeze," Josie said with certainty. "Fingers. Each one separate. I thought it was *your* hand. I recognized it, you see. The shape, the touch. I was so sure it was you," she said in a faint voice.

"No." He blew out the match. "Not me."

"Then what?" Hesitantly, Josie looked around at the room, but it didn't frighten her. Its rich grandeur remained inviting, wickedly tempting. She stood up. "What touched my face?"

"I don't know. But I'm going to find out." His grin was devilish. "A real mystery, sweetheart, isn't it?"

"Do you have any enemies, Ryder?" Josie said as she wrapped her arms around herself. She walked back toward the workroom. "Can you think of anyone who might try to work a...a con on *you*, Ryder? Who might want to achieve some peculiar kind of revenge by making you think you were losing your mind? I mean, since several of the episodes have happened here.'' She waved her hand in a circle.

"That was my first thought. Before the rest of the episodes.'' He pointed toward the computer. "I ran through the possibilities. Checked what people were doing. Anyway, Josie, if a magician wanted to get revenge, the most effective revenge would be to steal one of my illusions and tart it up, make it better and more exciting, have everybody raving about what *he* was accomplishing. Make people forget that the concept and execution had originally been mine. Now that would really make me nuts.'' One eyebrow rose in self-derision. "Anybody who knows me at all knows that. No, I don't think it's likely that someone's out to get me with a convoluted scheme. Something else is causing these phenomena.''

The energy pulsing from him pushed against Josie, and needing to put space between them, she wandered back toward the computer. The combination of the room's opulence, the late hour following a long, distressing day, and all the spinning, humming power coming from Ryder was wearing her down, weakening her in some essential way.

Even knowing it wouldn't be a smart move, she still wanted to curl up on his leather couch and pull the blanket over her. She wanted to drift off to sleep watching the rippling silk panel of the magician and the panther.

With Ryder's deep voice murmuring in her ear all night long, in her dreams beside her.

The thought stole through her. It was as if she'd heard an actual voice, as if Ryder had taken up residence in her brain, beguiling her with her the echo of her own need.

A pamphlet on the computer table stopped her. Picking up the booklet, she flipped through its pages. "Software to track down all kinds of information about people, Ryder?'' She should have been angry, but after everything they'd been through, his earlier trespass no longer seemed important to her. Events had pulled the plug on her anger. She discarded the leaflet with a twist of her wrist. "That's how you found out my mother's name."

"Yes." The prism lights of the chandelier fell across Ryder's face as he walked through the sitting room area. "And I'd do the same thing again, Josie. You know I would."

"I know." She pushed the pamphlet away from her with the tip of her finger. "It's the way you are. Curious." She knew her smile was rueful. "You think you'll never go back on the stage, Ryder, but you'll always be a magician. You have that kind of complicated, puzzle-solving brain."

"I reckon." He followed her to the computer and booted it up. With several key punches he brought up a screen filled with information about her. "We're all bits and bytes in some computer, Josie. This information is available to anyone who really wants it. I did."

"I don't like feeling…exposed, I guess, is the best word. Good grief, Ryder," Josie said, chagrined as she peered at the amber screen, "you even have the name of the first boy I dated here."

"That wasn't in the program," he muttered, his face flushing. He pushed a delete file command and the screen went blank except for the cursor's friendly nudge. "I was—"

"Curious," Josie said again. She didn't know whether to laugh or stomp on his foot. "I ought to sue you for invasion of privacy."

"Probably," he said. "I'd testify on your behalf." He gave her an unapologetic half smile.

She turned her back on the lure of his knowing smile and walked toward the stack of mirrors. The silvering had been etched away from the edges of several of them.

"Props for the Arbor Illusion." He cupped his hands on her shoulders, moved her in front of one of the mirrors mounted across the corner of the alcove. "Stay there," he ordered.

Behind the mirror he placed one mannequin of a woman in a spangled ball gown. "My assistant," he drawled.

Reflected in the mirror, part of the room seemed empty, but as Ryder touched a switch that drew the mirror away diagonally, the woman seemed to appear suddenly in the room because of the etched-away side of the mirror. "Stage lighting would cover the movement of the mirror."

Josie could see how a figure could seem to float into view.

Before returning the mirror to its original position, Ryder stood another mannequin, this one in a tuxedo, in the corner opposite the mirror. "Me," he said. "Actually, my double. The mirror makes it look as though I'm over there—" he pointed to the mannequin "—but really—" and he stepped behind the mirror, moving the female mannequin out of the way as he slid the mirror to its original position "—I'm here."

The ball-gowned mannequin disappeared, becoming Ryder when the mirror was pulled partially back.

"Clumsy, performed this way, with all the mechanics showing," he said as he came up behind her.

In one of the other mirrors, his reflected eyes watched her. Not touching her this time, he lowered his head and bent his knees as his mirrored mouth moved along the reflected image of her cheeks, her neck, his breath cool against her.

In the mirror, the woman's green eyes grew large, misty, her mouth parting as Ryder's sleek dark head slipped along the curve of her shoulder.

No mannequin. A real woman—herself. Unrecognizable in the dazed, yearning woman in the mirror.

"And this is the old version, not a high-tech, sexy one with lasers and gimcrackery," he whispered, his breath growing warmer. "I love the way you look in my house,

Josie, in my magic mirrors." His eyes met hers, hungry, his loneliness a mirror of her own. "See how beautiful you are, Josie Birdsong?" And still he didn't touch her.

Josie couldn't move. She remembered too well what had happened earlier in the kitchen when she'd touched him, but she couldn't escape the two of them in the mirror, his dark head moving over hers. She didn't want to escape.

A strand of his hair slipped against her throat, the brush as intimate as a kiss.

"A basic version of what I showed you earlier. An old trick."

For a second, Josie thought he meant the incident in the kitchen, but then he stepped back, his mirrored image vanished, and once more she was alone.

The reflection of herself, soft and expectant, waiting, and alone, sent a shaft of sadness and hunger through her. She turned away from that self.

She'd learned to live with her loneliness.

Without Mellie, the world was empty.

Josie understood reality. Although she might believe sometimes that no one else had ever grieved the way she did, that no one else could comprehend her loss, she knew she wasn't alone in her desolation.

The parents of five other children were with her on that barren plain.

So, too, were the parents of Eric Ames.

And the circle of time would move on, taking them and their grief with it.

Every day people learned how to cope with loneliness and emptiness. She would, too. That was part of life. Going on. One foot in front of the other. One day at a time.

Ryder snagged the end of her skirt, stopping her. "Josie, what made you think the dogs were rabid?" He was frowning.

Shrugging, she said, "Their eyes, I think. Why?"

"When I opened the door, you were angry, yes, but there

was something in your face, a look of terror underneath all that anger. I'd forgotten about it until a minute ago. What was strange about their eyes?''

''The color looked strange. Not right. And the dogs seemed to know what I was thinking before I did. They appeared so...calculating.'' She managed a tiny laugh. ''If they'd been rabid, I guess they would have looked crazy, not with that animal intelligence that scared the liver out of me.''

She left the workroom and returned to the main area of Ryder's sanctuary.

There, following the lines of the bookshelves, she walked around the room. At the opposite end from Ryder, an old pine corner table filled the area where the shelves ended and the next wall began. An unimportant-looking dun-colored pot rested on the table.

In all the riot of color and richness, the plain pot was out of place, its earthy brown faded and monochrome. The homely ordinariness of the pot caught her eyes and drew her closer to examine it.

Of a shape to fit into her hands, the pot was rounded even on the base. The figure of a bird about four inches long formed the top of the ball shape of the pot. The whole object was no bigger than four or five inches from top to bottom, side to side. Because of its shape and closed top, Josie couldn't imagine what it would have been used for or what its purpose would have been, other than decorative. Leaning toward it, she saw that the tail of the bird was open like a spout, its feathers and wings indicated with primitive streaks and shallow indentations that looked as if they'd been poked into the clay with the end of a pencil or stick.

Although she didn't touch it or the table, the pot seemed to rock slightly in its holder.

Trying to determine the purpose of the object, Josie took a step closer. With a suddenness that made her cry out, the rug in front of the table skidded out from under her foot. Pitching toward the table and the bird pot, she flung out her arms with a helpless cry of alarm.

The table listed, tipped, and the pot rattled against the wooden surface.

She knew she hadn't bumped into the table.

She was falling, the pot was rolling toward her, faster and faster in a blur as the floor rose up in front of her face.

And then Ryder was there, cradling the pot with one hand, his other arm around her. Her knee was millimeters from the floor.

"You okay?"

"Is the pot all right?"

Their words collided over the beak of the ocher-colored bird with its bead of an eye.

Josie cupped her hand around the smooth surface of the bowl. The clay was warm, and her fingers lingered on its smooth shape, tracing the wings of the bird.

"I can't believe I was so clumsy," she whispered, alarmed that she'd come so close to breaking an obviously treasured object. "I'm so sorry." She pushed away from Ryder. And found she couldn't.

His fingers dug into her waist. His eyes narrowed, shone with the glittering light from the chandelier that seemed to whirl above her with dizzying speed. Even as she stared at him, the skin across his cheekbones tightened, flushed with heat.

"Ryder! Let me go," she whispered, troubled, yet clinging to him. "We don't want this."

Around her, over her, in her, she heard the beating of wings, their fluttering growing powerful and strong, and she was terrified. The experience in the kitchen was pastel in comparison with the dark pounding now inside her body, the hunger to lie down on the floor and ease her need, ease the hunger she saw in Ryder's eyes. "Let me go!" she said, knowing if he didn't release her in that instant, she'd never let him go, and, oh, she didn't know for one beat of her heart if she wanted him to listen to her or ignore her. And that was the most frightening truth of all. "Ryder!" she said, despairingly. "Please!"

With her words, he slowly straightened. Looking down at the pot he still held, he returned it to its support on the table. "Jesus," he whispered. His hands were shaking. "What the hell was I thinking of? After all I said? Damn."

"Your eyes, Ryder. They frightened me. I frightened myself, because I didn't *care* whether you let me go. Ryder, I'm so frightened," she cried, putting her hands over her burning cheeks.

He stepped back from her and rubbed his eyes. "God, Josie, I thought the images were the result of some kind of shared telepathy, that's all. But this is something else. I can't believe what happens to me when I *touch* you, Josie." Backward, backward, he moved, appalled. "I swore I wouldn't harm you. And I don't understand what's happening to me, but every oath, every good intention flies out the window. Desire, lust, I recognize. This is something else. Stronger. Like a part of me I would keep under lock and key. Josie," he said urgently, "I'm afraid of what I'm going to do to you. Get away from me, sweetheart, for your own safety. *Now!*"

His hands were behind his back as he retreated from her.

In the mirrors around them, Josie saw her own eyes, as wide and horrified as Ryder's.

All around them in the silk panels, the figures moved, stirred, a restless, living band.

And in the mirror in front of the table with the cards on it, she saw the glow of tiger eyes, hot and fierce and yellow.

CHAPTER NINE

Like the tiger eyes in the mirror, the headlights of Ryder's car stayed in her rearview mirror all the way home.

He'd insisted.

Flinging open the door of his magic room for her, he'd stepped back while she ran, the growl of tigers loud in her ears. He'd thrown one of the scarlet pillows across the room. It hit a book, knocking it to the floor with a crash that made her jump.

She'd been halfway down the hall when he caught up to her. He stayed at one end, she at the other, the stacks of magazines and books taking on a life of their own in the dim hall.

"Josie, listen to me. If you think for one damn minute I'm letting you out of here by yourself, you're out of your ever-lovin' mind." His drawl was all grits and gravel, rough with urgency and strain. "I don't intend to get within three feet of you, but you're not going off by yourself tonight."

If Josie had doubted Ryder's motives before going to his house, she no longer did. He had been as staggered by the day as she had been. And if she'd doubted the reality of their shared visions, she no longer could.

The tiger's eyes had been like the eyes of the dogs. Like the eyes of the grackles.

Evil walked unchecked in her world.

She'd never been afraid of the dark before, but driving down the winding roads to her house, she locked her doors and felt ridiculous. The power that had been unleashed in Ryder's room didn't know the meaning of locks and bolts. That power that had let her hear Mellie's voice after months of longing for her child, the power that had generated the glimpse of Eric Ames—that power wouldn't stop at her feeble barriers.

And that power had seduced her into hoping that there was a possibility of finding out what had happened to Mellie.

Not a ghost come to comfort, after all, but a tiger power, red in tooth and claw.

Negotiating the curves of the road, Josie steered her car with hands that shook. Every turn of the wheel threatened to wrench the wheel from her slippery grasp. Her teeth chattered with a fear beyond anything she'd ever known. The moments two days ago in her yard were a picnic compared to the primal fear that ruled her now.

The tigers come at night.

The line from a song kept running through her stunned mind.

The tigers come at night.

As she pulled up the dirt road to her house, she was terrified that she would see yellow eyes glowing at her from the woods or from the interior rooms of her house. And she could have wept for the relief spreading through her when she saw that Ryder followed her.

She hadn't realized she dreaded that long, dark approach so much until she'd made the turn.

Turning off the key, she waited, sweating with the windows of the car up while Ryder's sleek car rolled up behind her. The low purr of the car's engine was a comfort beyond measure in the thick blackness of the hot night.

Watching his lean form exit from the ghostly glimmer of his car, Josie looked toward her house.

Her cabin had never looked so isolated and unprotected. All the years she'd lived here and never been afraid, and now she didn't think she could walk through the front door of her own house.

Ryder bent down to the window and peered in. In the

darkness, his pale face appeared like an apparition in the dark, floating in front of her as she turned and unlatched her door. As she stepped out, he moved back.

This night there would be no more accidental touches. No more momentary brushes of hands, lips. He gave her as much room as she did him, each watching the other warily.

"I'm going in first, Josie." Striding up to the door, he didn't wait for her to give him the key. A piece of metal flicked once in his hand and the door swung open.

Josie ran after him, her shoes slipping on the rough ground. She didn't want to let him out of her sight. In spite of everything that had happened, in spite of the fact that it was Ryder who seemed to focus whatever power whipped between them, she felt safer with him.

"The light switch is on—"

Light flashed in her living room, kitchen, bedroom, as she stayed half in, half out of her small house.

"Why the hell do you live out here so far from town, Josie?" Ryder asked as he came slamming back into the house from the back porch. Her porch light glowing behind him cast his shadow forward, toward her, large and overpowering.

He must have seen her reaction because he stopped so abruptly that she heard the squeak of his shoes against the floor. She had no idea how he'd managed to get his shoes on and catch up with her before she flew out of his house, but he'd done it.

And, oh, God, was she grateful.

"It's the only house I have, Ryder," she said through clicking teeth. "Some of us don't have vacation houses and condos and—oh, Ryder! I'm scared," she finally wailed, everything catching up with her and snapping the last, frayed remnant of her self-possession. Except for the night she'd run wild in the woods, screaming for Mellie, Josie had never broken down, never let anyone see her weak, but now, with the lights of her house blazing around her and the woods dark in front of her, the perimeter of her lights struck her as pitiful in the face of what stalked them.

"Aw, Josie, please, sweetheart, don't cry. I can't help you if you do, sweetheart." Like the night on the porch, Ryder's voice came low, husky, the mellow sound running along her jangled nerves like honey dripping down a spoon. "Listen to me, Josie, just listen," he crooned, and the dark woods vanished in the flow of his voice. "Breathe, Josie, slowly, slowly, and take a step inside, sweetheart. I won't let anything hurt you, sweetheart. I won't hurt you. This way, sweetheart, one step more," he whispered, and his whisper brought peace, light, safety. "That's it." His voice rose to its normal register, and she saw him standing between her kitchen and the back porch.

She stepped inside and shut her front door, clicking the bolt. "You hypnotized me the other night, didn't you, Ryder?" The calm center inside her would hold a bit longer, and she owed that certainty to him.

"Partly. The rest of it was this...this *power* that runs between us, Josie. I couldn't have hypnotized you otherwise. I'm not Svengali, no matter what you may think at the moment." The lines around his mouth were deep gouges in the light of her kitchen. He looked as if he were holding on by as thin a thread as she.

"I wondered." She stayed where she was.

"I don't want to leave you here. By yourself," he said and rubbed the back of his neck. "But I don't know if you're safer with me or without me tonight." His laugh was harsh. "God, Josie, I must wear the mark of Cain somewhere on my body. Sandi. Now you." Harder and harder, he struck the doorframe with his fist. "Tell me what you want."

"Not to be by myself, that's for sure." Her teeth no longer chattered like maniacal maracas. "I'm not afraid of you physically, Ryder. You have to believe that."

He looked at her. His fist fell to his side. "How can you not be?"

"I don't know. I'm sure, inside somewhere, that you wouldn't hurt me. I can't explain why, but I'm positive that I'm safe with you. All the way home the thought that you were right behind me, keeping me safe, kept me from going off the road into a ditch."

"You're not safe with me, Josie." His face was pinched, dark with emotion. "I know exactly what was going on inside me. I wouldn't have intended to hurt you, but having you was the only impulse ruling me. Twice as powerful as the incident in the kitchen and growing stronger by the second. I don't know what would have happened next. Maybe nothing. Maybe the greatest sex either of us has ever known. Maybe something would have come springing out of the mirrors at us. For the first time in my life, I didn't want to find out the answers. I couldn't risk you that way." With his back braced on the doorjamb, he slid to the floor, sitting on his haunches looking up at her as he repeated, "Tell me what you want me to do, Josie."

"Would you stay here? On my porch? Or in your car? Somewhere close at hand? But not too close." She clung to the doorknob. At the moment it was the only thing giving her enough strength to stay upright. If she sank to the floor like Ryder, she didn't think she'd ever rise again. They'd be found someday, both of them, petrified on her floor. "Tonight I'm afraid of the dark, even if you aren't. I need someone to be with me tonight. I need you here, Ryder."

"All right. I'll stay. Throw me a blanket— Yes, damn it, Josie, I'm *cold*. Even here in your house with no air-conditioning, my bones ache with the cold." He glared at her. "Get me a damned blanket and stay as far away from me as you can. Because you may not be afraid I'll hurt you, but hell wouldn't burn hot enough for me if I did." He groaned and stood up.

"Thank you." She took five steps inside the living room

and frowned. "Somebody's been here." She sniffed the hot air that had been enclosed inside her house all day. "Somebody walked into my house," she said, outraged.

"How do you know?" Ryder didn't move.

"I can *smell* something," she said, bewildered. "Only a trace of…I don't know. It's gone now." Turning her head, she sniffed the stale air again. "Nothing."

"I told you your locks weren't worth the metal they were made of, Josie. Hell, any idiot could be in here and gone out the back door by the time you got to the kitchen."

"You're incredibly reassuring, Ryder. I can't thank you enough. You've really calmed my last, lingering fears. Golly gee, I think, after all, I'd rather be by myself." Her teeth were starting to chatter again as she walked around her living room looking for evidence of anything missing. "Bye-bye, Ryder. Lock the door after you've gone—oh, no," she cried. "No!"

"What?" He came down the short passageway but stopped just short of her.

"My picture of Mellie! The Christmas one. It's gone!" Somewhere between tears and rage, she found the last reservoir of strength and stormed toward her phone, Ryder backing away with her advance. "I'm calling Stoner, and by heaven, he'd better get here within five minutes, or—"

The jangling ring of the phone jerked her to a halt. She looked at the stubby appliance that squatted on the counter in her kitchen like a malevolent presence.

Ryder stared at the phone. At her. "Josie?" He looked at his watch. "It's two in the morning."

The phone shrilled insistently.

"Do you want me to answer it?" He went to the counter and waited.

"No. If it's Mellie, your voice would scare her. I'll get it." Josie didn't want to pick up the receiver. Didn't want to hear the static of a bad connection.

* * *

Ryder watched her walk to the phone. Her eyes were enormous, filled with dread. He wanted to pick up the damned phone and fling it through the window. Anything to erase that expression from her face.

But he was helpless.

"I'm here, Josie. Answer it."

She lifted the receiver, put it to her ear, waited. Her normally tanned face lost color as she held the receiver for a full minute before replacing it carefully on the base. "Static." Her lips stuck to her teeth. She'd gone dry mouthed.

He knew the feeling. "This has happened before, hasn't it?"

"Wrong number. Bad connection. Static." She went into her bedroom and returned, bringing a blanket and pillows with her. "Here." She heaved the stuff in his direction, waiting until he caught it before turning back to her bedroom.

And then she turned to him, her eyes dark and enormous. "I'm afraid to open my window. Afraid to be in my own bedroom by myself!"

He wanted to take her in his arms and shelter her from the distress racking her. And he couldn't. The power that surged through him when he was with her seemed different at his house, stronger, more carnal, but he wasn't taking any more risks tonight. "Josie, I'll sleep here on the floor outside your bedroom. Right across the threshold. Like a medieval vassal, okay, lady green eyes? I won't let anything past me. I promise," he said, knowing the promise was worth spit, but willing at that moment to throw himself into the void if it would take that look of despair from her, if it would give her back that mischievous independence that fueled her.

"You will?" She swayed on her feet.

"I will." He waited as she gripped the door until she had her balance.

"Wait. I have to call Stoner." She looked as if a breath of air would topple her to the ground.

"It'll wait, Josie. Tomorrow will be soon enough. You've hit the wall. Go to bed. I'll be here."

"Good."

She didn't even turn back her bedspread. Leaving the window to her bedroom closed, leaving all the lights burning, she curled up on the narrow bed and shut her eyes.

Keeping his word, Ryder checked her house again and locked the back door that he'd opened in order to check the back porch. He, too, left the lights blazing away. It seemed to be a night to let the light shine, shine and push away the dark.

He considered gathering her pot lids and stringing them in front of the doors and windows, but the thing he feared wouldn't come by way of doors.

Wouldn't come through windows.

What he'd do if the power came into Josie's house, Ryder didn't know. All he knew was that nothing more was going to threaten Josie.

He'd brought danger into her life. He wouldn't let anything else strip her of her pride and courage.

He'd die first.

Lying on her floor and breathing in the scent of her that lingered on the blanket, he was startled by the intensity of his thought.

For the rest of the night, he listened.

He heard frogs croak wearily, needing water. He thought he heard a dog howling in the hour before dawn, believed for insane moments that with the intensity of his concentration he could even hear the leaves in the woods moving, rustling with an unseen wind and the soft sound of raindrops.

He knew there was no wind.

No rain.

Nothing but the sauna heat that still left him cold.

As sunlight edged across the floor, Ryder heard Josie's fretful breathing, heard her turn once on her bed, whimper.

The need to comfort her stirred in him, urged him to go to her, told him that it would be all right. Teased him with the false hope that he could control what was between them.

Ryder stayed under the blanket, keeping her safe. Safe from whatever stalked them.

Safe from him.

This night, at least, he had kept her safe.

What the day would bring to them both, he couldn't predict. But he sensed the world outside edging ever closer to them, bringing the wind and the darkness.

Ryder turned to face the bedroom where Josie lay sleeping.

He would guard her.

Care for her.

And they would face the darkness together.

Solitary by choice, alone by design, he stirred. The image of Josie by his side brought with it a curious peace, and for a brief span of time, Ryder slept.

With the sun high in the sky and burning through the closed windows in the morning, Ryder opened the ones near him while he stirred eggs in a skillet. Locating her coffeepot, he'd thrown in an extra scoop of the ground coffee he discovered in the freezer. For the first time in ages he was hungry. He knew they needed food.

Bleary-eyed and wan, Josie straggled through the door. Slumped at the table, she stared at the plate of eggs he shoved under her nose. "Ryder, I don't think I can eat. I'm sorry," she said.

"Eat." He handed her a mug of coffee. "Drink."

"I don't drink coffee," she said with no energy to her statement. "I drink tea."

"So live a little dangerously," he goaded.

That penetrated her foggy consciousness, and she stared up at him. The purple shadows under her eyes were the sole color in her drained, exhausted face. "You don't think I've been living dangerously?" she said, a trace of her usual animation struggling to the surface, sinking back under the exhaustion. "Gee whiz, Ryder."

He nudged the cup closer. "Come on, Josie. You need something to cut through the mugginess. You'll be able to think clearer with a little food fueling you."

She lifted a lump of scrambled egg on her fork. Put it down. "Ryder, I really can't." Fatigue shone in the deep green of her eyes. "I'll throw up."

He saw the faint tremble in her hand and wanted to cover the small, callused palm with his own. "All right." He handed her a piece of dry toast. "Eat, Josie. We have things to do." He took a mango from the bowl on the counter and methodically peeled it and sliced the deep orange fruit into long strips on a saucer.

Josie broke off a piece of the toast. Nibbled. "I called my friend at Angel General from the bedroom phone. The people injured yesterday are improving. Some broken bones, nothing that won't mend. That's a relief."

"Yeah," he said, sliding the mango toward her. She'd eaten half a slice of toast. "I called Stoner. Told him someone had broken in. Reported the disappearance of Mellie's picture."

"And?"

"And he said that he'd be out as soon as he could get away."

"Think he'll bother?" she asked, picking up a thin slice of mango and biting off the end.

"Maybe." Ryder walked to the open back door and stared toward the woods. In the heat-heavy noon hour, the leaves were still, dust covered. "I watered your garden, Josie." He didn't tell her he'd also checked around her garbage for signs of the rattlesnake and found nothing.

Her garden with its struggling green plants moved him unbearably. He understood its symbolism. "Josie," he said, watching the darkness of the woods, "do you expect to find Mellie alive?" He regretted the bluntness as soon as he'd said the words.

Her fork clinked against the saucer. "No."

"I don't, either," he said and turned around. "And I don't expect the police to find the Ames child alive."

Unraveled in sleep, her dark hair slipped around her face, hiding her face. "I know," and her voice was infinitely sad. "Things have been set in motion. We're on a carnival ride that's broken loose." She crumbled up bits of toast, the crumbs sprinkling the leftover mango like cinnamon. "What do we do now?" Her expression was hopeless. "Is there anything we can do, Ryder? Because I look around, and for the first time, I don't know how I'm going to keep going." She looked blindly at him, her eyes unfocused and empty.

"We don't have a choice, Josie. You realize that, don't you?"

"I don't think we've had any choice from the beginning."

"So." He tapped his fingers against her countertop. "Here's what we'll do. I want to talk to the trainer of that elephant that went berserk yesterday."

"The trainer?" she said slowly, the plates tipping in her hand. "Why?"

He held up his fingers, bending each one down as he ticked off the incidents. "The tiger. The dogs. The snake. All these attacks." He shrugged as he pulled the back door shut. "I'd like to know if anything had occurred with that elephant before. Before the parade. Anytime." Knowing it was a waste of time, nevertheless, he snapped the latch closed. "The trainer's handy. I'd like to hear his version. I was watching you during the parade. I saw you fall. I merely wondered if the movement startled the elephant. If something like that explained the elephant's behavior."

"Someone bumped into me." She placed the saucer on the counter.

"No one was near you, Josie." He stared at her. "I saw the child at the curb. She was hard to miss. I saw you talking for a while to some big, beefy guy." The man had leaned in too close to her for Ryder, but he'd decided that was her business, not his. "You moved down the block a bit as the parade turned the corner. That was it."

"I felt someone's elbow in my back." She shook her head. "I know I did. Like a jab."

"Okay. Maybe I looked away." He was certain he hadn't. "Or the parade might have blocked my view. Anyway, I want to talk to the trainer today. The circus organizers may close up shop early because of the accident. Today may be the only chance. I won't go without you, though." He would give her whatever protection he could. Whatever she'd allow.

She jumped as the pounding on the door reverberated through the small house.

"I'll get the door," Ryder said as she hesitated.

She was right on his heels when he went to the door and unlocked it.

As Ryder opened the door, the scrawny man smoking a cigarette looked up, saw Ryder and flipped the cigarette onto the concrete step. With jerky, scrubbing motions, he stubbed the butt out on the step. "I'm looking for Miz Conrad. She in?"

Josie stepped out from behind the door. "Yes, Mr. Milton?"

Her face was closed off, and Ryder instinctively stepped slightly in front of her, between her and the man she'd called Milton.

"You got a coupla minutes, Miz Conrad? I sure would like to speak with you. I come all the way out here on account of I ain't explained." He cast a furtive look at Ryder, edged closer to Josie. "You know, Miz Conrad. About the bus and all. I never did explain to you how it was." He kept shifting back and forth as he stood on the stoop.

Josie's hand fluttered, lay still against her skirt. "That's all right, Mr. Milton. It's not necessary."

Sensing the turmoil in her, Ryder moved even closer, keeping his body between her and the open door.

"I'd rightly 'preciate it, ma'am, if you'd let me come in for a minute, if it ain't too early?" He looked quickly at her rumpled clothes and then away. "I been trying to get up the nerve, and when I seen you yesterday at the parade, I decided I been putting it off too long. I got to explain, Miz Conrad." A desperate note crept into his high-pitched voice.

Strain showed in the tight lines around her mouth as Josie turned. "Ryder, this is Henry Milton. Henry, Ryder Hayes."

Her manner was distant, more formal than Ryder had yet seen it, and he didn't understand her attitude toward the man. At worst the man was shabby, but he seemed innocuous. Even so, Ryder didn't move.

"Come in, Mr. Milton," Josie said. Holding herself stiffly erect, she motioned the man in. Her gesture was jerky.

"Pleased to make your acquaintance." Wiping his hands down his green work pants, Milton nodded to Ryder and scraped his shoes against the mat before stepping into the living room. "I won't take long, Miz Conrad. I promise. But I gotta get this off my chest."

With an abrupt nod, Josie indicated a chair for Milton, and he sat down on the edge, one hand resting on each knee as he looked earnestly from her to Ryder and back again. "With school starting up in a coupla weeks—"

Looking as if her legs had buckled, Josie sat down. The

line of her spine went as rigid as a steel rod. Ryder drifted over to her and stood behind her. Looking down on the defenseless crown of her head, he wanted to rest his hand on her shoulder, let her know he was there, tell her she wasn't alone.

Instead, standing like a sentinel at the gates of hell, he folded his arms across his chest and faced Henry Milton.

"Yes?" She choked out her question.

"I couldn't let the year start and not tell you it wasn't my fault that day."

A shiver ran along Josie's shoulders, and Ryder touched her once, quickly, and folded his arms again.

"I know."

"Your Mel, she got off the bus like always, and I watched her go down the road, this way, you know, like always," Henry Milton said, leaning forward with a kind of misery that spoke to Ryder.

Her hands jerking up as if to ward off a blow, Josie flinched. "I understand."

"I *always* waited until I seen her get to your door. But some idjit at the back of the bus yelled something and I turned around. When I looked back down your driveway, I thought she was inside, Miz Conrad, and I drove off. But she was only a few feet away. I wanted you to know," he said. "What happened wasn't my fault," he said with dogged insistence. "Because I waited."

"Yes." Josie rose to her feet. "Yes, now, if you don't mind, Mr. Milton, I have an errand, and I have to go."

"You know—"

Interrupting him, Josie said, "Thank you for stopping by. I see that you're not to blame. I appreciate your concern. Thank you. You've been too kind."

She walked out of the living room so swiftly that Henry Milton stared after her, caught in midsentence. "It wasn't my fault, you see," he said to Ryder. "But everybody's blaming me for that kid disappearing, and now with the boy—''

"Eric?"

"Yep. Three of them kids rode my bus, see, and with everybody riding a hair trigger, I don't want nobody thinking I had something to do with it. You know," he concluded vaguely. "And I liked Mel, too. She was a sweet one. Never sassed me. I thought Miz Conrad ought to know."

"Why'd you wait so long to tell her about that last day?" Looking toward the bedroom where Josie had disappeared and quietly shut her door, Ryder decided Henry Milton wasn't as harmless as he seemed.

"I done told the police, of course, one of them detectives, but I never said nothing to Miz Conrad. I felt bad about the little girlie."

Ryder suspected that Henry Milton's motive had less to do with Josie than with the precarious job market. "You saw Mellie go to the door?"

"Not exactly. I mean *almost*. She was heading down the driveway, more or less." He scratched his jaw. "Sorta."

With each detail, Milton's insistence that he *always* waited until Mellie reached the door became less believable. There was an odor about the man of lies and desperation that made Ryder want to pick him up by the scruff of his scrawny neck and pitch him out the door.

"What you mean is that you saw Mellie leave the bus, and that's about all you really did see, right?" Ryder could scarcely imagine how Milton's story had affected Josie. It was a cruel story, and Milton's watery blue eyes hinted that the bus company would be wise to run a check on the man. "What you mean is that you didn't wait until Mellie got anywhere near her door, right, Mr. Milton?"

"Sheesh. Don't get your shorts in a knot, bub. I been feeling guilty about the girlie and thought I'd help Miz

Conrad, and now you done acted like I shoulda kept my yap shut.''

"Might not be a bad idea," Ryder said, his hand flat against Milton's back lifting the man onto tiptoes. "What did you see that day, Milton?" Ryder asked casually.

"You tell Miz Conrad I'm sorry, hear?" Milton said, ignoring him in the spasm of coughing as Ryder kept moving him forward. "I done the best I could. You tell her that!''

"I'll tell her," Ryder said. "Goodbye, Mr. Milton, and I wish I could say it was a pleasure meeting you, too.''

"Huh?" On the step, Milton looked dumbfounded. "Yeah, sure. I done my duty, though. You tell her that, Hayes." He stomped off to his pickup truck.

Waxed and polished to a high gloss, the blue paint of the truck shone in the sun. Resting its jowls against the open window of the truck, the sad-eyed beagle watched mournfully as Henry Milton stomped and coughed his way to the truck. "Let's go, Beans. Don't nobody around here appreciate when a man's doing his civic duty." He lit a cigarette and coughed, the sound a sharp bark of congestion.

Beans let out a long howl of sympathy.

The engine turned over smoothly, a rich rumble of juiced-up carburetor and valve.

As he pulled out of the driveway, Milton gave a long, appraising look at the woods. Beans's ears flapped in the wind of their exit.

Thoughtfully, Ryder watched as the man stopped at the main road. The road where he would have stopped the bus every day while he *always* waited for Mellie to reach her door. From the road, the front door would have been visible. But the woods were only a few feet away from the main road at this point on Josie's property.

It had been unusually cold in January. Frost warnings. Mellie would have been wearing a coat. A jacket.

Ryder stayed on the step waiting and thinking until Milton turned onto the road.

Dust rose behind the blue truck like a curse.

CHAPTER TEN

"**I** hate him." The passion in her voice bubbled up from underneath and spilled out.

Ryder saw how animation revived her and was glad.

"That he could come here and tell me that *story* about Mellie! I could kill him, I could." Sheets, pillows, pillowcases flew around her. "I hate him. I'll never forgive him." Her voice was a monotone, flat. Her fury showed not in the voice but in her jerky movements, her doubled-up fists wound tightly in the sheets as she stripped them from the bed. "If I ever see him anywhere near my house again, I'll swear out a warrant."

Leaning against the doorjamb, Ryder shifted.

Looking up, she glared at him. "Don't you say one word to me. And don't you dare defend him. I know he's pathetic. I know I shouldn't hold a grudge against him, but I do! I do! And I can't help hating him because he was the last one to see Mellie and if he'd waited two minutes—one, even—she'd be here with me!" Josie tied the linens up with one knot and threw them toward the doorway. They landed at his feet.

Pacing in front of the closed window, Josie threw him quick glances while she stormed back and forth. "If I could forgive him, I would. But I can't. He's a weasel and a worm, and if there's a heaven, they'll slam the door in his face, and I—"

"He's a jerk," Ryder said mildly. "And he's not telling the truth."

She whirled on him. Her skirt whipped around her legs, and her hair belled out, settled in the airless room. "How do you know?"

"What was Mellie wearing that day?" He knew she would remember.

"Red tights. A navy skirt and shirt. A red-and-navy jacket," she recited by rote. "Why?"

"Because he saw her go into the woods. He saw the color of her jacket or her tights in the woods. That's why. It was cold. A lot of the shrubbery was killed in those December and January frosts. There would have been bare spaces. He saw her go into the woods. And I think he saw something else, too. But he's afraid to tell because he doesn't want to lose his job."

"Why would he lose his job?" She sank onto the edge of the bed. Her hands gripped the edge of the bare, narrow mattress.

"He drinks. Or used to. Either way, he's scared. And he's afraid that people are blaming him for what's happened to the children."

"They searched the woods," Josie said, numbed, and his heart ached for her. "For a week. They combed through the woods all the way down to the river. Stoner told me so. He organized volunteers and they divided into sectors. It was as if she'd never been."

"Do you think Milton would have harmed Mellie? Or Eric?" Ryder added, watching her closely.

"A lot of us have a darkness inside we're not aware of. Who knows what anyone would do?" She bent over her knees, toward the floor. Her hair swung away from her face, brushed the old boards.

"Where were you that day, Josie?" Ryder watched the sunlight on her face turn her skin to velvet peach, glisten in the tiny beads of perspiration along her lip. "You weren't here, were you?" He didn't accuse her. Wouldn't. Not Josie. He knew her too well. Only an act of fate could have prevented her from being home for her daughter. Something had kept Josie away that day.

The sun splashed across the bare boards of the floor, turned the varnished old wood mellow with light.

Stirred up by her vigorous action, dust motes caught the blaze of sun and turned to diamond dust.

"I was five minutes behind the bus. I'd even left work early, but a sailboat went through to the gulf. The bridge tender raised the drawbridge. I was the first car in line. I was stuck in traffic." She pulled her legs up onto the bed and wrapped her arms around them. "Five minutes." Her laugh skewed up, up toward a level of despair beyond imagining. "For want of a nail, the shoe was lost. For want of a shoe, the horse." She stared at him over the green of her skirt. "You know the rest, Ryder."

"For want of a horse, the war was lost. Five minutes, Josie. And if Henry Milton had waited as he was supposed to—"

"But he didn't. And I wasn't here. When I'd *always* been here before. So of course I hate Henry Milton and can't stand to see him." Acid burned in her words. "And the rest, as they say, is history. One of the reasons why I'm not crazy about history, Ryder. We can't change it. You and I have that in common, don't we? Guilt and recrimination."

"Psychic twins, Josie?" he suggested lightly.

"Guilt's a powerful bond. Beats the heck out of superglue, I bet."

There was nothing he could answer. She was right. They were bonded by guilt and by a carnality that threatened to burn them both to a cinder. "Hey, green eyes, if there is such a thing as a psychic bond, I'll bet a year's income you and I are welded by now."

"These last three days beat the heck out of those group encounters that charge you a fortune to get in touch with your inner self, I guess." Her laugh was shaky, but she'd managed it. "Demon snakes. Rampaging elephants. Phantom phone calls." She pulled a strand of hair over her shoulder and ran her fingers through it, untangling the silky stuff that slipped through her fingers like cool, dark water.

"Are you afraid of Milton?" he asked, thinking about the phone calls and the snake that had been coiled up on her step. Henry Milton was a country man. He wouldn't be afraid of snakes, even rattlers.

"No," she replied slowly, her brow furrowing in thought. "I don't like him. I'm uncomfortable around him. But I don't like many people lately, so that doesn't say anything about Henry, believe me." She stood up, went to her dresser and moved the copper pennies into a star before she turned back to him. "Should I be afraid of him?"

"You've had those phone calls. They might not be wrong numbers. Or interference."

"It doesn't matter. I won't change my phone number." Josie stacked the coins up, toppled them over with a touch.

"All right." Ryder didn't like Milton, but whether or not that made the man a killer was another matter. "Seemed a bit too coincidental for me that he showed up today after all these months."

"You don't believe him?"

"Yes. No. I definitely don't believe in coincidences. We've had too many of them for my taste, Josie."

"And you want to go to the circus," she said as she walked toward him, bringing with her the faint, fragile scent of dying roses.

"That I do. Will you come with me?" he asked again.

"I'm not going to stay here," she said and looked around the steam box of a room. "And I don't have the nerve today to be outside by myself. Without someone around, anyway. Right now, I can't bear to stay in this house." She nodded vehemently. "Oh, yes, Ryder, I'm going to go to the circus. Give me ten minutes and I'm out of here." She grabbed a pair of shorts hanging on the back of the door near him and pulled out a white T-shirt and a blouse that made him think of strawberry soda pop, fizzy and pink.

He waited in the kitchen while she took a shower. He heard the water go on. Off. On. And she was out, her face scrubbed and shiny, her fizzy pink blouse knotted at her stomach over the shirt. Her legs made the shorts seem nonexistent, but Ryder decided he liked the effect, that long, long length of tanned skin. But it wasn't only the length, he thought, studying them as she raced back to the bedroom.

Her legs had a strength to them that made them beautiful. Like Josie herself. The tapered loveliness of muscle and skin was a wonder of nature, and she reminded him of a delicate, perfect hummingbird. Small and strong and exquisitely beautiful. Ryder didn't think anyone had ever shown her just how beautiful she was.

Watching her flash and dart around the sweltering house, he wished he could be the one to show her.

"We might as well leave your car here and take mine," he said as she stood on the doorstep looking at the two cars uncertainly.

"I have to change. And if it's late by the time we're finished, Josie, you know I won't let you come back here by yourself. Not while there's so much unfinished business." He opened the passenger-side door for her.

"I should insist on taking my car. For form's sake, you understand. To prove I'm a not a woman who uses a man. And because I don't want you thinking I'm a wussie." She wrinkled her nose at him. "That most of all."

"All right," he said solemnly, "I won't think you're a wuss." He waited while she slid into his car, her legs lovely against the cream leather. "I'll still respect you tomorrow."

She'd covered the purple smudges under her eyes with one of those lotions and creams women worked wonders with, and anyone who didn't know what she'd been through in the past three days sure wouldn't see it broadcast on her face. You had to look for the tiny traces of strain, the evidence of tears shed.

The shine of unshed tears.

And Ryder suspected those tears were the most bitter of all, the wormwood and gall to her soul. Those were the tears that called forth tenderness from him, those the tears that made him want to shelter her, comfort her in the old ways men and women had comforted each other throughout time.

When he stopped to shower and change at his house, he insisted she stay outside. In the car with the engine running. With the windows up, open a crack for air. "Lay on the horn if anything at all happens, hear me, Josie? Don't even think twice about it. Just blast that horn and take off down the road."

"What about you? What about your car?"

"Hell, I don't care about the damned car, Josie. I was going to leave it at the parking lot all night, anyway, so that I could ride with you yesterday."

Later when he returned after one of the fastest showers he'd ever taken in his life, she tipped her chin toward the roof of his car and then asked, "Do you believe in evil, Ryder?" She leaned her head against the window while she waited for him to answer. She'd pulled her hair up into some kind of twisted knot on top of her head and secured it with two bright hair combs the color of ripe tangerines. "Real evil?"

The tires swished against the concrete pavement. "Evil? Yeah, Josie, I reckon I do."

"I never used to." She was silent. The leather seat whispered against her skin as she shifted closer to the door. "But I believe in it now. I can feel it, Ryder."

"Me, too, Josie."

"But it doesn't frighten you? The unknown? The unknowable?"

"When I thought I was going crazy, I was frightened. The idea that my *self* was turning against me scared the living daylights out of me." He waited a moment before adding, "And now I'm worried about you. About what could happen to you if I can't protect you. If I'm responsible for introducing evil into your life. That terrifies me, yes."

"You felt responsible for Sandi, too."

"This is different, Josie."

"How?" She pursed her mouth pensively. The indentation in her bottom lip cried out to be touched, to be kissed. "You've tortured yourself for months over your sense of responsibility for Sandi, Ryder. I don't want you worrying about me. I'm not your responsibility, understand?" Her small, round face was endearingly earnest. "I don't intend to be the cause of another session on the rack for you if something happens to me. Do you hear me? Nobody's responsible for what happens to me except myself. We're both consenting adults, so to speak. And since I'm choosing to take part in this witch-hunt, why should you worry about me, Ryder?"

Because I'm beginning to care too much, Josie Birdsong, that's why. Because I look at you and see all the things I've missed in life and never knew I'd want someday. And now it's too late.

"I reckon," he drawled, "it's because I've been dying to play Caveman Charlie all my life, sweetheart. A kind of vestigial remains of the male instinct to serve and protect."

"Oh," she said sweetly, and the kissable indentation vanished, reappeared. "Like an appendix?"

"Yeah," he muttered. "Something like that, I expect."

Josie slipped her shoe off and tucked one leg under the other. "Good night, sweet prince," she said with a wrinkle of her nose. "You do your male stuff and get us there. But if you get lost—"

"I know. Wake you up, right?"

"Gosh, no, Ryder. I'd get lost in a paper bag. I was going to suggest stopping at a gas station and asking for directions." Her expression was sweet innocence.

"Of course." He slapped his forehead. "Damn. I should have figured that out for myself. One of those missing genes us guys lose out on, huh?"

"You betcha."

She used her hand as a pillow against the window and door. "Us wimmenfolks got all the really good genes. Try to remember that when you start feeling like thumping your chest and strutting around, okay?"

"I'll try my feeble best, Josie. But, you know, being a guy, I can't vouch for how successful I'll be, but—"

"Shut up, Ryder," she said, her voice silky with amusement. "You can't quite manage the humble-male role. You'll need to practice the meek shtick some more. You don't have quite the right servile look in those eyes."

"Whatever you say, Josie."

"Arrgh. Let me go to sleep. Please. I'm about this far—" she held a thumb and index finger a quarter of an inch apart "—from committing terrible violence on your person if you don't let me go to sleep. For five minutes. That's all. Please?" She closed her eyes.

The brilliant sunlight wasn't merciful. Deprived of her essential self, her animation, her face looked worn and drawn, even with the makeup masking the shadows.

With her eyes shut and her sassy tongue silent, she looked so small and helpless that Ryder felt as if he were invading her privacy by looking at her.

She was so tired that he wanted to tell her she didn't have to work so hard at being cheerful, he didn't care, but if that was how she wanted to play the game, he'd match her, shot for shot.

They didn't speak for the rest of the trip to the circus grounds. Josie fell asleep with her cheek pressed against the car window. Her left hand slipped out from under her cheek and fell palm up next to him. Carefully, quickly, like a thief, he brushed the back of one knuckle against a line of scratches and calluses.

She worked so hard on that damned garden.

Turning off the Trail, he watched for the signs indicating the way to the circus grounds.

Maybe she was right to keep the atmosphere light. Maybe it helped diffuse that sense of hovering evil and darkness for her. Maybe it would help him ignore the craving to touch her, a craving he suspected was tied in with everything else.

Keeping the mood between them light wasn't working for him. He couldn't close his mind or his senses to her anymore.

He'd lost the ability to distance himself from her pain and sweetness.

Whether or not he could find that ability again was going to be interesting.

Whether or not he wanted to, ah, that was the real question, he decided as he pulled into the field that had been turned into a temporary parking lot.

"Wake up, sleepyhead."

Hearing the voice, Josie stirred. She didn't want to wake up. Much more pleasant to stay where she was with the low voice murmuring near her like the soothing sound of a river. For the first time in a long while, she felt safe. Protected.

A cold finger poked her bare arm. Ryder.

"Come on, Josie. Time's a-wasting, and we got off to a late start." The finger ran down her arm, brushed her palm.

She sat up. "We're here?"

"Yes. And I didn't get lost."

"Oh, goody. Would you like a medal?"

"Of course. The larger the better. You know how us guys are about the issue of size." He shot her a bland look. "Vanity or something, I reckon."

Josie delighted in the way Ryder kept his face impassive in the face of her needling, but his mouth would give a small twitch. She'd learned to watch for it, and half the pleasure of razzing him came from seeing whether she could provoke that twitch.

The noises and smells of the circus grounds assaulted her, overwhelming her senses, confusing her. Too much noise after the long months of solitude. First the parade and now all these sensations. She moved closer to Ryder as he shut the car door after her. She couldn't get a deep breath in all the color and noise. "This wasn't a good idea, Ryder."

He frowned. "We don't have to stay."

"Give me a minute, please?" Looking around, she tried to accustom herself to the wall of sound. Shrieks, drums, rumbling engines. Flags hanging limply from the main tent.

And everywhere, people. Rushing, screaming. Excitement turning their expressions grotesque.

People with children.

She hadn't seen this many children all at once since the first day of school a year ago come September. Not even at the parade. The small whimper that escaped embarrassed her and she clamped her hand over her mouth.

"Sheesh, Josie, I should have thought." Ryder bent over her, his lean body curving into her, and she sensed that he wanted to take her in his arms, shield her from the onslaught.

Truth was, at that moment she would have gone willingly, devil take the consequences.

"It's the kids, isn't it? Aw, sweetheart, come on. We're leaving." He touched the bend of her elbow, turned her back toward the car door he'd opened.

"No. I'm all right. I'd forgotten how quiet my place is. Was. This is good. I haven't forced myself to do anything except go to work and go home. That's the problem. It's all a little overwhelming. But it's good for me," she added. "If I don't quit being a hermit, I'll start hating the whole human race. I mean, look at how I took off after poor Henry Milton. He's harmless."

And her reaction to Ned Dugan. But she didn't tell Ryder about the creepy feeling Ned caused. It seemed too personal in a way she couldn't identify.

"I want to stay, Ryder," she insisted as she saw that she hadn't convinced him. "Where do we go to find the trainer? How do you know he'll even talk to you?" Generated by Ryder's continuing silence in the face of her nervousness, Josie's words poured out of her.

"Josie," Ryder said gently, "you keep amazing me. I thought you were this reticent earth woman who'd dance naked down the street before she'd say more than three consecutive sentences. And I'm usually such a good judge of character." He shook his head regretfully, but his sideways glance teased her. "I thought maybe the other night was an exception, but you really are a talker, after all, aren't you?"

Startled, Josie glanced at him and recognized the truth of what he was telling her, a truth that went deeper than she was prepared to deal with. "Must be your fault, then, Ryder," she said, scuffing the ground. "I've never been much of a chatterbox with anyone else. Except Mellie, of course. But she talked constantly. I picked it up from her. If you want me to hush up, I can. Easy as pie. Say the word."

"The word." His mouth twitched, once, at the left corner, and sounds faded from her consciousness in the tenderness of the look in his eyes. "But that's all right, Josie. I like listening to you." He lifted a hand toward her hair, as if he was going to brush a strand back, and the tenderness and kindness in his eyes blinded her, dazzled her with its affection.

If Bart had ever once looked at her that way, she would never have let him walk away. She would have fought tooth and nail to save her marriage for a look like the one Ryder gave her now. Affection. Compassion. Emotions more powerful in their way than the wickedly seductive physical hunger that had swamped them last night. These emotions had nothing to do with conquering and surrendering. This tenderness made her want to go to him and offer him herself, her heart, her soul, in return.

She blinked.

Seeing something in her expression, Ryder bent closer, his eyes darkening. And then he stepped back, and she felt as if an enormous magnet pulled her with him, all the little electrical impulses in her cells pointing toward him.

"On second thought, let's stay, Josie." His voice was gruff. "We're better off here."

Better to share that moment in public than back at her house.

Or his.

They both left the words unspoken.

Going in front of her to make a path through the milling people, he led them toward the big top and the wagons around to the back. Twice, shoved from behind by the energy of the crowd, Josie bumped into him. His light gray linen jacket was smooth and cool against her face, his back strong and wide enough for a woman to lean against, and she wished they were back at her house, even his, and could forget all the reasons that kept them apart.

With the cool, crisp fabric of his jacket rubbing against her cheek, Josie longed to know if she could make his lean body burn with that incredible heat again. Wistfully she wondered if she had the power to make him lose control, to need her so badly that only her word would stop him.

The strength of his male response to her made something deeply feminine in her nature hum, as though he'd turned on a switch in her that no one had known was there. Except Ryder. She was beginning to wonder if, indeed, all that heat came from outside them as Ryder suggested.

She wasn't so sure.

The question lingered, invited her to find the answer. To see if there was a shore beyond the sea of grief.

Such a risk to take in the face of everything that threatened. She stared at the straw-packed, dusty ground where thousands had walked before her.

And kept a careful distance from Ryder.

Outside the enclave of train cars where the trainers apparently stayed, an empty field had been turned over to a model-airplane exhibit.

Throngs of adults and children ringed an open area where airplanes with nine-foot wingspans swooped and soared. Tugging the hem of his jacket, Josie stopped Ryder. "You go ahead. I'll wait here. I'd rather stay outside, anyway, even in the heat. I'll stay right here by this stand." She indicated the cold-drinks-and-cotton-candy stand. As he hesitated, she said, "It's broad daylight, Ryder. There aren't any elephants, or dogs, or snakes anywhere in sight. I'll be fine. Really."

"You're sure?"

Josie nodded. The field of planes was visible from the train car. "I'll scream like a banshee if anything happens. But I want to be outside. Really."

An eyebrow lifted in question, he shrugged. The gray jacket moved with him as if it, too, had been custom-made to fit the wedge of his shoulders, the lean muscles. "All right. But I won't be long. I'm going over to that car." He pointed to one with large bales of hay and straw near it. "Jacob Bloom is the man I'm looking for. I called from my house while I was getting dressed. Nothing like portable phones. Technology, Josie. Miracles."

His tucked-in half smile made her heart turn over.

Ryder was a man who would wear well over the years, a man for the long haul. Ryder was a man who would keep a woman on her toes. He would tease and razz and nag, but he wouldn't let her forget for an instant that she was a woman and he a man.

A man who could make a woman smile and forget, for

long, wonderful moments at a time, the clouds and darkness.

His gray back, somber in the riot of color, moved away from her.

Josie wanted to call him back, cling to him.

A woman was truly lost if she clung. She'd learned the hard lesson that a woman needed to know that she could stand alone. Because, whether she willed it or not, the time would come. She would need her own strength.

But the promise of a strength shared, even briefly, oh, that promise cast a spell a woman would find difficult to resist.

And for that reason, if no other, Josie turned away, turned to the field of brightly whirring, dipping, soaring planes.

One brilliant yellow plane circled, rose, shrieked to the sky, and in an instant came dive-bombing toward a steel blue, stubby plane sedately circling around the field. Like a hornet, the yellow plane buzzed in, swung away, coming closer and closer to the blue target as the onlookers squawked and yelled in excitement.

Drawn by the drama in the chalk-dust white sky, Josie meandered closer, making sure that she stayed in view of the train car Ryder had indicated.

Ten men wearing orange-striped vests were in charge of the field. A sign indicated that the model-plane society of Angel Bay was contributing all proceeds to the pediatric wing of the hospital. Onlookers had a choice of flying the planes in a pattern and landing, taking off and guiding the planes around until the end of a five-minute time limit. On the side closest to Josie, two men were in charge of the aerial combat, selling chances to guide the blue or yellow plane as each dodged and attacked.

Begging their parents for permission, children swarmed around the adults lined up for a chance at the controls of the yellow plane. The man in charge of the blue plane had his line of customers, too, but it was the yellow plane's vividness and sharklike design that drew the bigger crowds.

Josie herself felt an itch in her hand to try the controls. But she wanted the blue plane. Its squatty solidness appealed to her for the same reasons her ugly phone and Ryder's homely bird pot did. Their ordinariness called to her.

Glancing back, she saw that if she got in line, Ryder would be able to see her. The train car was clearly visible to her, so she took her place in line and dug out three dollars for her chance.

Although she didn't know the man in charge of the blue plane, she recognized Chuck Woolverton in front of the other line of yelling, screaming kids and adults. Pocketing the money from the eager participants lined up to try their hand with his plane, Chuck nodded to her, his gaze shifting to the thirteen-year-old who waved a ten-dollar bill at him. "Sure, kid, you're next. But hold your horses. You have to wait until the planes land. You can pay for one turn a time, and then you have to get back in line. One turn, one chance. Five minutes a shot."

"But I don't want to go to the back of the line. Let me have an extra chance, Woolly. Besides, I helped paint it. Nobody'll care."

"No way, son." Woolverton caught Josie's eye and looked away, obviously harassed by the boy's insistent demand.

"Fair's fair, Woolly," the boy whined. "Give me an extra minute on the Mustang, then, 'cause I can take the blue dude. That B-25's a dinosaur. Don't be such a hard nose, Woolly."

"Not today, Doug. Can't do. Rules is rules. You know that." Usually a low-key patient man, Woolverton looked as if he were ready to bolt and run as his frazzled glance met Josie's and fell again to the boy. Turning, Woolverton looked over his shoulder at the woman operating the yellow plane.

As he turned, Josie realized that Woolverton was the short, thin man Stoner had been talking to at the parade. A local mechanic who specialized in rebuilding car engines, Woolverton had fixed the valves in her car in February, not charging for the repair, and Josie knew she should feel grateful to him, but she couldn't.

His kindness had seemed patronizing, a kind of pity, and she'd stayed away from him ever since, made uncomfortable by his gushing attempts to express sympathy. She'd sent him a check.

He hadn't returned it.

But he hadn't cashed it, either, and her checkbook still carried that amount, an unwelcome reminder every time she paid a bill or cashed a check. Hostility toward the man stirred in her again, even now, and she shifted, facing away from him.

Being with Ryder had made her aware of how isolated she'd become, how rusty her ability to interact in a normal way with normal people. Josie told herself she should go over to the man and apologize for the way she'd treated him after his generosity, but she couldn't make herself take the first step in his direction.

Even watching his casual touch of the boy's shoulder make her flinch.

When her turn came, she listened to the instructions.

"If you crash, you pay cash. Got it?" The man handed her the controller. "Don't get cute and whip it around until it gets smashed or augers into the ground, lady. That's my advice. You're not going to have much chance against the P-51, anyhow. Just circle the cow pasture and have a good time."

Waiting until her teenage opponent was ready, Josie had the eeriest sensation that she was being watched. She'd had the same feeling at the parade. Both times, the sensation of being singled out in a crowd had been eerily uncomfortable.

The hairs on the back of her neck rose, and she turned,

but the whistle shrilled the beginning of the time limit, and
people were screaming and clapping as the yellow shark
plane came streaking low and fast at her plane still on the
ground.

CHAPTER ELEVEN

Coming out of the emptiness of the sky, the attack of the plane seemed vicious, personal. Uneasily scanning the crowd for the source of that primitive alarm, Josie had her back to the landing field. Screams alerted her, drawing her gaze back to the planes, away from the shifting, moving throng of merrymakers, and she pushed levers frantically, for some reason compelled to get her blue plane airborne, to escape from that unseen watcher.

Even caught up in the frenzy of the moment, she knew her reaction to the diving fighter plane was excessive, but she reacted to it the same way she had to the dogs. To the snake.

She didn't feel like sitting around waiting to be victimized.

And, mortified, she realized that she didn't like the self-satisfied smirk on the teenager's face. The look that dismissed her.

With an intensity that astonished her, she shoved the controls up, sideways, leaving the ground with a lurching, bobbing takeoff that exhilarated her. She laughed, excitement rising in her with the droning lift of her plane, a fat bumblebee blue in the hot, white sky. Like herself, a tiny speck in all the vastness, running.

It was like being a kid on the playground again, running all out in a game of fox and hounds, the adrenaline-pumping, heart-pounding childish dread of being caught sending her racing for safety. The freedom of playing with a toy released something in Josie that had been bottled up forever, it seemed, and she laughed again as the boy groaned when his plane passed too far to the left, his miscalculation letting her escape by a hair.

Red liquid squirted from under his plane as he roared by. He thought he'd caught her. The water-soluble-dye spot on the ground marked his error.

Josie wanted to win. Seized by a sense of competition she hadn't known since she was ten, she wanted to defeat the yellow plane. She knew she couldn't. She'd been warned. Her plane was a bomber, it didn't have the maneuverability of the other plane, and she was unskilled. Again, though, as she manipulated her plane in a large circle with the other plane zooming up over her, preparing to dive toward her, she surprised herself. She wanted to mark that whining, buzzing nuisance.

The boy zipped his plane in, close, released the dye marker, and took off before she'd completed her turn with the stubby, wallowing little plane she'd chosen.

One hit.

She couldn't win.

The rhythmic chanting of the crowd distracted her, and she moved the wrong control. Her plane listed to the left, right, slowed down.

The second hit came so fast she didn't even realize that her plane had been marked until the crowd roared.

She had one more chance, but her plane slipped sideways, wallowing, and she didn't have the skill to manipulate it into a move that would let it escape the yellow streak coming up fast.

And then Ryder was there, his arms around her, enclosing her and swallowing her smaller hands up with his, his long, agile fingers sliding the controls she still held so fast that Josie laughed again with the sheer pleasure of seeing her little plane dart close to the ground and fly low and fast, as the other plane swung in and missed.

The sun was warm on her face and arms, on her legs, chasing away the night terrors as she followed the flight of her plane as it flew west, toward the enclave of animal trainers, rose, circled and came roaring back toward her. This heat and noise and crowd excitement were real, not that otherworldly cold and terror of the night.

The whoops of the crowd cheering her and Ryder made her laugh once more, and she turned to him. Standing close at her back, his gaze fixed on the blue plane, he was smiling. One strand of his hair hung onto his forehead, and the muscles of his face and body were relaxed, loose. He was not the man she'd first seen, not the man of the narrowed eyes and flushed face who'd followed her down to the floor as eagerly as she'd gone there.

Like her, Ryder, too, was playing, intent on the swoop and soar of the toys, and when he abruptly looked down at her, he laughed right back at her, his eyes bright with a lightheartedness she could never have imagined in him.

"Let's get this dude," he said, mimicking the teenager who'd yelled when the blue plane had managed to avoid the last hit. "He needs an attitude adjustment. Somebody needs to teach him the proper respect for his elders. What do you say? Want to?" Working the controls, Ryder took one step closer. "It'll be fun."

She felt the brush of his thigh against her, and in the hot sunshine, the open field, and the crowd of laughing, cheering revelers, she surrendered to the frivolity, surrendered to the moment. It was as if the spring wound inside her so tightly for months and days had snapped, freeing everything tight and tense and sad in her to float away as free as the balloons in the sky overhead. "Get 'em," she said, laughing and easing her grip as he guided their joined hands over the controls.

And because of the clever working of his hand over hers, Josie had the sense that she, too, was controlling the plane. She began to feel the movement of their plane through the controls, began to understand what the plane could do. Oh, she knew they still couldn't win, but with Ryder behind her, keeping her safe inside the strength of his arms, she no longer cared.

The game was enough.

So in those fleeting moments, knowing that they had stolen the seconds, knowing they were running out of time, Josie relaxed back against him, let herself fly with the stubby little plane shuddering through the pale sky.

Ryder's cheek, smelling of soap and shampoo, was close to hers. "Watch," he whispered into her ear. "Don't look away, Josie. This is going to be fun. Trust me." He turned and gave her a grin so brimful of devilment as he lifted his eyebrow in that deliberate way he had that she wanted to stand on her toes and kiss him.

Kiss him because it was daylight and the sun was hot inside her.

Kiss him for the joy of the moment he was giving her.

Kiss him for the joy of touching him.

She knew he saw her intent because his grin spread to his eyes, darkened them with a glint that would sweep a girl off her feet and make a woman remember that love wasn't always an illusion.

Even in a world dark with shadows, it was the miracle.

She rose on her toes, ready to share with him her sense of remembered innocence, that joy she'd forgotten existed.

The crowd shrieked, groaned. Letting the moment pass, both feet firmly on the ground again, she looked back at their plane.

Ryder worked the controls rapidly as the yellow plane zoomed up behind them and closed in on the blue plane.

As the teenager worked into position to make the final hit and the whistle shrilled, indicating their time was up, Ryder angled the nose of their plane down to maximize speed and then, with the shark plane almost on the blue plane, pushed the vertical control until the blue plane rose straight up, shuddering and stalling as the yellow plane, miscalculating, zipped by, missing them.

And Josie screamed as the spot of red dye from their plane plopped onto the Mustang. "Yes!" She leapt into the air, arms to the heavens. "Yes!"

"Way to go, sweetheart." Ryder's arm was around her waist and his lips grazed her ear, a stolen kiss for a stolen moment, and the sweetness of the kiss, the sweetness of the moment, was as rich as the water she poured onto her parched garden every day.

The crowd surged around them, enjoying the unexpected victory as much as if they'd been guiding the plane.

The boy's petulant face as he turned to Chuck Woolverton was the only discordant note in the tumult.

"Hold on, Josie," Ryder said. He left her and strolled toward the teenager with a deceptively easy, slouching saunter that caught up to the boy before he realized Ryder's intention.

Even in the afternoon heat, Josie missed Ryder's presence at her back.

She felt vulnerable without him. She couldn't remember if she'd ever allowed herself to feel that way with anyone.

They'd leaned on her, instead.

Turning off the remote control, she handed it to the owner and went toward Ryder and the boy, coming up on them in time to hear Ryder's "Good work" as he extended his hand to the boy.

"Yeah. I screwed up. I shoulda won." The boy kicked the dirt at his feet. Dust puffed up, powdered his shoes.

"Do this often?" Ryder lifted a shoulder in the direction of the planes.

"Why?" the boy said, his expression truculent. "What's it to you?"

"Nothing." Ryder turned enough so that Josie could see the boy and gave her a quick glance that cautioned her to stay where she was. "Thought you looked as if you'd had a bit of practice. You made some pretty slick moves."

She wondered what Ryder was up to. She'd thought he

was merely being a good sport, teaching the overconfident teenager a lesson of a different kind.

The boy flushed, kicked the ground again. "Yeah, well, I'm in the club. I shoulda known better than to fall for that trick you pulled. Me and Woolly and Hank—" he pointed toward one of the men working the planes "—us and a bunch of the other dudes get together and work on the planes and take 'em out. Like a club. A society, I guess, of plane builders."

"Next time, don't underestimate your opponent," Ryder said, and his voice was even, his expression calm. "Doesn't pay to get overconfident. Leads to miscalculation."

"Yeah." The teenager finally stuck out his hand and shook Ryder's. "Like I said, I screwed up. Next time, I won't. But you did good. Nobody's ever gotten away with that stunt on the B-25." His smile was chagrined.

"Kind of like playing with a stacked deck, was it?" Amusement rippled over Ryder's face.

The boy rolled his eyes. "Yeah, but I fell for the trick. See ya." He looked toward the line of people waiting for their turn on the blue plane and grinned at Ryder. "Now they think they can do the same thing. See ya," he said and sauntered off with a swagger toward the growing crowd waiting for a chance to see if they could sucker the yellow plane's operator.

Ryder's gaze followed the boy as he went first to Woolverton and then joined the second line.

"What do you see, Ryder?" She was watching them, too, and couldn't figure out what had put the contemplative expression on Ryder's face.

"Lots and lots of people. Magicians watch folks, study them. Like actors. All part of polishing the act." He slicked his hair back and straightened the sleeves of his jacket. "Well, Josie, I learned diddly from Jacob Bloom. As far as he knew, Beatrice was a saint among elephants. A little peevish if he didn't feed her on time, a mite peckish—his word, not mine—if she was overly tired. All in all, I've wasted your day." He sighed and, like the boy, kicked the straw-strewn ground. "Sorry."

"You didn't waste my day," she said softly. "It was a good afternoon. Thank you."

He sketched a bow, his gesture elegant and theatrical in the midst of the circus heat and dust. "A small thing, of no significance, but you're welcome, Josie Birdsong." As he looked at her, his expression became contemplative, tinged with regret. "I wish I'd given you pearls and rubies for your memory collection instead of a sun-baked field with a smart-ass kid trying to chase you down with a model airplane. But you're not a pearls-and-rubies woman, are you? That's a compliment, in its way," he said with a half smile as he tapped her chin. "But I can see you in pearls." He shaped make-believe pearls out of the air, draped them around her neck, down between her breasts.

Though there was nothing there, the movement of his hands in the air made Josie feel the weight of the heavy pearls against her bare skin.

"And rubies." His fingers flicked, flashed, and he dropped a candy-size red stone into the V of her T-shirt. The stone was cool, but her skin heated against it as he smiled gently at her.

She dipped her hand in and retrieved the glowing stone. Holding it up in mock confusion, she asked, "Am I supposed to wear it like Shanna the belly dancer?"

"Yeah." He grinned. "I could see that." His eyes let her know exactly where he envisioned the ruby, and his eyebrow quirked roguishly. "Yeah, that would be a sight to see."

"Hmm." Her cheeks burned as hot as the color of the faux ruby's fire. She tucked the stone into her shorts pocket. "I don't think so."

"Well, who knows?" As though the silliness with the airplanes had freed something in him, too, a reckless energy crackled through his words, captivating her and lifting her bruised spirit even higher. "Come on, Josie," he said and snagged the tail end of the bow on her blouse, tugging her with him. "I want to show you something Jacob mentioned. I think you'll find it interesting."

His ground-eating pace left her breathlessly hurrying after him, and she braked, stopping him. "Whoa, Superman. I can't fly." She lengthened her stride, and he shortened his as they continued down one of the side paths toward a tent with mobile bulletin boards outside it. "Speaking of which, why'd you come help me fly the model?"

"You looked like a little kid, frustrated, ready to stomp your foot and throw a tantrum, Josie," he said, his expression so innocently puzzled that she almost believed him.

"Listen, Ryder, I never, ever throw tantrums. Never have, not even when I was a grubby little kid. I might throw a bucket at you, but a tantrum? Nah."

"My mistake." He grinned at her again. "You should have seen yourself, though, Josie. You were out to smash that poor kid. I don't ever want to get on your bad side, that's for sure. Not if you have a bucket close at hand. You're a dangerous woman, that's for sure. A take-no-prisoners lady." He ducked as she kicked a soda can his way. Scooping it up, he flipped it back her way, with only a bit of a spin on it.

He could have thrown it so that she couldn't have caught it.

Josie knew that, and she smiled at him. His answering smile was companionable, inviting her to join the game. An impish impulse making her arch the silver-and-blue can high, she snapped the pop can back his way.

And, flexing his powerful thighs and calves, he leapt, circled, and caught the can with a one-handed catch, pitching it into the enormous black recycling can as he landed. "Hey, green eyes, guess what? I didn't have visions when

I was helping you crunch that poor little kid and his nifty airplane. Did you?''

She hadn't thought about it. Absorbed in the chase and capture, she'd been engrossed in the whir and buzz of the planes. ''You're right. Nothing happened when we touched. That's odd.''

''Every other time, we've seen something. Right?'' He was walking backward, facing her as they neared the tent.

''Well, not every time.'' She couldn't meet his eyes. She shoved her hands into her pockets. The ruby stone was cold against the smooth warmth of the shard of green glass.

''Why not? Have you thought about last night any more, Josie?''

Oh, she had. She'd thought about evil. She'd thought about the way Ryder's touch had ignited her, made her blaze. And after Henry Milton left, she'd thought about Ryder and the tiger eyes and hunger a lot.

And she'd remembered that with Ryder blocking the entrance to her bedroom she'd slept and not dreamed of the stalking figure. She hadn't had the nightmare.

After everything that had happened, she'd expected to.

She had dreamed of Mellie, heard her calling endlessly to ''hurryhurryhurry.''

''Well, have you?''

''Yes.'' She looked at the ground, not quite able to face him. ''But last night was different from all the other times. I didn't have any sense of evil in what happened between us, Ryder.'' Oh, no, the hungry wildness he'd made her feel had nothing in common with evil. ''It was the tiger eyes. There was evil in them. That was what scared me, not you. Why?''

''Well, Josie Birdsong, champion pilot, I'm trying to figure out if there are any rules to what's going on, or if it's all random. Chaos. Whether it's day or night doesn't seem to matter, so I'm fooling around with some ideas.'' Without looking behind him, he two-stepped out of the way of a group of spangled and spandexed performers coming up behind him. "What was going on in your mind? What were you feeling right before I came up, Josie? Were you scared? Angry? What?"

"I was excited," she said slowly, remembering how the contest had started. "No, wait. At first I felt...threatened. Almost as if the plane were alive, like a bird, an animal." She fumbled for words, trying to convey that peculiar sense that had sent goose bumps down her arms. "I don't know, but I felt as if it were after me. Goofy."

"Maybe. Maybe not. What else?"

"And for a second or two, I had that feeling again that someone was watching me." She frowned. "I almost didn't get my plane into the air because I turned around to see who was staring at me." Thinking about that unseen pair of eyes, Josie shivered. "It was so much like what happened before the elephant broke away yesterday. But then the planes were looping around and the crowd was screaming at me, and I...I was caught up in the game. I wanted to win." Abashed by her admission, she shrugged and made a face. "And I'm supposed to be an adult."

"Brat."

She glanced up. Seeing Ryder's teasing expression, she laughed. "Anyway, I had fun." She lifted her arms to tuck a trailing end of ribbon back into her hair. "I don't see any pattern. We've been in different places, different times of the day or night."

He stopped abruptly. "And our emotional states have been different." With each word, he took a step closer to her. "Anger, exhaustion, fear. This was the first time, Josie, that the feelings weren't negative ones. Think about it, sweetheart." He circled her, came up beside her.

"That our emotional states offer a pathway to whatever is happening? The stronger the emotional state, the more...*open* we are to the influences around us? The more vulnerable? Is that what you think?"

Shading her from the sun, he stepped in front of her. Because he was backlit by the sun, his face was in shadow and she couldn't see his expression. "It's the best explanation I've come up with, Josie. You made me think of it when you said last night that what we had in common was guilt and recrimination. I kept thinking about that. Both of us have been walking around under a killing load of guilt. You said there was a bond between us, like superglue. You may be right." He stepped back and the sun flashed into her eyes, momentarily blinding her. "And the other emotion that erupts between us is pretty obvious. Desire is powerful, Josie. And I've never wanted anyone the way I want you. As if you were the air I needed to breathe." He was backing away again, disappearing in the glare. "Desire like that leaves me very vulnerable, sweetheart."

Watching his dark form move away from her, Josie thought of her dream, thought of all the ways the young boy had been vulnerable. No wonder he liked being by himself. Safer. If you didn't take any risks, you weren't hurt. If you didn't let anyone into your heart, your heart wouldn't be torn apart. Control. Ryder had organized his life so that he was always in control. That way nothing could come leaping out of the dark to surprise him.

There were all kinds of tigers that prowled by night. And by day.

"Ryder," she said, coming up close to him, "we can't protect ourselves absolutely. It's impossible. We're all vulnerable in one way or another. That's life." She held her hand out, palm up. "We can't keep anything. Except in memory. Except in our hearts."

His hand shaded his eyes. "Philosophy 201, Josie?" he drawled. "No pain, no gain?"

"That's about it." She followed him into the spacious tent where wood panels had been laid to form a floor. With the vaulted effect of the tent's roof, the overall impact was cathedral-like. Floor fans circulated the air, and high up overhead, a ceiling fan mounted to struts drew the air up and out. The quiet humming of the fans and slow movement of air conveyed a sense of tranquillity after the raucousness of the circus outside. Twenty or thirty people roamed slowly around the tent, their voices hushed. The contrast with the hectic atmosphere outside was restful.

Working in her garden gave her that same sense of serenity and rightness. Of peace.

Grouped in the center of the dim interior, simple wooden boxes held carved panthers, owls, snakes. The fabric panels of the tent were hung with pictures. Oils, watercolors, photos. Easels displayed larger, framed paintings. "An art exhibit? What did you want me to see?"

"Take a look, Josie."

She did.

One oil painting showed fantastically colored will-o'-the-wisps and explosive sprays of ball lightning. In the forefront of the painting, a mythical snake rolled like a hoop across the swampy ground, the stinger in its tail threatening and enormous.

In a watercolor, delicate and gauzy-winged dragonflies hovered over a wounded snake. As she looked closer, she saw that filaments came from the dragonflies as they fluttered their wings and sewed up the injury. All the colors were pastel, subtle, and the impact was as if she'd stepped into a fairy tale. "Oh, Ryder, this is lovely," she said. "Mellie would love—"

Ryder watched the realization of what she'd said widen her eyes. He could see how the picture would entrance a small girl. There was such a playful look to the insects as they went about their task. He went to Josie and put his arm around her. He sensed that whatever found its way into the world through them couldn't harm them here.

She resisted the light pull of his arm, but then, as if the air had gone out of her, she leaned against him. Cupped by his arm, her shoulders were not much larger than a child's.

Whenever he touched her, he was struck anew by her slightness, her smallness, her delicacy. "You don't talk about your Seminole heritage, but I thought you might like this, Josie Birdsong."

Glancing up at him, she smiled, a watery smile that wobbled. Unshed, the tears welling in her eyes magnified their green flecks. "She would have loved this. It makes me think of her." Turning to the watercolor again, Josie stretched out her hand, not touching the picture, simply moving her open palm over it as if to absorb the loveliness.

"I know," Ryder said, his heart shattering like a glass ball.

He stayed by her side, walking with her as they looked at the sculptures and paintings. An enormous, coiled rattlesnake carved from a cypress knee had her stepping back, but the impact of the carving was powerful. In another oil that captured her attention, rainbows and stars were scattered across a purple-red sky where a heavy wind moved, bending the trees before it. Small creatures huddled near the pine trees, and from the earth an enormous serpent crawled forth bearing a deerskin pouch.

As they paused, a slim woman came up to them. "This is a painting representing the death month," she said. "December, more or less, if you're interested. Actually," she added, pointing to the streaks of paint that made the wind, "January is the Little Wind Month, so there's a bit of artistic license in the picture."

"It's...unsettling," Josie said.

"The souls of the dead are going to the spirit world. When a spirit dies, or an object is broken, the spirit is released. Some of the spirits here—" she pointed to shapes in the background "—are lost. They will remain for a time on earth, hostile. Even dangerous. Until they make their way beyond the sky. That's why we believe you must break camp and leave when a death occurs. The spirits walk among us and they are powerful."

"This is yours?" Turning to the black-haired woman, Josie shifted under Ryder's arm, the slippery ribbon in her hair tickling his nose as she did. "You painted this?"

The woman nodded. "Are you interested in our history?"

Josie didn't answer. She'd said she wasn't interested in history, and he suspected that the explanation to her aversion had many reasons, and one was connected to her heritage.

"If you have any questions, I'll be happy to answer them," the woman said. "My name is Betty Cypress. Take your time. I have all day." She walked back to the temporary desk where piles of paper lay among bits of wood and leather.

"Why don't you talk about your...history, Josie?"

She moved away from him, stopped in front of a small painting where a coffin of split logs rested on a leaf-strewn ground under a thatched shelter. In the open coffin lay broken shards of pots, pipe stems snapped in half, and a dismantled, broken shotgun. The accompanying card explained that breaking the articles released their spirit in the same way that the man's spirit had been released to find his way or not to the spirit world.

Restlessly Josie turned away from the painting.

"I'd like to know." Catching the ends of her hair ribbon, Ryder let the silk wind between his fingers. "Tell me, Josie."

"It's unimportant."

"Nothing's unimportant, sweetheart. If it hurts so much that you can't talk about it, it's important. Why? Are you ashamed?"

She whirled on him, her legs a flash of smooth skin and her fizzy pink blouse a blur of color.

He inhaled, and the scent of roses and rainwater moved into his lungs.

"Don't be silly, Ryder. We never talked about being

Seminole in my family. My grandfather—his father had been trained as a shaman and Papa was supposed to learn the medicines and herbs so that he could follow in the tradition, too—was forced to leave the clan because he wanted to learn to read and write.''

The pink of her blouse warmed her face, its vibrancy and color warming him even as he stood next to her. ''What did they do?''

''They repudiated him because he decided to forsake the old ways for the white man's tricks. My grandfather was furious. He wouldn't let my grandmother or mother ever talk about anything connected with the old days, the old ways. That's all. Because the subject was so secretive with my grandmother and mother, I've never talked about my 'heritage.' It doesn't feel as if it's *mine*. It belongs to her.'' Josie swung around and pointed to Betty Cypress. ''Heritage has meaning for her, not for me. I'm an outsider. I don't have a 'heritage.'''

''I see.'' He thought of the way she lit her candles at night, the herbs he'd seen drying from hangers on her porch, thought, too, of the way she loved her garden, loved the touch of the earth itself against her ungloved hands.

''Ryder, it's no big deal. It doesn't have anything to do with me. I live here, in the present. Not the past.''

''Whatever you say, Josie.'' Ryder touched her hair gently, brushed the sleek silk at her neck. ''Beautiful hair, sweetheart. Part of your heritage. Your past. Part of you.''

''I know. But how can I claim something I've always rejected?'' She wandered to a mask made of cypress bark. The calligraphy card underneath indicated that the mask was like one used for the fall hunting dance. She glanced at the price and blinked. ''History's expensive, I guess.''

''Sure. Look at the price that's already been paid.'' He placed his palm against her back, guiding her to another picture that showed a modern Seminole male wearing a hat with an egret feather in the band.

His nose was high arched, his face broad, his lips thin. Dressed in a multicolored, horizontally striped shirt and long khaki pants tucked into calf-high leather boots, the man stood with his arms stretched out to the sides, his feet apart. In the open pouch between the man's feet Ryder could see bits of green stones and feathers, herbs, snake fangs, bones. In one hand he held a bow and arrow, the arrow snapped in two. From his other hand, a stream of water poured from a large clay pitcher onto the ground.

In the water were reflected the bent figures of modern Seminoles moving toward cities, away from the woods and swamps behind them where trucks and bulldozers stripped the trees and palmetto bushes to sand.

At the very back of the stream of water a modern city, small and flimsy, rose on the barren ground.

On his shoulder a small, beautiful ground dove perched, its mouth open in a call.

The card under the painting read simply "Assi Yaholo (Osceola) on the Trail of Tears: Past and Present."

Josie stooped to read a second card and crooked her finger to tell him to come closer so that he could read it. The card explained that the painting wasn't historical, but allegorical, the Osceola of the painting a representation of the Seminole shamans, the ground dove a harbinger of death and the open medicine bundle symbolic of the loss of the Seminole culture and the resultant death of the tribe. Without the supernatural powers of the medicine bundle that had been stolen from it by the white man, the tribe would die.

In the corner of the painting, the artist's signature was barely legible, but leaning over Josie, Ryder made out the wavery lines of the name.

J. Birdsong.

Her back stiffened against his hand. "What on earth?" Frowning, she bent closer, staring at the painting of the man. "I wonder who that could be?" She squinted at the face of the man. "He almost looks familiar."

"Aren't you just a little bit curious, Josie?" he asked. "I am." He touched the back of her neck where the dark, silky hair whorled up over the lovely curve of her head. Her neck was warm and soft, smooth.

He was curious about that lovely curve, too.

Curious to know if it would feel as beautiful to his touch as its sleek hair felt against his finger.

And standing there with only the tip of his finger touching that delicate bit of Josie's skin, Ryder considered the workings of fate. Of coincidence.

Past.

Present.

Those silvery threads winding in and out of their lives, drawing them closer, bringing Josie to him.

Past.

Present.

The murders.

Reality. Illusions.

Evil.

And desire.

He sensed that the threads were all intertwined, leading them somewhere.

If he and Josie could follow those elusive strands to their beginnings—

In that cathedral of Seminole paintings and sculptures, Ryder wondered if life might still hold a chance of absolution.

CHAPTER TWELVE

The moon was full and bloodred, its light shining fitfully through the open flaps of the exhibit tent.

Walking with them to the entrance, Betty Cypress looked out at the sky. "A dark moon in a dark sky," she said as she shook their hands. "Not right," she added, frowning. "A bad moon."

But going down the midway with Ryder close at her side, Josie saw how the electric lights lit up the night so brightly that it was easy to forget about the enormous red moon hanging low overhead.

Before they left, they asked her about the painter of the Osceola painting, telling her about the similarity of names and about how Josie's grandfather had been turned away from his clan. Betty explained that the painter was a young Seminole woman who lived along the Tamiami Trail.

"Johnnie Birdsong's a Big Cypress Reservation woman, born there, but she went to college. She teaches English to the migrant children down the road from Angel Bay. Because she lives so close, we were able to talk her into letting us sell some of her stuff. But I don't think she could be any close relation to you," she'd said, turning to Josie. "All her clan have lived for years on Big Cypress and Brighton. She was the first from her family to leave the reservation. Although—" Betty studied Josie's face "—you have a look of her about you. Here," she said, handing Josie a series of cheaply printed pamphlets. "If you're interested, these brochures give quite a bit of information about Johnnie. There's some background on the themes that reappear in her paintings, too. She's a complicated woman."

Looking at other pictures the woman had done, Josie saw the deep, angry bitterness in the dark tones and the subjects. Betty explained that, coming from the Big Cypress Reservation, a federal reservation, Johnnie Birdsong had grown up seeing every day the results of what had happened when her people had been pushed farther and farther into the swamps and marshes.

Her bitterness had been bred-in-the-bone. Earned.

The land set aside for her people, for instance, more than 42,663 acres, was virtually unusable for much of the year. Flooded during the rainy season and under water most of the time, it had few stands of pine or timber, few areas suitable for cultivation. Other areas near Big Cypress had been taken back, used for drainage projects when developers decided that land was usable, after all.

Looking at Johnnie's pictures, Josie saw her own heritage and was ashamed that all those years she'd turned away from it.

She could have been Johnnie Birdsong, drinking the bitter wine of a nation that had been virtually destroyed, its land, its religion, its people taken from it.

Before they left, Ryder bought the picture.

He bought the one of the lost spirits, too.

Now, leaving the midway for the parking lot, he handed her a butcher-paper-wrapped package.

"What's this?"

Visible from the midway the garish lights blotched Ryder's skin with reds and greens.

"For you."

Peeling back a corner of the brown paper, Josie saw the translucent colors of the dragonflies watercolor. Her hand closed around the edge, gripping the painting tightly. "Oh, Ryder, why?"

"Because," he said. "Just because, Josie, that's why."

Words left unsaid trembled on the air like butterfly

wings, filling her with a sweetness she'd never known. "What can I say?" She held the picture close to her heart.

Reminding her of the delight Mellie took in fireflies and dragonflies, its loveliness eased her soul. If she'd had the money, she would have bought the picture.

For Mellie.

Because in its beauty, her daughter still existed. Her spirit. That knowledge was balm for an aching heart.

When they arrived at Josie's house, the moon had turned to dull red-gold. She heard the phone ringing as Ryder turned off the ignition. "Hell," he said and leapt out of the car, popping the door and lifting the phone receiver before she got there. Right behind him, she raced for the bedroom and picked up the receiver there.

From the kitchen he stared at her as they both listened to the slosh of sound through the wires, the static. He hung up first, shrugging.

"I don't like these calls, Josie."

"Neither do I." She returned to the kitchen. "It's so hot in here that even you must be warm by now." She touched his face. Cool, bristly. Like before. "Guess not. Have you always been so cold, Ryder?" she asked, letting her hand stay against his angular jaw.

"Not until last January when—" He rubbed his eyes. "Josie? We checked my room for drafts. It's me. The cold comes from me. That's all I know. No matter how hot it is, I'm cold."

"Except that one time."

"Yeah." His eyes held hers. "Oh, yeah." Cupping his hand over hers, the way he had when they'd flown the plane, he turned his mouth to her palm and pressed a warm, open kiss that turned her bones to water.

"Yeah," she mimicked, and couldn't keep looking into the darkness.

He cleared his throat. "I'll get the pictures out of the

car. We rushed in here so fast neither of us thought about them.''

Josie watched him vanish through her doorway. Over his shoulder, she saw the red-gold bottom of the moon glowing against the tops of the pines in the woods. When he drove away in his car, she would be alone again.

Alone with her memories and what-ifs.

Alone with this electricity running strong through her body, calling him.

It would be worse this time.

Something had shifted inside her.

The sense of benediction she'd felt in the art tent remained with her, guiding her responses in much the same way Ryder's hands had guided hers. She wanted his touch against her, against her skin, his touch guiding her.

But she didn't know how to tell him.

Didn't know how to ask for what she needed.

She turned on her portable fans but left the windows closed except for the kitchen where she was. If the heat wave didn't end, if something didn't happen soon to make her able to sleep with her windows open or out on her porch, she would have to leave her house.

Last night she'd been unconscious to everything while she slept. But the house was stifling, the heat from the day lying so heavy that it was hard to breathe even with the fans going full blast.

When Ryder returned, carrying all three pictures, she took the dragonfly painting and held it as he pounded a nail in her bedroom wall. Lifting the wire strand over the nail, he straightened the picture while Josie propped the others up against the couch and turned off the lights for coolness, lighting the candles she kept around the rooms of her house.

The tiny candle flames flickered against the darkness pressing against the walls of her house.

''Here.'' She handed him a glass of wine and sipped from her own as she regarded the Death Month picture with its lost souls. In candlelight, the picture seemed more powerful. "Why did you buy these two pictures, Ryder? They make me uncomfortable."

"They talk to me, Josie." He shrugged and downed his wine. "They make me believe. Whether I want to or not. What I see in them talks to me in a language beyond words."

The one of the lost spirits especially disturbed her. The idea that the souls of all those creatures and some of the man-made objects were hovering between this world and the spirit world, their spirits hostile to the living made her want to cover the picture, but she couldn't.

The colors of the rainbow drew her into the picture. The longer she looked at the rainbow, the more she saw how those colors shimmered and gleamed in the candle shadows. She walked closer to it, touched it, traced the arc of the rainbow. "It's growing on me, I guess. Think of all those restless souls, Ryder."

"I'm a restless soul, Josie." He set his glass down on the floor and stood up. "Restless and hungry."

"For what?" she whispered, seeing the answer in his eyes, knowing they were both lost and looking for a safe place. "Tell me what you want, Ryder." She walked over to him and put her hands on his shoulders. "Let me give you peace tonight, Ryder. I need to."

"For me? Or for yourself, too, Josie? Because I don't need you to throw your body on a sacrificial altar." He ran the back of his hand along her neck, up over her ear. "I'm not feeling anything except totally positive emotions right now, Josie." His voice was strained and low. "God, they're positive, sweetheart." He placed her hand over the thunder of his heart. "Feel how positive, Josie?"

"And I'm not angry. Or afraid. There's nothing negative in my feelings right now, either." Slipping her open hand under his jacket, she traced the line of his shoulders. "Oh, Ryder, I don't want to be alone tonight. I don't want to dream and wake up in my bedroom by myself. Stay with me. For me. If you want.''

''I want,'' he said, his words urgent and as solemn a vow as any she'd ever heard. ''I want, more than you'll ever know, Josie. But I'm afraid to take. I don't want to make love to you as a kind of psychic experiment, sweetheart.'' His laugh was shaky and his fingers trembled against her neck. ''Maybe before. Maybe in the beginning. But not now. This is a curiosity of a different nature, green eyes, a curiosity that's burning me up on the inside while I'm cold as ice outside. It's a curiosity I'd rather die than satisfy if it means harm to you.''

She stroked the back of his neck lightly with her fingernails, and he shuddered. He was yielding all his male power to her, and the wonder of it drew her closer, made her trace his mouth with her finger. And every time she touched him, she felt the touch inside herself.

Tipping his head back, he shut his eyes. ''Ah, Josie, that feels so good.'' But even then he didn't touch her.

His hand rested in the slope of her neck, and she turned her mouth and kissed the tip of his thumb as it brushed against her earlobe.

And over his shoulder, she saw the moon, red in the darkness of the woods.

Caught in the candle flames in front of her, the lost souls marched endlessly toward the rainbow, seeking peace and salvation.

Leaning against his chest, she slipped his jacket off. The shushing sound it made against the wood floor slid along her nerve endings, set them jangling. ''Oh, Ryder,'' she whispered against the white cotton of his shirt, ''there's no evil in this room tonight. Only peace. Only rest.'' Brushing his hair back from his broad forehead, she stood on tiptoe, letting the strands slide again and again through her fingers. And then, deliberately, knowing what she was doing, she let her hands move over his shoulders, down his ribs, over the powerful muscles of his haunches, learning the shape of him through the expensive fabric of his custom-made clothes.

The waistband of his slacks was narrow, loose, the slim leather belt as supple and sinewy as the man. As she flipped the metal tongue, the belt hissed through the loops, fell to the floor, and she lifted the fine cotton free, letting her hands go beneath to touch his cold skin that seemed to warm as she stroked it. The zipper rasped against her hand.

His groan reverberated deep inside her. ''God, Josie, sweetheart. If tigers came leaping through the door right now, I wouldn't care what they did to me. This moment would have been worth the price.'' His heart was pounding so hard against her seeking mouth that she could feel its thunder on her lips.

And he remained utterly unmoving in spite of the fine trembling running like a current over his skin, letting her explore him, giving her the power and the control over the engine of his body, over himself.

Trapping his hands, the cuffs of his long-sleeved shirt were buttoned, and his shirt hung over the back of his slacks, white against black. Darkness and light. Knotted around his neck, his blue-and-silver tie lay against the taut muscles of his rigid chest, his naked skin a canvas for the storm-cloud colors of the tie.

The effort it took him to remain passive showed in the tension of his muscles, in the straining cords of his neck. Running her fingers down the length of his silky tie, she tugged him closer and bent to his midriff, kissing the ridged muscles along his rib cage. His slacks thumped to the floor and he took one step forward, coming closer to her, one bare thigh slipping between her legs. As she stroked the long line of his spine, tracing it down to the silk of his boxers, his thigh rode higher, shifting and moving against her until she gasped.

His answering chuckle was wicked and delighted. "This is the picture I'd like to keep in my scrapbook."

"What do you see, Ryder?" she murmured, letting her lips trail along the midline of his chest.

"Only you, Josie." He opened his eyes and looked down at her. There was humor in their darkness, heat in their depths. "Are you enjoying yourself, sweetheart?" His chuckle was raw, rough.

She smiled up at him. "Oh, yes, Ryder. Very much."

"Good. Because I sure as hell am." He stooped and kissed the tip of her nose. "God, Josie, you smell so good. I'd know you in the dark."

"And I'd recognize you, too." She breathed in the spicy spell that was Ryder, his skin, *him*. "Anywhere." Delicately, she touched the tip of her tongue to one hard nipple.

He jerked, rigid as a rubber band stretched to its limit. "It seems to me that turnabout's fair play." His hands were suddenly free of the handcuffs of his shirt, and the loop of his tie was around one of her wrists. "Is it my turn to play, Josie?" he muttered against her ear, and the vibrations curled her bare toes.

"Not yet," she whispered. "Not quite yet."

"I don't think I can stand much more, sweetheart." He groaned again as she trailed her palm over the length of him.

She glanced down and smiled. "Oh, I'll bet you can. If you try. Please try, Ryder."

And he did.

She would give him that.

He tried, but she found that, after all, she did have the power to break him. But in the moment when he groaned against her seeking mouth and bent down to sweep her up, victor and vanquished meant nothing. All his beautiful muscled strength was there for her pleasure, and even as he yielded to her, she yearned to surrender to him, the giving and the taking so closely related that her body, his, no longer had meaning to her in the exquisite pleasure of touching and being touched.

Somehow her wrists were around his neck, the loop of the tie holding them, and she was sitting on his knee, close to his chest, her legs dangling on either side of his waist. And the subtle shifts and thrusts of his thigh against the seam of her shorts created a tension inside that made her edge even closer to him, and when she did, he took her mouth under his, deepening the kiss even as she rode him, the deep thrust of his tongue rasping against the tender lining of her mouth and creating shivers so deep that she clung to him, after all.

But even as she clung to him, needing the stroke of his hands, the rasp of his tongue against her breasts, he held her as tightly. She never knew when he slipped off her blouse, only realized it was gone when his cool fingers tugged her nipple and spread across her bare back.

Suddenly, the ribbon in her hair fell around her neck and her hair tumbled down, sliding against her back, tickling her skin as he draped it over her breasts and brushed the strands across her nipples, her stomach, across his mouth.

"Oh, Josie, I wish you could see yourself. What a beauty you are, sweetheart." He kissed her belly button, and the gentleness under the urgency of his touch melted her, made her stomach ripple against the heat of his mouth.

"I do," she murmured, seeing herself in the way he touched her, stroked her. And she saw herself, too, in the glow of his eyes, in his delight in her. How could a woman not feel beautiful when a man looked at her as if all the pleasure in his world came from touching her? "You make me beautiful."

Sliding both hands under the waistband of her shorts, he eased them off, replacing them with his hands that suddenly grew warm against her as he pressed and parted, his touch rougher now, harder, the urgency carrying her with him. He cupped the back of her neck with one hand and her fanny with the other, lifting her tight against him as he lay back on the floor, bringing her on top of his hard chest.

His hand pressed against the V of her thighs, stroked her there until she dropped her head back, helpless in the grip of that shattering pleasure.

And then, while she trembled against him, he flexed and sat up, cradling her in his lap as he parted her and rode with her to the floor, entering her with one strong thrust that bowed her up against him and started the spiral of pleasure all over.

The candles sputtered and burned as if air stirred in the airless room.

He turned, taking her with him as he slipped his hands under her hair, draping it over his chest as he lay back with his knees bent, supporting her.

The ruby stone glittered between his fingers. Trailing over her lips, down her throat, over the outside curve of one breast, letting it graze her nipple, he brought the glowing stone down her ribs, circling and circling closer to her navel until he pressed the stone into the oval indentation.

Its fiery glow gleamed on her skin, and his hand beneath it turned her to fire.

Her skin was slick against his, and as she bent, nipping the cord of his neck, his skin suddenly burned with that remembered heat and he thrust harder and harder in her, taking her faint whimpers with his mouth.

And she burned against him, incandescent in the dark.

The air moved over her, caressed her naked back as Josie lifted her head and stared at the picture of the rainbow and stars and lost souls.

The last candle guttered out, and in that darkness, the bloodred moon shone through the closed windows.

The voice came.

Half sitting, Ryder rose and scooped her hair forward, wrapping it around one fist. "Josie," he muttered, "hold me. Don't be frightened. Please, hold me. It's happening again. But you'll be okay. Josie, don't turn me loose. Or I don't know if I can find the way back.'' His grip was tight against her scalp, his face pained.

With her gaze fixed on the painting, she held him tightly as the darkness grew heavier, swirling and pushing, the movement of its shadows palpable.

This time she didn't fight the dark. She let herself follow the shadows. Somehow she knew that if she held on to Ryder, she would be safe. He would be safe. She saw what he saw. The red shoe in the sand. A stand of pines, one twisted and shredded by wind and salt water. The small hand coming from a humped mound of sand under the twisted pine.

She cried out.

"Don't let go, Josie!" Ryder's fist tightened in her hair, and she knew he needed her, needed her to keep him in the vision.

"I won't," she moaned, but she wanted to, oh, she didn't want to see what was coming next.

The images swirled, and once more she saw the boy's pug nose, heard his plaintive cry, saw the child's hand underneath the sand this time, and she saw the palmetto bushes and sea grapes, the sea oats. Saw the shiny black shoes of an adult walking away, the welts in the sand the shoe heels left.

Too clear, everything that she saw.

Almost saw a face to go with those shoes.

With her gaze fixed on the painting of the lost spirits, she was cold now, as cold as Ryder.

Bone-deep cold.

The images vanished.

"Devil's Island," she said. "Not Santa Ana. Santa Ana doesn't have tall pines." And her voice trembled like the wind chimes her mother had kept on their porch during her childhood, the vibrations constant in the slightest breeze. "I think." She couldn't stop shaking. "Or Madder Me.

Madre Mia. One of the islands. He's there. And we're too late.'' She was trembling. ''Ryder, I'm so cold, so cold.''

Carrying her in his arms, he rose and took her into her bathroom. Turning the faucet all the way to hot, he waited until steam filled the tiny room. Adjusting the faucet, he stepped right under the shower head with her.

''We'll call Stoner.'' He let her trail down the length of his body and even under the steam and hot water his skin was cold now to her touch.

''He won't believe us.'' Her teeth chattered.

''He doesn't have to. And we don't have to tell him everything. We'll think of something, Josie, sweetheart. We're going to find Eric Ames. It may not be too late.''

But she knew it was already too late.

With the water streaming over them, they held one another, sheltering each other from what was to come.

When Ryder dried her with a shabby towel he found under the sink, he couldn't bear the blanched color of her skin, and he rubbed hard, trying to warm her as he'd tried so long to warm himself.

Finally, he gave up and grabbed a sweatshirt out of her drawer and pulled it over her wet head. ''Hold still, green eyes. This isn't going to hurt,'' he muttered, tugging the shirt on even though it stuck against her wet skin.

''Ryder,'' she said, her teeth clicking together in a frenzied rhythm that had him pulling the shirt and twisting her.

''Yeah?'' He yanked the shirt down. ''What?''

''You need some clothes on, too.''

He glanced down. ''Damn.''

Huddled on the toilet lid, she shivered. ''I'll be fine. Go get dressed.''

''Right. Don't move.'' He hit the living room in mid-stride, reversed direction and was back beside her. ''We're going for an early-morning ride, Josie, over to the islands. And then we're going to come back and tell Stoner we saw something he should check out.'' Ryder had no intention of giving Stoner any more details about the source of their information than he had to.

"Okay. Okay." She stood up, and he caught her up in his arms again as her knees folded. "Sorry." She buried her head against his shoulder. "Oh, boy, Ryder, no wonder you thought you were going crazy. I couldn't stand a week of this, much less months of it."

"The images weren't specific until I came here. Saw you. And then things snowballed." Grabbing the thickest towel he could find, he scrubbed her hair hard, trying to dry the heavy mass. "Josie, do you have a hair dryer? We've got to get this stuff dry, or you'll never get warm."

She shook her head and wet strands flopped against his face, stinging him. "I usually go outside. Is it morning yet?" she asked, her voice a woeful plea.

"Almost. Come on. I'm taking you out on the porch."

"Good idea. I like my porch."

They sat curled together in a wooden rocker on her porch until the sun blazed bright and hot. Josie's arms around his neck were the sweetest chain he'd ever been bound by, her slight weight in his lap the most welcome burden he'd ever known.

Holding her against his heart, watching the sun come up with its harsh light, Ryder felt as if he'd come home.

When they reluctantly returned inside, Ryder settled her on the bed facing the dragonfly painting while he refolded the towels he'd yanked out of her cabinets in his frantic search. "Josie, you don't have to go with me if you don't want to." He stacked the towels back in the cabinet carefully, noticing that even her linens smelled of roses. "I can make up a story for Stoner that won't involve you. I can convince him."

"You could. I don't doubt that." Her teeth had quit clickety-clacking, but her lips were blue and bruised looking. "We'll do this together, Ryder."

"Whatever you say." Rummaging through her chest of

drawers, he pulled out a pair of shorts and panties. "How're you doing?" He sat down next to her, the shorts and panties dangling forgotten from his fist.

"I'll be better when this is behind us." She snatched her clothes from him. "I can dress myself, Ryder. I'll be out in a minute." She was pushing him away, setting up boundaries around herself, and, on the outside, looking in at her pain and distress, wondering if she'd let him past her barriers again, he'd never felt so lonely in his life.

He thought he'd wanted a solitary life. Uncomplicated. No ties. Free.

And he discovered that freedom was a loneliness beyond anything he'd ever imagined. Like the song said, freedom was just another word for nothing left to lose.

He left, shutting the door quietly behind him.

Even through the closed door, he heard her sobs.

It was a sound he'd never forget.

Waiting for her, he watered her garden again and watched the water pool on the dusty surface, running off to the trenches she'd dug between the rows where it finally disappeared into the parched earth. With its roots drying in the heat, one seedling listed to the right. He straightened it and patted the dirt tight around the threadlike roots. Maybe it would survive.

He hoped so.

When Josie came out, she'd untangled her hair and pulled on jeans and a long-sleeved shirt. The swath of her braid was doubled and twisted close to her skull so that she was all big eyes and cheekbones, the strain showing in the drawn lines around her eyes and mouth.

"I'm ready." She locked the door behind her, her glance at him stubbornly insistent. Josie would maintain some illusions.

Stark, plain in her faded jeans and white shirt without the brave mask of her wild colors, she looked not much more than skin and bones housing an inner strength that blazed in her dark eyes and made them brilliant with determination.

He thought he'd never seen anyone, anything, so beautiful in his life.

"It's a beautiful day for a boat ride, Josie. A picnic," he said grimly. "I've come to take you to one of the islands for a walk and a look at the flora. And fauna. We'll see what beasts have been roaming the islands of Angel Bay. Will you accompany me?" He held out his hand, wondering if she would trust him now.

She took his hand, her fingers closing tight about his, and it was as though she'd turned on a current that flowed from her to him and back, growing stronger and more powerful, that energy surging through both of them, a shared power that would see them through the next hours.

Looking around her as if in farewell, she said, "You're right. It is a lovely day for a picnic. Madder Me is the closest. It has some unusual trees and picnic areas. Why don't we go there, Ryder?"

They did. On the way to his house and the powerboat he had there, he passed a convenience store and picked up a wedge of cheese and crackers. A bottle of wine. He knew they wouldn't eat the cheese. Wouldn't drink the wine.

Props.

Setting the stage.

Circling to the back of his house, he parked the car under the shed and opened the car door for her. Her smile was strained, an effort of will only.

"Your house isn't the problem, Ryder, and we both know it now."

Standing at her side and looking back at the elegant, decaying lines of his house, he tucked her right arm close to him, close to his heart. "No, but I don't want to take you inside. Not yet. Later, maybe." He wanted there to be a later for them.

Wistfully, she stared at the house. "It could be so beautiful. A home. If you didn't mind plowing your fortune into it. If you wanted a place to live. A place with roots.''

''And history?'' he asked, brushing his hand over the smooth satin braid.

''Yes, a place with a history.'' There was a note of melancholy acceptance in her voice he'd never heard. ''A past you could hand down to your children. Their heritage. A gift you could give them. Roots.''

''I can see that.'' And he could. Could see a dark-haired, dark-eyed, sturdy girl with tanned, bare legs racing across a green lawn where there were now only weeds. Could see a skinny, red-faced boy hanging upside down from an oak tree dark green with leaves where there was only a dusty tree dying in the drought. ''Someone could turn this old run-down, decrepit house into a home.

''Wait for me, sweetheart. I'm going to make a costume change. For our performance.'' Unbuttoning his hastily donned shirt as he left her, he couldn't resist looking back at her as she waited for him.

He liked the picture she made there in his yard. She was sitting under the oak, her head tilted back and the long, sweet curve of her throat catching the sunlight filtering through the leaves.

Off in the distance he heard the mournful call of a dove.

When he returned in jeans as faded as hers and a long-sleeved white T-shirt, he gave her a quick look and extended his hand to her. ''Show time, Josie. Curtain's going up. Ready?''

''As I'll ever be,'' she answered. Taking his hand and rising, she gripped his hand, her apprehension showing in the way her fingers tightened against his.

Turning away, they went down to the dock that jutted out into the Angel River. They motored slowly out into the current, Ryder guiding the rudder and sending them toward Madre Mia and Devil's Island.

CHAPTER THIRTEEN

Cutting through the water, the boat generated a wind that whipped color into Josie's ashen cheeks. Ryder headed out of the river and into the gulf, aiming first for Madre Mia. In between Devil's Island farther out and Santa Ana close in, Madre Mia was a hangout for local motorcycle gangs who camped overnight for beer-and-drug parties. Few people went to Madder Me without a damned good reason. He'd gone once shortly after buying his house. The hairy giant who'd confronted him had been a teddy bear, but Ryder didn't think most folks would make a habit of picnicking on the island.

It wasn't a safe place.

He thought it seemed the most logical choice to search for Eric.

Easier to slip there in the dark and return home unnoticed if that's what you wanted to do.

"You doing all right, sweetheart?" He leaned forward and tapped Josie's shoulder.

Placing her hand over her ear, she indicated with a questioning look that she couldn't hear him. Throttling down the motor, he repeated the question, and she nodded.

He worried about her with an intensity he'd never felt toward anyone, and he wanted to see her smile again, wanted to see her sassy and prickly, wanted to see that tiny gleam in her eyes when she needled him.

Carnal.

Tender.

She brought out contradictory emotions in him.

The carnal heat of his need for her had terrified him with

its power to make him lose control, horrifying him with the thought that *something* was acting through him to harm her.

But the sweetness of her inexperienced seduction had pierced him with tenderness, the sexuality of those moments in her tin-roofed cabin woven into some other emotion that reached down into his soul, showing him what life could be.

And she made him laugh.

Tapping her on the shoulder again, he gestured to show that he was going to circle the island first. Pantomiming the twisted tree they'd seen, he pointed to the thick pines in the center of the island.

She shrugged. Damp with salt spray, the white sleeves of her shirt were transparent against her slim arms. She turned to look at the pines and her profile, windswept and sculpted against the black background of the trees behind her, pierced him with its vulnerability. She seemed to him in that moment as precious as any art treasure he'd ever wanted, her strength and loveliness as fleeting as the rainbows captured in morning dew.

She was a woman to be treasured by a man who would appreciate the value of her courage and strength.

Ryder knew how rare she was.

But he was a man of tricks and deception, a man who hid behind shadows and misty lights, creating fantasies. A man who knew little about treasuring a woman like her.

She deserved reality, not illusions.

Josie deserved magic.

And he didn't think he knew how to give her that.

He swung the boat toward the strip of white sand sloping into the sparkling water. The scrape against the bottom of the boat, the squawk of sea gulls.

The slop of water against the sand.

It was too early in the day for those who would come by dark to litter the white sand with beer bottles and cans, with the trash of their wildness.

"Come on, sweetheart. Nobody's here. Just you, me, and the birds."

"I hoped we'd find people here. Someone who could tell us if they'd seen Eric. Or anything," she said, her voice going low and soft.

"Me, too," he said as she stared at the empty beach. "But anyone here wouldn't be eager to share information with us, so we're no worse off."

He swung the anchor into the shallow, clear water where white sand reflected dazzling light and turned the gulf into liquid crystal where shimmery gray minnows darted and flashed, nibbling at his jeans. Helping Josie out of the boat, he swung her over to the shoreline, keeping her jeans-clad legs as dry as he could.

Walking closely at her side, he pushed aside underbrush as they slogged through marshy ground and gray-white sand. The ominous sense of waiting for the other shoe to fall kept him silent in the oppressive heat. Away from the shore, they slapped at "no-see-ums" and mosquitoes in the hot, windless interior of Madder Me as they searched futilely for over an hour, their eyes shifting, moving, watching for the twisted pine, for the stretch of sand they'd seen.

It was early afternoon by the time they left Madre Mia and headed out for Devil's Island, making a body-pounding circuit first. Coming around the ends of the island, the confluence of the currents from the gulf, bay, and river crashed into the island and churned up a heavy chop over the white sand, leaving the water dark and murky.

Spray flew up, splashed onto both of them. The boat rode the waves sloppily, slamming back into the troughs between them and jarring Ryder as he angled the boat toward a thick growth of sea grapes where he turned off the motor as the boat bounced in toward shore. "Sorry, Josie. This is rough. Almost as if a storm's out in the gulf somewhere. We're both going to have to wade to get into shore."

"Not many people bother coming here. The currents and

undertow are nasty. Not a good place to go shelling.'' Her arms were folded tight around her waist. ''I don't like this place, Ryder.'' She stared out toward the horizon where the sun was red and huge over the dark water, and then looked uneasily at him. ''It does look like a storm. We ought to hurry. I sure wouldn't want to be caught out here overnight.''

''Do you want to go back?'' Ryder didn't want to spend the night on Devil's Island, either, but he didn't want to leave it unsearched. Unless Josie asked him to. ''It's your choice, Josie.'' His earlier words, the ones he'd used in the beginning, now seemed weighted with meaning. He wanted her to decide. She had the most at stake. ''I'll do whatever you want, sweetheart. No second-guessing.''

''I know you wouldn't. I said you were a fair man.'' She unwound the anchor chain. ''I can't leave, Ryder, not without knowing if that child is here.''

They found the twisted pine on Devil's Island shortly before the red sun on the horizon dropped into the angry reds and purples of the gulf.

There, in a patch of brackish water, the toe of one water-soaked red sneaker poked through the muddy sand. He stepped in front of her. ''Don't look, sweetheart.'' In the dimming light he saw her eyes grow huge and agonized as she tried to push by him. He used his chest as a shield. ''Don't, Josie. You don't need to prove how tough you are. Enough's enough.'' Ryder pulled her away, toward him, folding her against his chest. He'd seen the small hand. ''We're going home. Back to Angel Bay. We'll tell Stoner. He can handle it from here. We don't have to go any closer.''

''I can't leave her here,'' Josie wailed, beating her small fists against his chest. ''I can't!''

''*Him*, sweetheart.'' He pressed her face into him. ''We haven't found Mellie. And we have to get Stoner out here.

We don't want to disturb any clues he might find. We're going to catch the son of a bitch who did this.''

Josie went still against him. ''This is a place of monsters!'' she cried. ''I can smell them.''

He rubbed his cheek over the smooth helmet of her hair and unfolded her fists, placing them flat on him, letting her feel the steady sureness of his heart beating in the darkness against her, giving her what comfort he could.

The reassurance of himself.

They returned to Angel Bay with the crimson glow of the sun following them across the water. Docking the boat, they went straight to Stoner.

Gripping Ryder's hand with desperation, opening herself to him emotionally, opening herself to whatever might come through their shared touch, their shared emotions, Josie kept expecting, hoping, to *see*. She stared at the dark road as Ryder drove to the police station. She shut her eyes tightly against the bright streetlights. She tried, she tried, to *see*.

To see Mellie. To find her daughter in the dark.

At the police station, she waited with Ryder. Watching the white face of the large clock over the duty sergeant's desk, she paced at Ryder's side up and down the hall outside Stoner's office until he arrived sweat stained and irritable from a crash-site investigation, a film of dirt and leaves dulling the shine of his shoes.

Sitting heavily on his desk, he knocked the dirt off his shoes into a trash can. ''Bad one,'' he said. Working methodically at his shoes, brushing the sand spurs off the cuffs of his black slacks, he didn't say anything more for several minutes. Dirt clots plonked into the trash can. ''Y'all found something?'' he finally asked, looking up at them wearily. Under the rolled-back sleeves of his shirt, the fur of his arms was thick with dust and dried sweat.

They told him. About their picnic. About the shoe on Devil's Island.

"Picnic?" Sitting in his chair, he swiveled, watching them. "All day?"

"Certainly, Detective," Ryder drawled beside her, his voice cool and imperturbable. "We were…carried away." He covered her hand with his, slowly stroking the vein on her inner wrist. "We lost track of the time." His smile was self-mocking, the lift of an eyebrow a beautifully executed male shout. He turned and gave Josie a meltingly tender smile.

There was no smile in his eyes.

But there was tenderness, a tenderness that gave her strength when hers had gone.

Stoner picked up the phone, spoke into it briefly, left, returned with a tape recorder. They repeated everything. Together, separately, together again.

And that was that.

Driving across the bridge toward her house, Josie squinted through the darkness toward the distant shape of Devil's Island and made her decision.

"Ryder," she said, turning toward him, "I have to stay with you tonight. At your house. If anything else is going to happen, I want it to happen now. Soon. I need the final answers. I need to know about Mellie. If being with you in your house will give me those answers, I want to be there. I'm not afraid. You won't hurt me. And I'm not afraid of your house, or of what might happen when we're there. I've been to hell, Ryder. I've been to Devil's Island. I've smelled the monster."

She had to persist, insist, beg, before he would give in, and then only with a reluctance that touched her heart. He was protecting her, but now she needed to face the darkness. Facing it with him at her side was the only path through to the morning, to the light.

"All right. Stay with me." He tapped the steering wheel rapidly as they neared the turnoff for her house. "Maybe that's the best idea, anyway. To finish it."

They went first to her house to retrieve his paintings.

In the light of an oncoming car, Ryder's face looked lean, grim. She glanced at the passing car as it slowed and thought she recognized the shape of Ned Dugan's large form. Leaning forward for a better look, she frowned as the car sped up, its red taillights winking and vanishing.

As she went to her bedroom to pack up a few belongings, the phone rang. With one hand on the open neck of the drawstring bag into which she was stuffing a minimum of underwear and T-shirts, she absentmindedly picked up the phone with her free hand.

"Hello?"

Static sloshing through the line like the tide rolling onto the sand.

"Who's there?" Her fingers were white against the phone receiver. "Who is this? I know you're there."

Static.

Nothing else.

Ryder took the phone from her and hung it up. "We're getting out of here, sweetheart. I really don't like coincidences like the phone ringing within minutes of your walking into your house. In these days of cellular phones, someone could be watching you from a car, from anywhere, watching and waiting for you to walk in."

Had Ned Dugan been in the car that passed them? And, if so, where had he been coming from? She threw a toothbrush into the bag.

He slung her drawstring bag over his shoulder, grabbed the pictures next to the couch as he passed it and shoved her out the door. Whipping the steering wheel through the turns to his house, he never changed his expression. Once he reached out and cupped the back of her neck with his hand.

With floorboards creaking and snapping underneath their feet, they went into Ryder's house.

She should have been afraid. The house was as atmospheric as it had been the first time she saw it in daylight. Nothing had changed.

Everything had changed.

"May I stay in the magic room?"

"Hell, Josie, you can stay in any room of my house you want. I'm just trying to figure out where I think you'll be the safest since I'm not letting you out of my sight tonight." Carrying the paintings in one hand, he rubbed the back of his neck. "Yeah. We'll see what happens." He shook his head. "Damn. I knew you had enough courage for any five men, sweetheart, but you sure scare the hell out of me. Well. The magic room it is."

He opened the door, turned on the light, and Josie watched the rainbow lights sparkle over the room as the round ball rotated overhead. Aimlessly, she wandered around the room, seeing things she'd missed before, standing once again for a long time in front of the magician and his panther. The panels shifted and rippled; the room was still cool, drafty.

Approaching the mud-colored pot that had intrigued her before, she said, "Where did you buy this, Ryder? It seems so different from everything else in the room."

Lifting it up from the pedestal, he held it out to her. "I found it in the trash outside the auditorium where I was working out the details of what had to be altered and built in the theater before that January show. I saw the pot as I was leaving. The light from the back door hit it as I opened the exit door, and the pot caught my eye. Worthless, I reckon, but I like it. I like the way it feels. Almost as if it were a living thing. Feel. It's almost breathing, isn't it?"

She touched the warm, smooth surface, stroked it. "I see what you mean. No wonder you kept it."

He sat on the floor next to the couch after he returned the pot to the pedestal. His jaws cracked with his yawn. "C'mere, sweetheart. You take the couch."

"Are you sure?" Josie slowly unfolded the blanket from

the sofa. "This room is so cold, Ryder. And so am I. Come up here next to me. All day, I've felt as if I would never be warm again. I need you to warm me now." She couldn't meet his eyes. Even after the way she'd touched him, let him touch her, she was unsure, shy with him. Unsure of herself.

"If that's what you want, Josie Birdsong." Still sitting on the floor, he curled his arm around her hips. "Are you frightened, Josie?"

"No," she said, shifting to face him.

He laid his head against her, resting it on her thighs. "Tell me if you are. Please. Because I'm so tired. I don't think I have the power to control anything tonight. I want to be beside you, inside you, Josie, and I want to keep you safe, too." He kissed her jeans-covered thigh near the inner seam.

In all the coldness inside and out, that small heat of his touch warmed her.

"You're in danger, sweetheart. Trouble is, I don't have a damned idea where the danger's coming from. From me? From someone out there watching you with evil in his heart? Or will the threat come from that *something* we've been sensing and tuning in to? I think I can protect you from myself. I know I can protect you from anything human that's stalking you. But—" He stopped, his mouth warm and damp against the cloth of her jeans.

"I believe we can protect each other," she said slowly, the certainty of that knowledge filling her. "We have so far, Ryder."

Taking her hand, he rose and lifted the blanket. "All right." He lifted her with one arm and sat on the couch. "So be it, sweetheart. Together, then."

And all during the long night, he lay with her.

Beside her, both still clothed and with the dried salt spray stiff on the fabric, he sheltered her with his body. Traced her face, her neck, the sensitive skin of her breasts and underarms. Touched her, gently, carefully, as she'd never been touched before, making her feel beautiful, making her feel as if she were the most important thing in the world to the dark-eyed man with the magic hands.

And inside her, too, the coming together slow and powerful, building a rhythm that beat through her with sweetness and tenderness and need as she moved to his touch, as she let his hands shape her and guide her through the darkness.

No urgent burning.

Only this exquisite, long loving, the elegance and control taking her slow and steady to a place where the light stroked her, turning her to molten gold.

The bone chill vanishing in this heat that was all prolonged touching, stroking, his mouth moving over hers, over her, with a delicacy that took her breath away even as his tongue touched her, claimed her and gave her peace.

Sometime before morning, they dozed.

In her dream, Josie heard the phone ringing, heard Mellie calling, "Mommy! Hurryhurryhurry!" The phantom figure was there, too, enormous, mythical, swooping overhead like the grackles, its eyes glowing yellow like the dogs' eyes.

She shuddered, wept, hurried after Mellie, and yet the phone rang, shrilled, until she opened her eyes and looked into Ryder's face.

His arms were around her, and he didn't move.

The phone was still ringing.

Ryder reached behind her to the table behind the couch and pressed a button.

From the phone speakers, static rasped into the room.

And then, soft, so soft, came the sweet voice. "Mommy?"

The sound of a click, of someone deliberately hanging up the phone, was clear.

Silence.

"My God," Ryder said, sitting upright and taking her with him.

Over his shoulder, she saw the earth-colored pot shiver, rock slightly in its holder on the pedestal. The bird seemed to sing in the stillness.

"It's a ground dove," Josie said. "Like in the painting. The picture of the shaman. When the ground dove sings, death comes." Her lips were stiff, but she wasn't afraid, only filled with the urgency of her dream. "Get the picture, Ryder."

He left her wrapped in the blanket and went naked into the hall to return with the Osceola painting. In the picture, the ground dove's beak was open as it sang its silent song of the death of the nation.

"Ryder." Josie stood up, her knees shaky. "Look at the pot, the smallest one. There, on the ground behind his medicine bundle." She touched the barely visible bird pot. Caught up in the story of the painting, she hadn't seen the pot when she'd first looked at the picture. Now, she pointed to Ryder's ocher pot on the pedestal.

They were the same.

"I don't like this kind of coincidence, either, Ryder." Holding the blanket around her, she walked over to the pot, standing near it but not touching it.

His mouth a tight line of dread, he came toward her.

"No, stay where you are for a second, please." She reached out to the pot, saw the faint, trembling movement, stepped back. "Ryder," she whispered, "come toward me, pick up the pot, and touch me."

He did.

The buzzing began at the back of her neck, shafted down her spine, the humming electrifying. Ryder held the pot in one hand, her in the other, his thigh against hers. "Don't leave me, Josie," he muttered. "Help me."

She saw the way his eyes narrowed, grew heavy lidded. Saw the red flush along his cheekbones.

Felt the heat buzz and hum over her.

And surrendered to it because of where it led.

To the truth about her daughter.

Like the fantastical ball lightning in the death-month painting, heat crackled and snapped between them, and Josie welcomed it, let it take her where it would.

This time the urgency was there, a pounding that shook them both.

But this time the urgency was threaded through with tenderness.

He took her standing up, her naked skin against the silk of the panther's body, and the growl of the panther was Ryder's growl in her ear. The hot slide of his hands over her was the slippery silk touch of the magician.

Fast, so fast that she gasped, he lifted her right leg and clipped it around his waist, holding her face with one hand, his other seeking her, parting her even as he entered and stroked hard and fast until she cried out.

There were no visions.

No voices calling her.

Only Ryder, filling her with himself, filling her with this piercing tenderness.

She touched her mouth to the damp, hot skin of his throat. "Go with me to talk to Johnnie Birdsong, Ryder. There are things she can tell us. Things we need to know."

"I will," he said, his mouth against her temple.

Stoner came to Ryder's house shortly before noon. "It's the Ames kid. We don't know anything yet except that he was strangled first. With part of his own clothing. There were knife cuts, too. But we'll know more after the autopsy. The FBI unit is coming in on this sometime tomorrow." He grimaced at Josie. "Lot of similarities to the killings, Miz Conrad. That's why the Feds have been brought in."

Josie left the room. She didn't want to know any more

of the details, but she heard the low murmur of their voices for an hour.

When Stoner finally left, they retrieved the pamphlets and brochures about the artist, checking to see if there was any information they could use to find her. Her phone number and address were unlisted, the brochures giving only a postal-box number.

Josie called Betty Cypress and asked if she would ask Johnnie Birdsong if it would be all right to give them her home number so that they could talk with her. "Could be a few days. She doesn't have a phone. I'll talk to someone who'll send a message down her way. She'll get back to you if she wants to. That's the best I can do, I'm afraid."

During the next week, they waited. And waited.

Sometimes the phone rang and Josie jumped, hoping it was Johnnie, hoping it was Mellie's voice.

Once the static came over the line.

Nothing else.

Josie went to her house in the mornings, Ryder like a dark presence standing guard as she watered her garden and tended her struggling tomatoes.

In the afternoons, they stayed outside at Ryder's. For hours they sat under the oak tree. Sometimes they talked, mostly they listened.

Listened to the occasional sound of the birds coming from the woods.

Listened to the heavy, hot quiet that lay over the land.

And Josie waited for the wind, for the wind that her mother had once promised would talk to her.

At the beginning of the second week, Johnnie Birdsong called. Her voice was musical, lilting, serene. Ryder said it was like listening to the sound of water moving in a quiet stream. He said, too, that if he only heard her speak for a moment or two, he would think at first it was Josie.

In the afternoon, Johnnie came to Ryder's house. She wanted to see the pot.

She was thin, and her face was broader and wider than Josie's. She was taller than Josie, too. Short, cropped hair, black and glossy as a crow's wing fanned back from her face. She wouldn't touch the pot. She merely shook her head. "This was part of an old medicine bundle. Sometimes if a woman approaches one of the bundles, the power of the spirits is too strong. Knocks her down. That's if you accept the old myths and beliefs." Her eyes twinkled. "I stand way back."

Josie remembered stumbling the first time she approached the pot.

The pot had been stolen last year from the burial place of one of the shamans.

"Everyone looked for the men who stole it. They were found and brought before tribal court this June during Green Corn Ceremony. Bad stuff happened. The thieves thought the pot was valuable. They thought they could sell it and make money."

"Did they?" Ryder asked, his expression intent.

"No, they found no one would pay for a pot with no jewels, so they threw it away. Somewhere along the Tamiani Trail."

"That's where I found it," he said. "In December."

"You were lucky if nothing happened to you. The spirits can cause great evil."

"I know." Ryder glanced at Josie, his expression sad, but resigned, and she knew he was thinking of Sandi. In bringing the pot into his life, he had unwittingly brought the restless spirit with him.

"It can cause great good, too, sometimes. Because the pot was lost and belonged to a very powerful shaman, Sam Osceola of the Panther clan, the tribe suffered and still suffers. His pot should have been broken. They didn't let its spirit loose. His spirit is lost, and trying to find rest," she said, stepping back from the pot. "The spirit will affect those around it. It needs prayers, offerings. It needs to go home. The men who stole it didn't know where they had left it. Or they would have returned it.'' Her voice was strong. ''You must return it to the burial ground, to the earth where it belongs. Or more bad things will happen. The spirit isn't evil. But it can cause great harm, I tell you. And the tribe has suffered enough. But you must return it. I can't do it for you.''

After Johnnie left in her bright green car, Josie went and sat in Ryder's lap. ''The spirit came to us when we were together and brought good, Ryder. Eric's body was found. I found you.'' She put her arms around his neck. ''And you gave me hope, the hope that I might reach Mellie somehow, or find out what had happened to her. I never felt a sense of evil around the pot, but I think Johnnie's right. We need to return it to Sam Osceola's burial ground.''

''Must have been those ancient shaman genes handed down to you, your heritage that saved you, Josie.'' He kissed her and held her so tightly that her ribs ached.

Then, lifting her up in his arms, he carried her outside to the oak tree and made love to her under the wide branches, his gaze never leaving hers.

They didn't speak of Mellie, who hadn't been saved.

The next day Stoner asked Josie to come to the station. With his first words her heart constricted and then beat so rapidly she had to sit down. ''Something you need to hear, Miz Conrad. We've made an arrest in the Ames murder.'' His voice was tired and discouraged. ''I've seen a lot in my life, but this is beyond me.''

Ryder took her to her house to change and then to the police station where he stayed by her side, his fingers wound between hers. They sat in a small, bare room with a two-way mirror. On the other side, Stoner faced a short, thin man whose head nodded as he smiled agreeably at Stoner.

"We found the Stellyte under Eric's fingernails, you know. And the traces of arsenic."

"That's in the compound I use to rebuild the engines. I'm very good at that. I work on the airplane engines, too, did you know that?" He leaned forward, and Josie saw his face.

"Yes, Mr. Woolverton, we knew that. Why don't you tell me about the other children now? Will you do that for me? It would help us out. Make things easier for us. You can do that, can't you?"

"Of course I can. I'll be happy to." He leaned back in his chair and glanced at the mirror.

Looking at Woolverton's face, Josie knew she was looking at evil. For a moment as he stared at the mirror, his eyes were the yellow of the wild dogs, the yellow of the strangely unified grackles, the yellow holding an intelligence not of this world.

As he continued to stare at the mirror, he told about the murders, his manner casual, helpful, but unemotional. Matter-of-factly, he detailed everything he'd done.

Josie couldn't keep watching. She put her head into her hands and gave a tiny sob.

Woolverton's head snapped sharply toward the mirror.

"Mrs. Conrad?" He stood up, Stoner going with him, staying close. He came close to the mirror, put his face right up to it, and for a moment, his eyes were hazel, confused, the evil absent in those instants. "You're in that other room, aren't you, Mrs. Conrad? I tried to tell you I didn't kill your girl. I called you, because I felt bad about what happened to her that day. I didn't kill her, though. I would never have hurt her. I only followed her into the woods because she was so pretty in her red jacket. I only wanted to watch her. She never even saw me, though. Funniest thing. She was playing, and she tripped. Hit her head on that big rock that's back in the woods near the cut through. She looked so pretty sleeping there. But she didn't wake up. So I covered her up, nice and comfy.''

Ryder's arms were both around Josie and she clung to him, to his strength that was the only thing keeping her upright at the moment with all that darkness closing in around her as she stared at the face of a monster.

"I kept her picture. I came to your house and took the picture because I liked her smile. I wanted to see her awake again. You can have it back, Mrs. Conrad. Because I've done a lot of bad things, I think, and I shouldn't have taken her picture. That was wrong.''

He told Stoner where Mellie's body was.

Later, Ryder went with Josie to the place in the woods where Woolverton had left Mellie that January afternoon.

Carrying a vase of flowers and the green shard Mellie had given her, Josie knelt at the spot where her daughter had laughed one last time, tripped and vanished, never knowing the pain or horror that Josie had feared.

An accident.

There was no sense of Mellie in the dusty, silent woods, no sense of that laughing, joyful child, and Josie sighed, brushed off the bright green-and-pink skirt she'd put on because the colors had been Mellie's favorites, and stood up.

"I don't know what I hoped for, but it's not here, Ryder. There's nothing here for me in this spot.''

As they left, Josie turned to look behind her, thinking, hoping she'd see that little shape that hurried before her in her dreams.

But no little ghost hovered hopefully there, waiting for her to find her.

Afterward, Ryder put the bird pot in his car and they drove up the Tamiani Trail to the spot Johnnie Birdsong had told them about. Walking far off the road, back deep into an area partially bulldozed and cleared for riverside condominiums, he found the place that had once been Sam Osceola's burial ground.

The Angel River was off in the distance, a shimmer of silver in the afternoon heat and dust. Ryder smashed the pot, the bird beak splintering first, while Josie dug a hole. Carefully, they each put a shard deep into the earth until all the pieces were covered with dry, parched soil.

Ryder's hand was under hers and as they brushed in the last of the sandy soil, his hand went utterly still and he looked up. Josie stared, too, out to the horizon where gray clouds gathered over the river, rolled silently toward them.

Under their joined hands, the earth trembled, seemed to sigh, and the sigh was the sigh of the wind moving lightly, lightly, through the dusty leaves of the trees around them.

The first drop of rain lay in the dust, rolled, rainbow colors splintering in its small globe.

And then the others fell, becoming a slow, quiet rain that washed Josie's face, carrying away tears as she saw the rainbow stretching from the river through the soft gray clouds to them. Coming to her through the clouds and rain was Mellie, her hand outstretched to Josie as she called, "Mommy!"

Josie felt Mellie's hand against her cheek, warm and *real,* felt her daughter's hand patting her belly as Mellie chortled, "Hey, sweetie-baby," felt Mellie's breath in the air as Mellie kissed her and closed her small hand over Josie's.

And then she was gone, her laugh trailing after her as she faded away, blurring until Josie saw only clouds and the rainbow. She looked down at her closed fist and the egret feather beaded with raindrops and misty rainbows.

"Aw, sweetheart," Ryder said, taking her in his arms. "I saw her, too. What a little charmer." He kissed Josie and she didn't know whether she tasted her tears, his, or the rain.

Under the soft gray clouds and the slow gray rain, on a

bed of pine needles, he made love to her, telling her with words and touch that he needed her more than life itself, showing her how much he treasured her.

"I love you, Josie Birdsong," he whispered, and it was the whisper of the wind in the green leaves.

"I love you, Josie," he said, touching her, and it was the touch of the wind against her bare breasts.

And in that moment of sweetest joining, with his eyes filled with her, Josie felt the flutter of wings above her, in her womb, and in that vision she could finally see the possibility of happiness, of joy, as Ryder gave her himself.

"Josie?" He lifted her above him, holding her up to the rain and sky.

"What, Ryder?" she asked, running her hands over his rain-slick body, loving him, erasing the shadows of loneliness from the child and the man.

His smile was wicked. "I have a very nice bed, back in my old, decrepit, run-down house. And I have a spot where a bunch of transplanted tomato plants would grow like weeds. What do you say, Josie? May I take you to my bed? To my home? Please?" he whispered, sending shivers down her bare back.

"A dry bed sounds lovely, Ryder, but not just yet," she murmured, leaning over him and tasting his mouth. "In a minute. Or two," she added as he gathered her closer and unpinned her hair.

"Uh, Josie, I ought to tell you about that red stone?"

"Mmm, yes, Ryder," she moaned when he tickled her navel. "That's another lovely idea."

"It's real, not a fake ruby, sweetheart."

"That's nice," she said and nibbled his ear.

For a long time there was only the slow, steady dripping of rain all around them, turning the earth green, renewing life, bringing the rainbow.

* * * * *

Every day is

A Mother's Day

in this heartwarming anthology
celebrating motherhood and romance!

Featuring the classic story "Nobody's Child" by Emilie Richards
He had come to a child's rescue, and now Officer Farrell Riley was
suddenly sharing parenthood with beautiful Gemma Hancock.
But would their ready-made family last forever?

Plus two brand-new romances:

"Baby on the Way" by Marie Ferrarella
Single and pregnant, Madeline Reed found the perfect husband in the
handsome cop who helped bring her infant son into the world. But did his
dutiful role in the surprise delivery make J. T. Walker a daddy?

"A Daddy for Her Daughters" by Elizabeth Bevarly
When confronted with spirited Naomi Carmichael and her brood of girls,
bachelor Sloan Sullivan realized he had a lot to learn about women!
Especially if he hoped to win this sexy single mom's heart....

Available this April from Silhouette Books!

Where love comes alive™

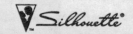

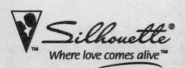

When California's most talked about dynasty is
threatened, only family, privilege and the power
of love can protect them!

THE COLTONS

Coming in May 2002

THE HOPECHEST BRIDE

by

Kasey Michaels

Cowboy Josh Atkins is furious at Emily Blair, the woman he
thinks is responsible for his brother's death...so *why* is he so
darned attracted to her? After dark accusations—and sizzling
sparks—start to fly between Emily and Josh, they both realize
that they can make peace...and love!

Available at your favorite retail outlet.

Is he tall, dark
and handsome...
Or tall, dark
and *dangerous*?

Men of Mystery

Three full-length novels of romantic suspense
from reader favorite

GAYLE
WILSON

Gayle Wilson "has a good ear for dialogue and
a knack for characterization that draws
the reader into the story."
—*New York Times* bestselling author Linda Howard

**Look for it in June 2002—
wherever books are sold.**

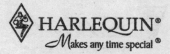

HARLEQUIN®
Makes any time special ®

BR3MOM